THE ATTRACTION ABACUS

Evelyn G. Foster

THE ATTRACTION ABACUS
A ROM COM

Heptagon Books

A CIP catalogue record for this title is
available from the British Library.

ISBN 978-1-0682004-4-1

First Published in 2025

Printed & Bound in Great Britain

Cover design by Adam Hay Studio, UK.

A big thank you to my test readers for all your invaluable input — Maggie, Hannah, David, Pat, Dawn, Al, Kitty, Lynne and Andy.

Also, a big thank you to Daisy Watt for her insightful developmental editing advice.

Chapter One

I tried to be positive when I worked morning shifts at the hotel, but I always slept badly. Waking up was even worse. Sometimes I took the bus to work, but more often I missed it, like that Tuesday morning. My hair was still wet as I left the flat, and I knew that a mad restyle was inevitable in the wind. Then, my best jacket snagged on the front garden gate, ripping a pocket, so my expectations for the day were set low from the outset.

It was early May, and the cold, easterly gusts around my ears seemed totally unjustified — immoral, in fact. I was walking quickly in fury, not out of conscientiousness, to get to work on time. My job had long since become expendable, and I chose to leave its fate in the lap of the Gods on days like this. As I stormed across the pedestrian lights towards the High Street, I nearly choked on a cereal bar. A coughing fit finally forced me to calm down. I passed Badger, our local street guitarist, who smiled and waved. I barely managed to smile back. Badger fully embraced his nickname, with his close-cropped hair dyed black and white. I was a regular contributor to his woolly hat, and I couldn't just ignore him, despite my irritation.

Our High Street here is like most others now, full of mobile phone outlets, charity shops and boarded-up windows. A few independents are hanging in heroically, but you feel like it's only a matter of time for them too. The shops were just opening as I reached the main drag, with their shutters clattering up around me. A cleaning cart beeped nearby. The pedestrianised square was filled only by pigeons, strutting about the pavement. In fact, I thought that I was the only living person around until I spotted Luke in the distance.

People say that you get a gut feeling when you first meet the important people in your life. I don't want to sound like a village hall spiritualist, but I really did. That strange sense of anticipation soon passed when Luke turned sideways. I could see that he was distributing leaflets or conducting some kind of survey or something. I was the only potential victim in sight, and he was directly in my path.

I stopped walking and pretended to check my phone. Was he insane? What idiot would start canvassing this early? My first piece of luck of the day presented itself: I had stopped outside Boots the chemist. Boots the chemist has two entrances, one on the High Street side and another at the rear, leading to the multi-storey car park. It was a slight detour, but still a passable route to the hotel where I worked. Fortunately again, Boots's door was unlocked as I pushed it. Ignoring the staff's barely disguised disgust at my early entrance, I wandered through the store, feigning interest in the meal deals for a few minutes, before heading out the other side.

Luke was standing directly in my path.

He had obviously circled around the block, past M&S, to intercept me. He was breathing heavily, so I knew that he must have run. Luke was around six feet tall, with a slim build. His eyes were blue, framed beneath a dark fringe, pushed messily to one side. There was short stubble covering his chin. Quite good-looking, I thought. I was drawn to the stupid grin on his face above everything else.

'I knew you'd try it,' he said.

'Sorry?'

6

'The Boots manoeuvre. Textbook avoidance.'

'Oh…'

Don't engage, I told myself. Never engage with a canvasser. Before you know it, you're signing off a direct debit that you'll snarl about for the rest of the year. He was smiling, though, and I always find it difficult not to smile back at smilers.

'Can I ask you a few questions?'

'Sorry, I don't have time.'

'Well, there are only three, and you've just answered one of them already. That didn't take long, did it?'

'I have to go…'

I was looking around now, checking to see if there were witnesses. The sucker spotlight was shining brightly on me.

'My name's Luke.'

A poor move on his part. It wasn't a question, and it was easier to ignore. I swivelled away, pointing my toes towards the road.

'I'm really sorry…'

'How's your love life?' he asked as I began to move. Surprise checked my steps, and he noticed. Luke was grinning now, challenging me to take offence at the question. The problem is I don't ever take offence, so the best I could do was raise my eyebrows. It wasn't a great reaction, though, weak and theatrical. 'There is a good reason that I'm asking,' he continued, reaching for the satchel hanging from his shoulder.

'I'm really late for work,' I replied, trying to sound officious now.

'Last question, I promise. Did you know that science can help you find your ideal partner?'

'Why do I need to find my ideal partner?'

'Maybe you do, maybe you don't. It's interesting though,

7

right?'

I don't know why I had instantly become defensive. Well, that's a lie, I do. The one thing that unites my family is their fascination with my love life, or lack of it. Being single is some kind of disease in their eyes. It was as if Luke had conspired with them beforehand and stage-managed the entire meeting. Also, I object to people saying "right" at the end of a question, as if I am too stupid to provide the answer unprompted. Finally, it was technically a fourth question, so I felt positively scammed by this point. It was incredible how much he had triggered me in such a short space of time. He was taking a leaflet from the satchel now. I could feel my face flushing.

'You might find the answers you need here... Evelyn,' he said, reading the badge on my lapel. He was grinning again as if he knew that he had rattled me, and saying *my* name aloud just compounded the irritation. To my frustration, I was smiling back, though.

'I'll pass, thank you.'

'It's only a leaflet. Dump it straight in there if you aren't at least a little bit curious,' he said, nodding to the concrete bin outside Boots.

'Actually no,' I said, taking it from his hand. 'I always recycle.'

The comeback was a minor victory that allowed me to walk away with a shred of dignity intact. I *was* curious, despite myself, but there wasn't a chance in hell that I was going to look at that leaflet while Luke was still in view, and I stuffed it in my bag without looking back. The smile began to slip from my face as I reflected on our conversation. It disappeared entirely when I imagined him having that same conversation with every other woman he bumped into that day. I started to walk faster again.

Luke was an arsehole, I concluded, but that wasn't my last encounter with him by any means.

The hotel I worked at was beside a roundabout at the edge of town. It used to be a Holiday Inn, but the new owner, Frank, bought it a few years before. His timing couldn't have been worse, opening just as Covid hit. He weathered the storm as best he could, deep cleaning with disinfectant between visitors and taking the kettles away from the rooms, etc. Frank loved taking the kettles away from the rooms. It saved on tea and biscuits. The height of Covid seems such a crazy time now. The restaurant felt plain weird with everybody walking around in masks and aprons. It was more like a bad science fiction set than a hotel, and I can't believe anyone bothered staying there at all. I guess we were all a bit stir-crazy back then and just wanted to do *something* — even sit in a mask in a restaurant by the side of a roundabout.

Frank may well be up to his eyeballs in debt now. He risked it all on one last roll of the dice, opening the hotel restaurant to non-guests and rebranding it as an Italian pizzeria, Francesco's. Somebody told him there was a good profit to be made from serving coffee in the mornings and pizzas after midday, so he tried both. *It's high margin, low effort, Frank.*

My job title was deputy manager. In reality, I was a zero-hour dogsbody. I had cleaned, cooked and served at various times, depending on the gaps in the rota. On that Tuesday, the other staff were already assembled in the restaurant for a meeting as I arrived. It was quite a spacious room — high-ceilinged, with dado rails and other original features still in situ, and the restaurant could accommodate around seventy diners at a time. The prints on the walls depicted beauty spots that were as alien to the hotel location as you could get.

You could tell what time of day it was by the smell. There was bacon in the air, and it instantly turned my stomach. Collecting breakfast plates was my weakness. I was sometimes hungover in the mornings, and the disgusting residue left on breakfast plates never failed to nauseate me. There was always the trademark cocktail of congealed scrambled egg and baked beans stirred together on one of the plates. What kind of sick person would mix them?

Frank was holding court in front of the tables. He gave me a "you're late" glare as I walked through the door, and I mouthed an apology back. Frank was a short, rotund man whose complexion was permanently red. It appeared as if his head might explode at any moment. He always wore a suit, though I don't know who he was trying to impress. I took my place between Pam and Rich, who shuffled along to let me stand beside their table. Pam's perfume was a bit too pokey for early morning, and I tried not to breathe deeply.

'First, some great news,' Frank said. 'Francesco's will be open to the public for coffee from next Monday morning. An extremely exciting development, I'm sure you'll all agree. So, brush up on your barista skills, and fine-tune your frothing!'

Silence. Frank cleared his throat.

'This has meant some changes to the rota, of course, so please check the latest sheet carefully.'

Groans.

'Are you employing more staff?' Pam asked.

'Eventually, yes, when things bed down a bit.'

So, no, we had already been "bedding down" for six months with no extra help. There were a few more grumbles, but Frank swiftly moved on to his next point.

'Secondly, I'd like to explore new ideas for the pizzeria.

We've had a few early negative reviews on *Tripadvisor*, claiming Francesco's is lacking atmosphere. Any thoughts on how we can improve it?'

Silence again. As I looked around at the other staff, eyes dipped away from Frank, it was difficult to determine who gave less of a shit. That's what our modern zero-hour, minimum-wage taskmasters don't get: this complete indifference is the price *they* pay.

'Well, I have a few ideas,' Frank said, unperturbed. 'Firstly, I think our staff need a new image. I'd like you all to wear black when you serve in the restaurant. It will convey a certain chic.'

There were a few stifled giggles, and then Pam spoke.

'I don't have any black clothes. Will you be paying for some?'

'We can discuss that on an individual basis,' Frank replied. Another definite no, but he wasn't finished yet. 'I am also installing some mood lighting, and an accordion player will perform on Friday and Saturday evenings.'

'Isn't that a French restaurant thing?' Rich asked.

'You have accordion players in *European* restaurants,' Frank corrected. 'But the continental theme has reminded me of another important point that I wanted to raise. I would like all serving staff to speak with an Italian accent.'

I was gobsmacked at this point, but as I looked around me, everyone else just seemed to be accepting the request. I didn't want to go there, but they gave me no choice.

'Frank, this isn't the 1970s,' I said. 'You can't put on fake Italian accents these days. You'll be cancelled for good.'

He sighed deeply, leaning back against the wall.

'How did I know that it would be *you* focusing on the negatives, Evelyn? I'm just trying to make this pizzeria the best it can be.'

Frank didn't like me much.

My shift seemed to last forever that day. Frank was obviously still sulking and lined up some crappy jobs for me in revenge. I didn't bite and just kept my head down. As I entered the last hour of my shift, Frank's mood seemed to sweeten. It was disturbing until I realised his motive when he cornered me as I left the kitchen.

'Evelyn, I need a huge favour. Helen has let me down tonight. We're short in the restaurant.'

'Sorry, I'm busy,' I said. I wasn't busy, but I was tired, and he had been a real tool to me all day.

'Please, I'm begging you. I wouldn't ask if I wasn't completely desperate. I'm running a coupon promotion tonight, and we're almost full. It's a make-or-break night for Francesco's. I need another person on service. I've already tried the others.'

Now I knew that he was telling the truth. Frank wouldn't ask me to serve in the restaurant unless he really was desperate. He didn't like me front of house at the best of times.

'I don't have any black clothes with me, and I'm definitely not putting on any accents.'

'You don't have to. Please, just help this once?'

'I'll need a taxi home. I haven't arranged a lift, and the buses will have stopped running by then.'

'Can't you… okay… fine.'

It was settled, and I took a quick shower in one of the empty rooms. Pam lent me some clothes that were a little big, but I didn't tell her that. Pam was always on a diet, and the information would not have been well received. As I was packing up my things, I found the leaflet that Luke had given me earlier.

Perching on the corner of the bed, I finally read it.

"The Attraction Abacus, opening soon. Let science find your ideal partner."

At the bottom, in small type, the leaflet mentioned that the company was recruiting. Their address was closer to my flat than the hotel, just off the High Street. The job also paid more than minimum wage, *and* it was only office hours. No weekends! Was I thinking about Luke, or how much I hated my job at that point? Definitely the job, but, either way, the leaflet didn't go in the recycling bin.

Chapter Two

I don't mean to digress here, but there are some things that you need to know about my life to make sense of the rest of this. I'll be as brief as I can, but my background had shaped my outlook significantly by this point, so it needs explaining.

You could say that my family were time travellers. Not in the literal sense, of course. It's not that kind of story. What I mean is that we were never truly *together* because of our differences. As a family unit, we were totally crap, really.

My dad, Ray, always lived in the future. Everything was going to be great tomorrow. He was incapable of enjoying any given moment without one eye on the next. If we were eating a meal in a restaurant, he'd be talking about the next course. The trailers were always more exciting than the film he was watching in the cinema that day. On a much-anticipated Spanish summer holiday, I remember him sweating at a beach bar, beer in hand, talking about what we would do at Christmas. He was trapped in a perpetual state of expectancy, never investing in the present for a second. I put this largely down to a sense of personal disappointment. His career didn't kick on as he had hoped, and it was this future success that would make everything better. What we had today was a pale imitation of what we would have tomorrow.

Dad was a frustrated actor who enjoyed some fleeting success in the late Eighties. People say that a bad teacher can scar you for life, but I think that we can often overlook the damage a good one can inflict. A drama teacher fatefully overpraised his performance of *Danny Zuko* in the school's third-year summer production of *Grease*. It launched him on a trajectory of self-delusion from which he never truly regained control. His teacher was an early adopter of the "you can be anything you like" school of thought. As anybody in their twenties, like me, knows, this theory has long since been discredited. After years of being fed this garbage, you wake up fifty grand in student debt, with a 2:1 in philosophy and photocopying staff rotas for the zero-hour hotel job that you've stumbled into. (I know you *could* email it to me, Evelyn, but I prefer a piece of paper in my hands.)

It's true there was Dad's purple patch in the Eighties (a bit part in the little-known soap, *The Country Dentist*), but this minor success only fuelled more false hope. Thankfully, it all happened before I was even born. My mum said that he was unbearable at that time, wearing fake designer glasses that didn't enhance his vision in any way and investing in a wardrobe of roll-neck sweaters. She'd already lost interest at this point, so God only knows why she started a family with him. I have an older sister, so it's difficult to dismiss us both as accidents. He took us all down with him, though. The more he chased tomorrow and failed to hold down regular jobs today, the more our lives degenerated. He squandered an early inheritance, and our family plummeted the property ladder in the Nineties, just as everybody else seemed to be climbing it. Finally, he blew all the equity entirely, and we ended up in my childhood home — the Alamo, as he referred to it. This tiny two-bedroom rental was where our family would make our last stand, supposedly. Only when we looked around, he had already left. I was ten years old.

When I later quizzed him about this early exit from my life, he glossed over it. It was best for everybody, he said, and we were still peas in a pod. Apparently, his creative juices flowed through my veins (I didn't like to think about that too much). Anyway, enough about tomorrow-man for the moment. The one thing that I took from him: never do anything that he did.

By contrast, my mum, Angela, always lived in the past. She occupied a world of photograph albums, emails to old school friends and bitter regrets. Her biggest regret was obviously marrying my dad. She maintained that her first boyfriend, Martin Abbott, remained the love of her life. She met Martin in her early twenties when they worked together in a local manufacturing company. She was employed in the marketing department, trying to make refrigerators sound alluring. Martin was studying to be an accountant, and their eyes met over an invoice with the wrong cost code.

Everything blossomed from that moment. They took their lunch breaks together in the staff canteen, and both joined the company pub quiz team that met on Wednesday evenings (*Licenced to Chill* — she still has the trophies). It wasn't long before they were dating, or "going out together" as Mum prefers to call it. Martin was squirrelling his money away into savings accounts to buy a flat. He estimated eighteen months before he could put a deposit down, with a fair financial wind. Mum still lived with her parents, but Martin crashed there most weekends. Everything was going just fine until my dad turned up with his unique brand of bullshit and unsettled everybody. Dad applied for a summer job at the company and weaselled his way onto the quiz team, claiming to possess an encyclopaedic knowledge of film. He had an ulterior motive, of course, always side-lining my mum when Martin disappeared to the bar. One often repeated conversation sealed her fate.

'Is this really all you want from life, Ange?'

'I don't see you setting the world alight.'

'A fair observation to date, but that's all about to change.'

'Really. So, what's the big plan?'

'I've been offered an acting role in LA this autumn. It's a huge opportunity. Do or die. You could come with me if you fancy living a little? We could see the bright lights and travel at the same time.'

This was her sliding doors moment. My mum was blissfully unaware that there was no actual acting offer on the table. Dad was using the inheritance that I mentioned earlier to fund the trip. He hoped that his talent would be spotted if he randomly hung around the streets of Hollywood for long enough. My mum agreed and resigned within a fortnight. Martin was mortified and refused to speak to her ever again.

It transpired to be die not do, of course, and Mum was re-applying for her old job back again within eighteen months. Martin had already moved on to another company. She had been suckered into the oldest trap of them all: the romance of the creative. It's not something that fools anyone after the age of thirty, but my dad had caught Mum while her brain was not yet fully formed. She had a future accountant in the palm of her hand but gave it all up for the promises of a flaky dreamer. Inexplicably, she stuck with my dad and married him two years later.

As her marriage later disintegrated, my mum became more and more resentful. Once she discovered the internet, *Facebook* was the real game-changer. Mum set up a fake account to stalk Martin, and it opened a window to the world that she was originally destined to inhabit. Her nemesis, Barbara, grinned back at her from increasingly exotic holiday destinations with Martin. Martin married Barbara in the Seychelles when I was

17

nine, and when they moved into their palatial new home a year later, it coincided with my mum's retreat into the Alamo. It was the final straw, and her laptop nearly decapitated Bruno, our Pomeranian, when she saw it.

'An open-plan kitchen with an island, Evelyn! I never knew that I wanted one until I saw hers. Now, it's all I can think about.'

It was a desperate time, but as Mum became resigned to reality, she gradually took control of her own destiny again. I was proud of her. Dad had left by now, and she worked hard at the manufacturing company, becoming a supervisor, then manager and finally associate director of marketing. She cut her hair short and dyed it blonde. She bought a convertible Mini and hit the gym. Her confidence was sky-high again, and I wish that was how it remained. The problem was that she didn't want to be alone, and a disastrous series of relationships dragged her back down again. The younger guys only wanted sex, and the older guys either wanted her money or somebody to look after them. Ten whole years were wasted in this hopeless pursuit of trying to find another life partner. After one particularly disastrous date, I found her halfway down her second bottle of Sauvignon Blanc on a Friday night, photograph albums open on the coffee table, sliding back into the past.

'Do you know what, Evelyn?' she said. 'By the time you finally figure out who you are and what you want from life, nobody else cares. I'd stay young if I were you.'

The lesson I took from her: don't listen to idiots like my dad.

Unlike my parents, my sister, Abby, lived in the all-too-present. Yoga, meditation, alternative therapies — you know the kinds of things. She's older than me, and her newfound Zen-like calm didn't extend to our childhood when we shared a bedroom. I was routinely terrorised back then, but she has conveniently wiped all that from her memory. To be fair, she was dealing with the same things as me, but with the chaos of puberty thrown into the mix. I looked up to her as an adult at that time, with her dark makeup, pierced nose and indie music, but she hit those difficult early teenage years just as our family life was falling apart. We have patched things up as we've got older. No longer sleeping in the same bunk beds really helped. I have even tried to join her "in the moment" since, but the meditation sessions just don't come naturally to me.

'Clear your mind. Just *be*, Evie.'

How can any sentient creature clear their mind? An ant farting distracts me when I am trying to meditate. So, I just lie next to my sister on the yoga mat, faking it, and wondering when she is going to exhale next. I don't know where this stuff takes you anyway. I'm probably missing the point, but until we manage to float away into another astral plain or cheat death, it all seems like too much effort. Abby has been through the whole card: aromatherapy, hypnotherapy, acupuncture — you name it. In fact, only conventional medicine could truly be described as alternative to her.

'Big pharma wants to control us all, Evie.'

She views a paracetamol as a little white conspiracy theory. She buys into *any* conspiracy theory, in fact. The government, the United Nations, the BBC; they're all in on it. In fact, the only reliable source of information is the *Furthest Down the Rabbit Hole* conspiracy website on *YouTube* (subscribe and buy our book now for £19.99 before *they* shut us down). Okay, what do I know, but I just wish that Abby was as equally sceptical about the latest crackpot cover-up as she is about the evening news, that's all I'll say. The lesson I took from her: really keep an open mind about things.

That just leaves me. Well, I guess I've occupied all their time zones at some point, but I've never really found my comfortable spot in the universe. Not yet, anyway. There *is* something I should mention about myself at this point, though. I have an undiagnosed condition that I call doom-dreaming. Doom-dreaming is an extreme form of daydreaming that first manifested itself around puberty. Doom-dreams are triggered at unpredictable times, but I am usually heightened with emotion of some kind when they occur, often, perversely, when I'm happy and things are going particularly well. This presents the unwelcome opportunity to grasp defeat from the jaws of victory. Doom-dreams are frighteningly vivid, to the point that the doom-dreamer believes that they are really happening. Sometimes, the doom-dreams are accompanied by a soundtrack in my mind, like a movie score, dramatising the whole experience, and often the same phrase repeats in my brain.

Past performance is no guarantee of future results.

I think I first saw these words on an investment advert somewhere, referring to the stock market, but for some reason they lodged in my brain and became my mantra. The words are a warning to me that, just because a doom-dream turned out okay once before, doesn't mean that all will be well next time. I shouldn't be complacent.

To explain with a simple example, imagine that you are taking a coastal walk and you come to the edge of a cliff with a sheer drop beneath. You might laugh nervously and say, "Oh, that's a long way down. I feel like I'm going to throw myself off."

Not a doom-dreamer. Oh no, a doom-dreamer will be face down in the grass, screaming, convinced that there is absolutely nothing to *stop* them from throwing themself off the cliff. As they

20

claw at the ground with their fingernails, their very grasp of reality is questioned. Can my legs really be trusted? Am I who I think I am? Is this world even real? I know that sounds weird, but I just wanted you to understand my little problem from the start.

Anyway, my dad was right about one thing. I have always been drawn to the creative. That's why I'm starting to write this novel. I don't have much free time, but my dream is to spend a few years in Goa completing it. I'll live in a beach cabin, tapping at my laptop as I look out to sea, and return a bestselling author, having cheated diphtheria and typhoid along the way. I'm saving hard, and I'm determined to make it happen. They say to write about what you know, and I came to know way too much about the Attraction Abacus. It certainly changed my life forever, but no spoilers about that for now. It's time to get back to the story of Luke and me.

I had to hand it to Frank; Francesco's did look better that evening. The lighting changes made the biggest difference, and the same old cutlery and glasses sparkled anew beneath the fancy fittings. There was no accordion player tonight, but Frank had changed the piped music, and it did add to the ambience. In fact, through squinted eyes, you could almost imagine that you were somewhere nice and not sitting at the junction of three major roads.

Pam, also roped into a double shift, gave me a skyward look as the first customer arrived at the second that we opened. There was always one. You may judge me at this point, but the customers that irritated me the most were the "niceys", as I called them. Their perpetual smiles and all their repeated pleases and thank yous really grated on a long shift. Give me the stroppy ones, any day of the week. Unfailingly older, the stroppy ones swanned into the restaurant in their smart-casual attire like they owned the place, scowling around for any minute detail to complain about. This was despite nearly always being on a mid-week coupon deal from the local newspaper. I saw them as a challenge and liked to push their buttons as far as I could without overstepping the mark. That's a lie. Frank had already given me four verbal warnings after customer complaints by that point. Legally, I don't think you can have four verbal warnings, but he struggled to hire staff, so tough luck, I say.

'You haven't been in the restaurant for a while,' Pam said during a break in the service. 'There's a new challenge: who can twist the pepper mill most over a customer's pizza without being stopped? Eight twists is the current record this week. Eight *full* twists. You must announce the attempt to one of the other staff as a witness before you try. Beat the score and you get an extra cut of the tips.'

I liked the sound of it. Frank's new pepper grinder was magnificent, almost half a metre long and made from solid wood. One turn alone was enough to unleash a storm cloud of pepper. As I weighed the grinder in my hands, I knew that this was a challenge that shouldn't be rushed and tried to formulate a strategy.

There were a couple of poor early bids for the title. Chris failed with a flat refusal, despite his ridiculous fake Italian accent. Pam was equally hopeless, dissolving into giggles as she even attempted it. Four twists were the very most she managed, and that's being kind. The tip pot was growing nicely.

My opportunity arose just after eight. Mr and Mrs Boyle, a couple of regulars, had the misfortune to cross my path. They were the ultimate niceys and perfect for my plan. After I had

22

served pizzas to their table, I returned to Pam and nodded at the pepper mill with a knowing smile. She looked at me in horror, trying to pull it away from my grasp.

'They're regulars, Evelyn.'

I grabbed the pepper mill, my eyes meeting hers. 'I'm going in.'

My efforts to distract the Boyles were *too* successful, if anything. I was chattering away about holidays, already fifteen twists of the pepper mill in, when I finally glanced down at my handiwork. It looked like a layer of volcanic ash covering Mr Boyle's pizza. Perhaps I had gone too far? All the same, I danced back to Pam with the pepper mill aloft. She shook her head in disgust. That performance would take some beating for sure. The celebrations were to be short-lived, however.

As I collected the Boyles' drinks from the bar, I was aware of a commotion in the dining area. Above the mellow backdrop of an Ed Sheeran cover was the unmistakable sound of a man choking. Edging closer, I could see Mr Boyle, red-faced and spluttering. All other heads in the restaurant were turned in his direction in silent concern. Mr Boyle coughed and gasped for breath. There was a ripple of anxious muttering from the other diners. Violent coughing again. Somebody asked where the nearest defibrillator was located, while another guy was moving in for the Heimlich.

Pam glanced my way in concern, but just as we considered calling an ambulance, Mr Boyle began to stabilise. After another minute of manic wheezing, his face returned to its previous shade of pink, and soon the familiar chattering lull of the restaurant was restored. Disaster had been averted, but I was still shaking. Pam could see the horror on my face and sent me to the kitchen while she fetched the Boyles' drinks. I was extremely grateful for the

23

reprieve, and by the time I returned, all was calm again.

I moved on to serve at another table, still reflecting on my brief flirtation with a manslaughter charge. The Attraction Abacus inappropriately sprang to mind. Recruiting now, the leaflet had said. Perhaps the universe was trying to tell me something? I think it was, because I instantly recognised the man who was sitting at the next table. It was Luke, whom I had met earlier in the street, dining alone. He was wearing jeans and a polo shirt, with his phone on the table in front of him. Had he seen the hotel logo on my badge when we had spoken that day? Did I have a stalker? Perhaps it was just a coincidence.

'I saw what you did,' Luke said.

'I'm sorry?'

'Let's just say that I'll pass on the pepper,' he said, grinning. 'Don't I recognise you?'

'No,' I replied bluntly. Either he knew that it was me, or he didn't. A stalking accusation might be deemed offensive. Plus, my timing was off that night.

'Well, you can't really answer that for me, can you?'

'Then it was a stupid question to ask,' I said.

'It wasn't a question.'

'Then why did the intonation of your voice rise at the end of the sentence?'

'I'm Australian.'

'You don't sound Australian.'

'I'm not.'

'Okay, I think I'd better go now, unless you need something else, sir.'

'I'm fine for now, thank you... Evelyn,' he said, reading my badge. 'Catch you another time.'

He had weaponised my name again, in an identical manner

24

to earlier. This time, I took it as a little clue that he *had* recognised me.

Chapter Three

Wednesday was my day off. I was still feeling bad about the Boyles, but I smiled when I thought about Luke, even though he was a dick. The recollection of the previous evening was the catalyst I needed to apply for a job at the Attraction Abacus. In fact, I even got up early. An hourly increase in pay would bring forward my Goa plan by a considerable time. If I were remotely mathematical, I could work out by exactly how long, but that part of my brain had already left early for the beach after my GCSEs.

Still wearing my pyjamas in the kitchen, I nursed a mug of tea, with a pad and pen in front of me. It had been a while since I had attended an interview, and it was a struggle to recall all the rubbish you're meant to say. Was it my imagination, but had interviews become tougher just as jobs had become crappier? Anyway, perhaps prematurely, I started to *Google* interview tips on my phone. A message flashed up from my sister.

'Dad worse. You should go and see him. A xx.'

'Which ward? xx,' I texted.

'Kipling. 3rd floor. West Wing. Don't leave it too long xx.'

It was typical of Dad's timing. He had been dying for some time, but just when I had the wind in my sails and a day off, he decided to deteriorate. I know that sounds cold, but you must appreciate our collective family's resentment towards him after his betrayal. I quickly submitted my application on the Attraction Abacus website and then decided to head to the hospital while I still had the entire day free. I threw on some clothes, grabbed some grapes from Tesco Express and was on a bus thirty minutes later.

I'd almost forgotten about masks. Fortunately, there was still one folded up in the bottom of my handbag as the bus rumbled up outside St. Cuthbert's. I ignored the falling crumbs as I hooked the mask over my ears. The West Wing was the oldest part of the hospital, constructed in an era when people were obviously keen walkers. The pine-scented corridors stretched for miles. In fact, the West Wing was all corridor and no wards.

Dad saw me, I'm certain, as I finally approached the entrance to Kipling, but he quickly looked away. It wasn't until I was just a few feet from his bed that he slowly turned his face towards me again. It was probably the most pathetic expression I had ever seen.

'Evie.'

'I heard that you're dying. I've brought you some grapes.'

I could see the smile lines above his mask as he wriggled higher on his pillow.

'Ah, grapes. The oldest hospital cliché of them all. You're better than that, Evelyn. My creative...'

'I know, your creative juices flow through my veins.'

'You've cut your hair short.'

'Yes, three years ago.'

'Are you still writing?'

'When I get the chance. Speaking of which, how long have you got left? I need to plan my leave, and I'd like to fit your funeral around a writing week.'

'Must you be *so* cruel?'

I didn't reply, pulling up a chair beside the bed. I took the grapes from the plastic bag, arranging them with the other two bunches on the cabinet. There was also some lemonade and a

27

newspaper. I positioned *my* grapes highest in the pile. They had cost me a couple of quid, after all.

'I see you've had a few visitors.'

The comment was a mistake. Dad loved an overblown analogy, and I could tell by the way he smiled and wriggled higher on his pillow that I had unwittingly triggered a new one.

'Indeed. This bed is just like the stage, Evie.'

'I should have guessed.'

'My visitors are only allowed bedside two at a time. I call them the double acts. Uncle Terry and Gill came first. I would describe them as poor stand-up. Too many hospital food jokes.'

'Nice that they showed their faces.'

'Yes,' he replied, glossing over the comment entirely. 'Sandy and Beth performed a two-hander Greek tragedy just after dinner. Somehow, despite *me* being the one dying, Beth's tears seemed to be more for herself. Their turn felt unconvincing and amateurish. It left me empty.'

'They aren't classically trained like you.'

'Yes, I should cut them some slack, I suppose,' he replied, adjusting the mask so he could breathe for a moment. 'And then your sister and her boyfriend came late evening yesterday. It was definitely a fringe performance from them. I think they may have been trying to indoctrinate me into a cult or something. She was waving a crystal on a chain above my head.'

'Ah, channelling the energy.'

'Apparently so, though I only felt indigestion. Anyway, it was quite a variety show. But you were always more of a solo performer, eh?'

'Thank you for reminding me of that, even now.'

'I just don't want you to end up alone, Evelyn, that's all.'

'It could be worse. I could marry somebody like my mother

did.'

'I'm serious.'

So was I, but it seemed too cruel to labour the point now.

'I'm quite happy, Dad. Honestly.'

'I've had a lot of time to reflect on things as I'm coming to the end. I don't want you to end up a lonely old spinster.'

'Spinster? That word doesn't even *exist* anymore. This isn't *Jane Eyre*.'

'Even so, you're pushing thirty, right? Time runs away from you before you know it. It's nice to share your life with somebody.'

I changed the subject quickly. Just because he's my dad, he thinks that he has the right to pry into my life. He lost that right twenty years ago, as far as I'm concerned. All the same, I could sense his frustration as we rattled through the standard hospital conversations. I knew that I wouldn't be able to sideline him forever. Our discussion about the view from the window was a real low point, and we both stopped bothering mid-sentence. He lowered his mask and took a sip of lemonade. I was shocked at how old he appeared without the mask, but I know hospitals have a way of making everybody look crap, so I tried to ignore it.

'Dad, I can't stay long.'

'You've only just arrived.'

'My hotel shift starts soon. I was only popping in,' I lied.

'You're too good for that job. Time waits for no-one. Trust me.'

So, we were back on this again.

'I've applied for something else.'

'That's amazing. Look, I know I haven't always been the greatest of fathers, but I've always wanted the best for you. I believe in you.'

29

'I know.'

'So, tell me all about the new job.'

'I've only just applied. Dad, I should be going.'

He ignored me, shuffling higher on the pillow again. I don't think he was really interested in the job anyway, and I should have noticed the twinkle in his eyes long before I did. There was another analogy on the way, and I hadn't moved fast enough.

'I won't hold you up much longer,' he said, taking my hand. I couldn't remember the last time he had held my hand. It felt odd, and it would have been a touching gesture if he wasn't trying to prevent me from escaping. 'I just want your opinion on something, as a writer. I've been lying here thinking that life is just like one of those weeks we had in Majorca way back then.'

'In what way?'

'Well, if you start by imagining that each day of the holiday represents a decade of your life.'

'Oh Christ, Dad.'

'The coach delivers you to the door of your hotel, and everything is new and exciting. You speak with the holiday rep, and you're going to do it all! Time moves so slowly in those first couple of days, and there's still the whole week ahead of you. The resort is your playground, and you have the energy of a young child.'

'Dad, it's getting…'

'Then, as you move towards mid-week, you realise that you need to watch your euros, and the holiday is slipping away faster. You've had a couple of massive hangovers already, so it would be nice to do something different, besides drinking by the pool, like a day trip or two. There's an excursion to "start-a-family-island", and you hop right on the boat. It's really great. More than you could ever have expected, but it hits your wallet hard.'

'I really must…'

'The holiday is just flying away now, and you only have a few days left. This really focuses your mind on what you still want to do. Flamenco night or the vineyard tour? You can't fit everything in. The trouble is you ate that dodgy paella at the Thursday evening buffet in the hotel. You have a bit of cash left, but in those last few days, you can't be more than twenty feet away from a toilet to spend it.'

As he stopped talking, I could see that he was really pleased with himself. He thought he was being funny, but I kept thinking of the carnage he had inflicted on my mum's life, so flippantly dismissed. The carnage he had inflicted on us all. It wasn't quite so amusing.

'I think that's your problem right there, Dad. Even in a week's holiday, raising a family would be more than a day trip for most people.'

A nurse saved me at that point. She needed to run a few tests, and it was the perfect opportunity to leave. I squeezed his hand and stood from the chair.

'Speak soon, Dad.'

He smiled, slowly lowering his mask for a moment. I wondered if it was the last time I would ever see him. He was probably thinking the same thing and had lowered the mask for dramatic effect, but it still hit me, nonetheless.

Despite all his failings, I realised that some part of me still believed that everything would turn out okay for our dysfunctional little family. I guess it was my inner child that clung to the hope of the most unlikely reconciliation. As I passed the other grey, gaunt faces lying in the ward, I finally realised that it would never happen. He was one of *them* now. Their holiday was over, and they had already passed through the airport departure gate.

I started to cry, and I didn't stop crying until I reached the bus stop.

A couple of weeks later, I received a text from Abby saying that Dad was worse. I couldn't bring myself to read the rest of the message and called in sick for a few days. I spent the whole time moping around in bed.

Frank made it such a hassle to claim sick pay, and I never had the qualifying days, according to his calculations. I didn't even bother this time. To be honest, I was just glad to be away from the hotel. I listened to a sad song playlist on *Spotify*, wrote a few terrible poems and ate too much cheese.

In between the bouts of melancholy, I experienced surges of fury every time I checked my emails. There was still nothing from the Attraction Abacus. I had been certain that I'd at least be offered an interview. It must have been that imbecile Luke's fault. He had darkened my name after the pepper incident. This fury was compounded by all the previous failed job applications I had ever submitted without the courtesy of a two-second rejection email in return. I worked myself up into a complete frenzy, daydreaming about an argument with an imaginary recruitment manager. As I finally stormed out of her office, knocking over the photograph of her butt-ugly kids on the desk, I almost fell out of bed.

I could take it no longer. I'm phoning them, I thought. I'm not just going to lie here and put up with this HR bullshit. Supposedly, they were too busy to respond to each application individually, but I resolved to waste even *more* of their time on the telephone so they would regret that policy. My face was still burning as I rang the Attraction Abacus number.

'Hello,' said a man's voice at the other end. He sounded surprised to receive a call. Was it Luke? I thought I recognised his tone, but I couldn't ask.

'Is that the Attraction Abacus?'

'It is, but we're not opening until next week.'

'I only wanted to know why you haven't responded to my job application,' I snapped.

'Your job application?' he mumbled. I could hear typing on a keyboard in the background. 'When did you send it?'

'About three weeks ago.'

'Three weeks ago! Are you sure?'

'Yes, on the 5th of May.'

'Right, I'm just putting you on hold for a second, madam.'

He didn't succeed with the call holding, and, after a loud beep, I could hear every word he said next.

'I knew that slimy marketing bastard had screwed the website up. I've got somebody on the line who sent in an application. I thought it was odd that we hadn't received a single one! How many others have we missed? There's only a week left.'

'That miserable little dick,' a muffled voice replied in the distance.

There was another beep, and the man was back on the call.

'Hello, madam, I *do* apologise for keeping you on hold. There appears to have been a small administrative error at our end. Are you still interested in the job?'

'Well… yes.'

'I don't suppose you're available for an interview today or tomorrow?'

'I can make it later today?'

'Two o'clock any good for you?'

33

'Yes, fine.'

'What's your name?'

'Evelyn Foster.'

A pause.

'Okay, great. We'll look forward to seeing you later.'

And that was that.

I should have asked at least half a dozen other questions on the call, but I hadn't been thinking straight. Fortunately, there was little time to worry about anything, so I just focused on making myself appear remotely presentable.

There was a café across the street from the Attraction Abacus. I arrived early for the interview and decided to grab a cup of tea first. From my seat beside the café window, I studied the exterior opposite. The Attraction Abacus had been opened on the site of a former solicitor's office, and the stencilled bedroom windows above the shop had not been replaced, still reading, "Turner and Williams". However, the shop facade below had been completely modernised, and there was a funky new sign in bright lettering. The frontage was entirely constructed from obscured glass, with a sticker on the window that read, "Looking for love? Science can help!" Beneath the words was a large cartoon of a scientist holding a test tube, with a red heart adorning the pocket of his white lab coat. Cheesy, but it didn't look like a bad place to work.

I must admit, the dating agency angle of the job appealed to me as much as the higher pay. As I have previously mentioned, the romantic side of my life had been a bit of a failure up to this point. I put this down to my relationship with my mum. There wasn't any weird *Miss Haversham*/*Estella* thing going on. She didn't poison my mind against guys, *per se*, but she didn't need to. I negatively experienced the secondary effects of *her* relationships, a bit like passive smoking, I guess. Also, Mum had always stressed that Dad had left us, not just her. I continued to carry this shared sense of rejection into my adult life. The net result was that I entered into any relationship expecting it to fail, as if there was some kind of hereditary weakness passed in our genes. Insecurity, I suppose.

As I finished my tea, I pondered the concept of dating. Did people still fall in love at first sight? Maybe I was just a product of my generation for even questioning the fact, but it seemed that dating may have replaced the falling process. Yes, you could instantly be attracted to somebody on a date, and, yes, you might also strike up a spontaneous rapport with them. You might even quickly establish that they liked you too, which must have been a crucial factor in the old falling process, unless you were a masochist. Would all of that have been enough back in 1950 when everybody was walking down the street and instantly falling in love with each other? Perhaps there was some other abstract spiritual factor at play? If so, maybe I had just missed it so far. That could be down to the information overload we have to deal with now. It could be lost in all the noise.

Spinster. Spinster. Spinster.

Dad's words came to mind again. I don't know why I let him get under my skin, but he did. My Goa plan was solid, and the last thing in the world I needed was a pretty face in my life stopping me from doing it all. With the thought of Dad, I quickly checked my messages. There was nothing new from my sister, which was hopefully positive. I would call into the hospital and visit him again later in the week, I thought.

'Evelyn?' said the guy sitting at the desk as I opened the door.

The room smelt of paint, and there were varnished pale wooden floorboards throughout. Image-wise, it tottered on the line between minimalist and derelict building. Maybe just about the right side. There was no sign of Luke. I remember feeling strangely disappointed. That was despite thinking he was an arsehole.

'Yes, sorry I'm early.'

'Not a problem. I'm Brian Asquith,' the guy said, rising and shaking my hand. 'Grab a seat in the meeting room, and I'll be with you in a minute. I'm just going to have a quick cigarette.'

Brian looked to be mid-fifties. He was tall and a few pounds overweight. His tight jeans were not flattering, and he disconcertingly hoisted them higher as he stood there. It was too much of something, though I'm not sure what. There was something familiar about his face, however. Perhaps he reminded me of an actor or something, with his slicked-backed grey hair and blue eyes? There was something else that I should have noticed at the time, but I didn't.

I settled at the desk in the meeting room while I waited. There was a single spider plant, with its leaves trailing sadly from a table beside the door. A couple of cheap prints were hanging on the walls, and I could see a certificate framed beside the only window. The room needed a few more personal touches.

There had been little time to think up to this point, but as I waited for Brian to finish his cigarette, I realised just how much I wanted the job. More to the point, I couldn't face going back to the hotel ever again. My stomach was churning by the time he entered the room, and I could feel my top lip twitching as I tried to smile. I had to say something, anything, as he took his seat in silence.

'I didn't think anybody smoked anymore,' I blurted, as Brian placed a folder on the desktop.

'Sorry?'

'I mean, it must be difficult to ignore all those horrible photographs on the packet. If there was a picture of a diabetic's foot on a chocolate bar, I'd think twice. You know, with all those toes missing.'

'Right.'

'And then there's the cost. Well, you might as well just burn the money and skip the lung cancer.'

'Okay.'

He cleared his throat, opened a folder and took out a pen. The functioning part of my brain stopped me at that point. I breathed deeply. Brian asked me questions about my background, gradually coaxing me back from the ledge. He covered my employment history, which didn't take long, and then tried to be polite about my degree. (Wow, the University of Portsmouth! Portsmouth's such a great place for a day out.) My lip was twitching less now, but I didn't like the way he was scribbling secretive notes. He noticed me trying to read them, holding the folder closer.

'My colleague will be joining us shortly, but I'll run through some background information now, if okay with you?'

'Yes, of course.'

'So, what do you know about the Attraction Abacus?'

'Only what I read on the website. From what I can gather, this is dating with a difference. It sounds intriguing, applying science to find an ideal match.'

'Dating with a difference. I like that,' Brian said, scribbling again, 'and yes, the matching is all based on science. I'm a scientist. That's my diploma from the British Society of Relationship Theory,' he added, gesturing to the certificate

37

mounted on the wall.

I chuckled, thinking that he was being ironic, but then I realised he was deadly serious just in time, turning the laugh into a cough. My sister had been awarded similar diplomas in numerous alternative therapies. The qualifications invariably involved a few hours of online lessons with a spurious institution in Milton Keynes and then parting with a hundred quid, with a worthless piece of paper in return.

'I see. What exactly *is* the science behind this?'

'An excellent question. At this point, I need you to sign this for us to continue,' he said, passing me a piece of paper from his folder. 'It's a confidentiality agreement.'

'How can I sign this when I don't know what you're going to say next?'

'What do you mean?'

'Well, you could be about to say anything, and I wouldn't be able to tell anybody.'

'Evelyn, this is standard business practice. You are about to be privy to some highly confidential information. It's only about the company.'

'I see.'

Reluctantly, I signed at the bottom. They hadn't even asked me to sign anything like this at the doctor's surgery when I started my summer job. Nothing could be more confidential than medical records, surely.

'Okay,' said Brian, eyeing my signature on the page as I returned it. 'The Attraction Abacus uses a highly complex algorithm to match our singles together. This algorithm is valuable company intellectual property, hence the confidentiality. I'm currently seeking venture capital to roll the Abacus out at scale. The shop here is only the beginning, Evelyn.

If you were to be offered the job, you would be coming in at the ground level of something big. This company is going national, potentially international.'

I was concerned now. It all sounded exactly like the world of hare-brained schemes that I had grown up in with my dad, or even at Frank's hotel.

We were disturbed by a knock at the meeting room door. When I glanced up, Luke entered the room. He was wearing a pair of black jeans and a blue short-sleeved shirt. There was a notepad in his hand. His hair was pushed to one side, in that trademark messy style. I noticed that his stubble was thicker today and wondered why I had bothered to dress up for the interview. Luke smiled at us both before taking a seat at the table. 'Sorry, I'm late.'

'This is Luke,' Brian said, giving Luke a little wink.

'Hello… Evelyn,' Luke said, pretending to read my name from his notepad. The joke was getting a little old, but at least he enjoyed it again. I shook his extended hand. It was surprisingly cold and clammy. 'Please just carry on as you were. I'll catch up.'

'So, how does the Abacus work?' I asked Brian, trying to ignore Luke's intrusion. It was trickier to concentrate knowing that he was listening.

'Good question. The algorithm computes an eligibility factor for each single, based on multiple criteria. We then compare this eligibility factor against other singles to find a good match. The premise is that you match with other singles within your factor range.'

'What kind of criteria are you talking about?'

'It's highly complex, but age, physical appearance, financial circumstances and personality traits are all examples. The point is that *everything* is factored in together to produce one overall score.'

'So, an old, ugly, poor person would score low?'

'Yes, well, no… not exactly. It's much more subtle than that, but you appreciate the general idea,' Brian said. I made the mistake of glancing at Luke, who was smirking at his notepad.

'How do you quantify somebody's physical appearance?'

'Science does it for us. We use scanners and facial recognition software. Symmetrical faces are considered more attractive.'

'This all sounds a bit Darwinian to me.'

Brian didn't seem to know what I meant, and I wondered if I had the right guy anyway and quickly shut up again. There was awkward silence for a moment.

'You're currently working at Francesco's, correct?' said Luke, looking at his notes.

'That's right.' He knew damn well that I was.

'How do you think your skills and experience from the hotel would transfer to the Abacus?' Luke's attempt to pose a serious question made it harder to keep a straight face. I just about kept it together.

'Well, I'm used to working under pressure to tight deadlines.'

'That's great,' said Brian, writing in his notepad.

'Definitely,' Luke agreed, pursing his lips. 'And how would you rate your customer service skills?'

Brian was still writing, but I had to look twice at Luke before I realised what he was doing. Luke was pretending to grind an imaginary pepper mill over his notepad, just out of Brian's eyeline.

'I like to think that my customer service skills are excellent,'

I replied, ignoring his gesticulations. 'I've worked with all kinds of people. Some are definitely more awkward to handle than others. You just learn how to deal with them,' I added, now smirking at Luke.

'Very true,' said Brian, finally looking up, 'but you have no specific dating agency experience?'

'Not as such. I am aware of the dating... scene.'

'The dating scene,' Luke repeated, nodding like an arsehole. 'How exactly are you aware of it?'

'Well, I'm not an active... participant, but I have friends... who use dating apps. I've learnt an awful lot from them.'

'You sound like a real expert,' Luke said. Piss-taker. Even Brian gave him a sideways glance. I sensed the interview was going badly now. Luke was scribbling away at the notepad.

'What did you just write?' I asked Luke.

'Just a note.'

'What does it say?'

Luke covered the words with his hands.

'So, why do you want the job?' Brian asked, knocking me out of my stride. Such a simple, obvious question, but my mind was suddenly blank. I'd practised which crayon colour I would be and the three things I'd bring to a desert island, but this instantly flummoxed me. Disastrously, I could only think of the truth.

'It pays a pound more an hour than the hotel, and I hate my job there.'

'This is minimum wage, Evelyn. It can't be a pound more an hour than your current job.'

'You're offering the minimum wage from *next* April in the ad, Brian.'

A silent pause.

'Oh, I see.'

I had never seen a human body actually deflate before. Brian wasn't writing anymore. I took this as a sign that I'd completely blown it. It was liberating in a way, and my mouth could move freely again.

'A bit of advice, Brian. What the pros do is take young people on as an apprentice. It's nearly *half* the hourly rate, and then you just ditch them at the end and get a new one.'

'You seem to know a lot about this.'

'I've been exploited on multiple occasions.'

Brian put the pad down completely now and folded his arms. He glanced from Luke to me. I felt like it was the first time he had *really* looked at me.

'In the spirit of our newfound... honesty, there is something else I would like to ask you,' Brian said, turning his head as if somebody else might be listening. 'There has been some early criticism of the Attraction Abacus from our test users. It seems that we're not catering for *everybody* quite correctly.'

'What do you mean?'

'Well, there are some... questions that we should be asking... for *certain* people.'

'Oh! Are these around gender identity or sexual orientation by any chance?'

'Yes.'

'Which one?'

'Both... all of it. We seem to have overlooked certain important *factors* in the algorithm. Could you help?'

'Well, I could, but it really isn't that complicated. Simply put, you just mustn't be a jerk. Have an open mind about things.'

'Have an open mind and don't be a jerk.'

As Brian looked at Luke and pondered the thought, I could

see the potential issues right there.

Chapter Four

I was offered the job the following day. It was a complete surprise, and I wondered if I had a marketing guy somewhere to thank for screwing up the website. I must have remained on a candidate list of one, given my interview performance. Or could it be that Luke had fought my corner, despite his attempts to trip me up? Either way, I had the job, and Frank was livid when I called the hotel to resign.

'It's poor form giving me four days' notice, Evelyn.'

'The job cropped up at the last minute.

'Jobs don't just "crop up". You apply for them. It's a big mistake leaving Francesco's now. The pizzeria business is flying.'

'I'm sorry, it can't be helped, Frank. I'm zero-hours anyway, and you haven't even written the rota for next week.'

'That's totally irrelevant. You're management. Don't expect a great reference.'

'I don't, but…'

The line was dead before I could continue. If Frank didn't owe me my final wages, I would have bitten back immediately. Fortunately, he had hung up just in time. Never burn your bridges, even the rickety rope ones over a cesspit.

I visited Dad again that evening. He had picked up again after his previous downturn. Our conversation was practically a replay of the first one, though he did seem pleased that I had been offered the job. I wasn't certain if I would visit again. It was difficult to know what else either of us could gain from the experience. He had been an absent father for over half of my life and made his choices. I had turned up at the hospital to say goodbye, despite it. That was surely the best he could have hoped for. It was clear that this could be a protracted ending, and we were just diluting the emotion now when we met. My mum still hadn't been to see him at all, so I didn't feel guilty. Well, that's what I tried to tell myself at least, but he still made me feel that way.

I knew the only way to get my final pay was to go to the hotel and collect it in person. I disliked the idea of facing Frank, but I needed the money, and there was no way that he would ever make the effort to post it. In fact, he would actively avoid doing so. I tried to time my visit so that my favourite co-workers would be on their break. It would be a chance to say goodbye to them properly.

It hadn't been that long since I had last worked at the hotel, but the place already felt strangely alien as I walked through reception. The smell was even different, and I finally realised that Frank's coffee shop was up and running. I hadn't considered the rota changes, and there was an unfamiliar sound coming from the old storage room that we used for our breaks. I realised too late that it was a baby's cry. Frozen in the doorway and unable to retreat now that I had been seen, I edged inside. Misha had brought her newborn son to show everyone, and the collected staff were all grinning at me as if they had been lobotomised as I entered.

After a fleeting conversation about my imminent exit (I was pleased about that part), the conversation refocused on Misha's new arrival, Noah. I tried to stay out of the way, but it seemed that we *all* had to test drive the baby, with the blanket-wrapped bundle passing from arms to arms. Despite my protestations, I was forced to complete the circuit. I had no little songs or silly voices to call upon like the others, and I just stood there rigidly, too self-conscious to even jiggle. I could feel everyone's eyes on me and began to sweat. There was a doom-dream brewing.

'There... you're a natural,' Pam said. If it wasn't Pam saying it, I would swear that she was taking the piss. It was difficult to imagine anything more unnatural than how I felt at that precise moment, and I continued to sweat more, holding the baby as if it were dynamite.

The doom dream is taking hold.

I nurse the baby in my arms, lifting it slowly higher. The others have stopped talking now, with a few chuckling nervously.

The smiles gradually slip from their faces altogether as I lift the baby higher, above my shoulders now.

Nobody is smiling at all when I hoist the bundle completely aloft above my head.

'Let's see what you think about these natural instincts,' I cackle, before launching the baby straight across the room.

Okay, so I wasn't serious.

But this was the exact problem with a doom-dream. I was mentally lured towards the worst possible scenario when I was uncomfortable. Crucially, having considered the totally inappropriate, I started to analyse exactly what was *stopping* me from manifesting it. I visualised the idea in my brain, and all the little neurons and receptors relaying the messages to my arms. If any of them screwed up and didn't realise this was just an inappropriate thought, I was in trouble.

Past performance is no guarantee of future results.

I tensed my forearms to reassure myself that I was still at the wheel. All was good. Thankfully, Noah started to cry, and Misha

46

took him from my arms at that point. I think he knew.

It's not that I don't like babies. They all look scrunched up and the same to me, but I don't mind them. It just takes me a while to get used to anything, and I like to do it privately and in my own time. I even thought that Bruno the Pomeranian was arrogant when I first met him, but I grew to appreciate his little swagger when we spent some quality time together. In any case, it was over, though my legs were still shaking.

Frank's face was beetroot purple when I entered his office. He hated doing the rota, or "effing" rota as he preferred to call it, so it wasn't the best timing. I was so wired with adrenaline after the baby-thing that I didn't care. He could see the craziness in my eyes and backed off.

'Here,' he said, tossing me a sealed envelope across the desk. I was amazed that he had already sorted my wages out unprompted. 'There's no sick pay in there. You didn't have the hours, and you were also an hour short on your last shift.'

So, that was the reason. He thought that he was stiffing me on a bit of money and had sealed it up quickly before I could argue. I never believed I'd see another penny from him anyway.

'Thanks for all the good times, Frank.'

'Whatever,' he muttered, without even looking up from the rota.

It wasn't the most touching leaving speech I had ever heard, but I grabbed my cash and was out of there.

I kept a photograph of a beach in Goa in my purse. If I were ever dispirited, I'd take it out to focus on the plan. I had it in front of me now on the plastic table surface. I was sitting in the café across the street from the Attraction Abacus. It was my first day, and I was early again. As I stared at the photograph, stirring my

47

tea, it occurred to me just how hopeless the interview had been, on all fronts. I hadn't asked what I would be required to do in the job, and Brian and Luke hadn't told me either.

I'm fairly computer literate. I can find my way around a spreadsheet, and I use word processors for my writing all the time, so it wasn't technology that concerned me. I guess it was just fear of the unknown. I felt good in my new clothes, though. I had bought a new skirt and top, and it was nice to think that I would even be able to keep them clean, unlike the hotel job. I'd also spent a bit more time on my make-up, something I rarely bothered with at the hotel.

Brian was smoking outside the Attraction Abacus as I crossed the road. I swear he was checking me out until he belatedly realised who I was and stumbled away from the wall, waving awkwardly. His panicked smile dissolved into a coughing fit, and I waited for him to regain his breath.

'Great to see you again, Evelyn. Grab a seat and I'll be in soon.'

There had been a furniture reshuffle since I had last visited. The room where I had been interviewed was straight ahead of me, though it had a new sign over the door that read, "Consultation Room". To the left of it was a desk with a large leather chair behind it. There was a jacket hanging over the backrest and a mug of coffee on the table. I assumed that was Brian's spot. To the right, there were two other desks, one directly beside the partitioned wall of the consultation room and another one in front of it, closer to the entrance of the office. Luke was sitting at the latter. He glanced up as I entered, grinning as always.

'You got the job then,' Luke said.

'Nobody was more surprised than me.'

'Your comprehensive knowledge of the dating scene probably swayed it.'

'Funny,' I said, advancing into the room. 'I don't suppose it was any thanks to you.'

'I was your biggest advocate.'

'I sensed that during my interview. Is that my desk over there?'

'That's the one,' Luke said as I passed his desk. There was an impressive illustration open on his screen. It was a picture of a woman lying on a riverbank with her hand trailing in the water. The screen was turned slightly so that I could see it, and Luke made a point of tweaking part of the background as I passed.

'Did you draw that?' I asked.

'Oh yeah, it's nothing. Just a quick thing.'

'Yet, you made certain that I could see it.'

'I just happened to be working on it,' he said, defensively. 'Why would I want *you* to see it?'

I bit my tongue. It felt good to see Luke squirm a bit at least, and he was definitely showing off.

Brian joined me shortly after, still reeking of cigarettes. He spent the first hour of the day trying to get the laptop on my desk to work. There were only four laptops in the whole place, but they didn't seem to like talking to each other much. As a message finally passed between our screens, it felt akin to the moment Alexander Graham Bell made his first telephone call. Brian certainly considered it an equal achievement.

My role was to be quite varied. Some of the information for the Abacus singles was captured online. Ultimately, there would be ways of obtaining everything online, but this wasn't possible until investment was secured, and the requisite technology could be implemented, so Brian said. I asked what would happen to my job at that point. He assured me that I'd be a director of a major tech company at that stage, but I just heard redundant. (I apologise for my negative thinking, but that was bitter experience guiding me.)

For now, the singles could complete some basic details online, and then they would pop into our office to complete the other parts. The entire application could be managed on-site if you were old school.

All on-site information was collected in the consultation room behind closed doors, and lots of new equipment had been installed within. There was a camera, mounted on a mini tripod, which was connected to the laptop on the table beside it. This was to analyse faces. There was also a set of scales and a height-measuring stadiometer adjacent to the window. I would later discover how controversial their use would prove to be, second only to the credit checks. There were also personality tests and aptitude tests to complete. These were neatly stacked in boxes beside the spider plant, which looked like it hadn't been watered since my last visit.

I would collate all this information, keying it into the central database, and then the Attraction Abacus algorithm would calculate an eligibility factor overnight. The system would process singles in the same factor range, spewing out matches. There was also an option to allow the algorithm to select a suitable date activity, based on the psychometric profiles of the singles. It all sounded very clever. During the morning, Brian dropped the bombshell that I would be reporting to Luke. I guess the job couldn't be perfect.

I had brought cookies for my first day. There was a specialist bakery, Cosmic Cookies, just along the street, and I had splashed out on a nice assortment. I wandered towards Luke's desk. This

50

time, he had a spreadsheet open on the screen.

'It's the Abacus project plan,' Luke said, noticing that I was looking. He seemed to think that I was interested in anything that he did.

'I don't suppose you have scheduled any cookie-eating time in there?' I asked, offering him the box.

'Are they from Cosmic?'

'Yep.'

'Long shot, but is there a pistachio and dark chocolate in there?'

'There absolutely is. My favourite.'

'Mine too,' Luke said, looking genuinely shocked. He stopped short of taking one, withdrawing his hand. 'Actually, I won't. I have a big gym session tonight.'

'I didn't have you down as a gym bunny.'

'What do you mean by that?'

'Take it as you will,' I said, carrying the box to Brian's desk. Brian was not so self-disciplined and had demolished most of a raspberry surprise while I stood there.

'Thanks, Evelyn,' he said, crumbs falling from his mouth. 'I wanted to ask you something. Are you doing anything tonight?'

'No… why?'

'Well, I thought it would be good to take you out for a welcoming meal.'

'That's a really nice thought, thank you.'

It wasn't what I felt like doing, but it seemed rude to say no. Also, Frank had never bought me a thing, so it made a pleasant change.

I headed straight out after work with Brian. Luke agreed to meet us there later after his gym session. The Thirsty Donkey was a gastropub with a pricey reputation. The atmosphere in the low-beamed bar area was exactly what Frank had been reaching for at the hotel. It was minimalist in design, with bare wood and stripped-back furnishings. My personal scientific theory: the prices charged in a bar are inversely proportional to the amount of stuff inside them. There were some quirky features throughout, with donkey-themed accessories and fittings scattered about, like the long-eared salt and pepper pots grinning at me from the tables. Brian wasted no time in ordering cocktails, and I began to relax halfway down a Peachy Keen.

'So, how did you hear about the job? I forgot to ask at the interview,' Brian said.

'Luke gave me a flyer in the street.'

'Really? The canvassing actually worked then,' he said, looking surprised. 'How are you getting along with Luke?'

'Fine.'

'He's a little cocky, isn't he?'

'I guess so.'

'A bit of a dick too.'

'Yeah, maybe,' I said, laughing.

'He's standing right behind you now,' Brian said, nodding over my left shoulder. I laughed again, thinking that Brian was joking and didn't even bother turning around. By the time I realised he was serious, Luke had joined us at the table.

'Here he is,' Brian said. 'Your supervisor, my son, and absolute dick, like you rightly say, Evelyn.'

Luke was grinning at me. I didn't know who to be angrier with. Maybe myself. Why hadn't I noticed the family resemblance before? Their features were so similar. Both men had blue eyes and the same-shaped noses that were long and angular. Brian's hair was grey, but his hairline was identical to

Luke's, high and bell-shaped on his forehead. Luke's hair was still dark, and he wore it differently, pushing his fringe to one side in that grunge style, but the underlying similarities were obvious now. And the stupid grins… yes, those stupid grins were the real giveaway, always smirking in anticipation of the next joke. How had I missed that?

I managed to regain my composure and make polite conversation. Our glasses were soon empty, and Brian immediately ordered three more cocktails. I offered to pay for them, but he declined. I sensed that Brian liked a drink, and he seemed like a man in a hurry.

'How was your first day?' Brian asked, with a rogue slice of orange tumbling against his teeth as he raised his glass. He was drinking an Old Fashioned from a tumbler, and the orange and ice seemed a constant hazard, sliding suddenly towards his mouth every time he tipped the glass. It made me nervous.

'Great, thank you.'

'Glad you've settled in okay.'

'What do you honestly think of the Attraction Abacus as a concept?' Luke asked.

Honestly. The word was my Achilles' heel, especially after a few drinks. My sister, Abby, said that my refusal to tell "little" lies was vanity disguised as integrity. It made me feel better about myself, whereas I should consider the feelings of the other person.

'Yeah, it could work,' I said, dunking a slice of peach below the surface of my drink with the stirrer. It was the best I could come up with, and I didn't want to meet Luke's eyes.

'Yes, but what do you *think* of it?'

Luke was really asking now, and I couldn't avoid revealing at least some of the truth.

'Well, there are aspects that I find a little… cold.'

'Cold, in what way?'

'Okay,' I said, setting my drink aside for a moment. 'The concept of the Abacus is fine, but just because somebody doesn't fit exactly within your eligibility range doesn't mean that you couldn't have a perfectly good relationship with them. I mean, I know that you run all the personality tests and stuff, but that's not everything,' I added. 'There's more to relationships than just matchmaking, Luke.'

'You mean love?' Luke said.

'Yes… I guess.'

I wasn't sure at what point I had become Danielle Steel, but I now found myself defending the unlikeliest of corners. It was probably just the cocktails talking, and I really shouldn't have drunk them on an empty stomach.

'So, we are talking about romantic love, Evelyn? The kind where you meet the one person you are destined to spend your life with, from a global population of eight billion people.'

'Well, maybe not just one.'

'As touching as that is,' Luke smirked, 'it's a long shot that most people will get that lucky. The truth is that finding the right person is a numbers game, and we are just narrowing down the field to make the search a little easier.'

'By eliminating people based on some arbitrary measure. That's harsh.'

Luke laughed. 'Life *is* harsh, and nothing is arbitrary. Your eligibility factor *is* a reality, whether you like it or not. People have unrealistic expectations when it comes to dating. We're approaching the dating scene from a totally new angle. It's not just about what you want, but also what you're offering.'

I laughed. 'Offering?'

'Yes, offering! If you're young and good-looking, you only need to turn up. Every relationship is yours to blow, but year by year you become less of a catch. That's life. But you can compensate in other ways, by being loaded, smart or successful. Maybe possess a sparkling personality,' Luke grinned, obviously referring to himself. 'The Abacus quantifies these little nuances and takes *everything* into account. It will make the search for that one in eight billion a little more realistic for all you incurable romantics.'

'Maybe.'

'Definitely. And remember, there are things we can *all* do to rank higher,' Luke said, draining his drink. 'Self-improvement can boost any Abacus score.'

'How do you mean?'

'Studying or learning new skills to enhance your career prospects, for example. Keeping fit or looking after yourself in other ways. Every day is a new opportunity to improve.'

'How inspiring!'

'There must be ways that you think *you* could improve?' he said, ignoring my smirk.

'I'm sure there are plenty.'

'So, why not be the best you?'

'Why not indeed,' I said, turning away. That was more than enough of Luke's life coaching shit, thank you.

I ordered a glass of water. There were still ten minutes before we would eat, and I knew that there was a danger I would become too outspoken. I still couldn't help confronting Luke on some of his views, and eventually, his condescension was just too much.

'Let's be honest, Luke. Guys are the real problem when it comes to dating.'

'In what way?' Luke asked.

'I think that there are three kinds of guys. There are those who blatantly think with their dicks. Honest, but gone in the morning. There are those who pretend to like you but are soon on their way if a better offer comes along. The worst kind, in my opinion. And the third kind, who really do like you. The rarest kind.'

'Interesting,' Luke said. 'I tend to think that there are two kinds of *people*. Those who pigeon-hole others and those who don't,' he added, sitting back in his chair, arms folded. Luke was literally hugging himself. He was trying to shame me, but the smug little knob was blind to irony.

'Two kinds, huh? Guess you are in the first category then, like me.'

Brian found this hilarious. Even Luke managed a smile. I drained the rest of my water triumphantly.

'So, how would you improve the Abacus?' Luke asked, serious now. Brian was sitting back, watching me hang myself with the rope that Luke was letting out.

'I would soften things.'

'What does that even mean, Evelyn?

'Well, the Abacus can feel like you're training for an Olympic event. Finding somebody that you care about isn't a competition, like you make it sound. It's not about scoring points. When we go on a date, we all turn up with our own little check cards. Does our date smoke, tick or cross? Does our date have tattoos, tick or cross? Does our date like dogs, tick or cross? The point is, there are no rights or wrongs. These are all personal preferences, and there are different reasons why we make our choices.'

'So?'

'So, how can there be an absolute score that fits everyone? The answers to these check cards are arbitrary and personal to each of us, and that's exactly what dates are for. To work through our personal check cards,' I added, gaining in confidence. 'But I think that we're *really* looking for something else.'

'What's that?' Luke asked.

'I don't think it's the person who completes our check card that counts. Your self-improvement stuff is all very well too, but what we're *really* looking for is the person who makes us want to tear up our check card and toss it away over our shoulder.'

Luke just looked at me in a confused way. Numbskull, I thought.

Chapter Five

As I began to recall snippets of the conversations the next morning, I curled deeper beneath my duvet. I had to face Luke at work after all my ranting, whether he had deserved it or not.

Luke was already sitting at his desk when I arrived at the office. I smiled awkwardly as he glanced up from his screen and took my seat. Neither of us spoke. Brian emerged from the consultation room a few moments later. He was wearing a suit and carrying a laptop case. His hair was sticking up at angles from the back of his head. He looked a little worse for wear, and I remembered the round of brandies he had ordered at the end of the meal. Thankfully, I had declined one.

'I'm heading out now,' Brian said, turning towards Luke. 'I'll be in London for meetings until two. There are a few punters coming into the office this morning. I talked Evelyn through the basics yesterday, but it would be helpful if you could shadow her today.'

'I have an essay I really need to complete later.'

'Just today.'

'Okay, fine,' Luke replied, glancing in my direction.

'I appreciate it, mate,' Brian said, disappearing through the front door.

The office felt doubly quiet in Brian's absence. Luke sighed and then rose from his desk, walking towards me. I pretended not to notice him, studying the screen in front of me. He dragged a chair beside my desk, and I could ignore him no longer.

58

'Just a quick word, Evelyn.'

'Yes, sure.'

'I can talk you through a few things today. It isn't that complicated.'

'Thank you.'

'But there's something else.'

'What's that?'

'It's difficult to phrase this, but here goes… Brian is passionate about this all working out. You know, the Attraction Abacus and everything.'

'Yes, I noticed.'

'But he can be a little blinkered in his thinking at times.'

'In what way?'

'Well, he has put a lot into this, personally. There's a great deal at stake for him, and it's not all financial. He *wants* this to succeed and can be slightly blind-sided by his optimism at times.'

'Okay.'

'These meetings with the investors today aren't the first ones he has attended, if you know what I mean?'

'I think so, but how can I help?'

'Just watch out for him, that's all,' he said, his blue eyes studying me across the desk. 'You know, like last night. He's generous, but the investment he is anticipating might never materialise. Everything is coming from his own pocket for now.'

'I'm not a free-loader, Luke. Brian invited me to a welcoming meal.'

'I know. I'm not saying that you are.'

'Then what are you saying?'

'Just watch out for him, that's all. I won't be around all the time.'

I didn't know how to reply, so I just sat there fuming. It was clear to me what Luke was implying, and I wished I'd never gone out for the stupid meal. He was definitely an arsehole.

Luke was on the telephone after I had dealt with my last customer that afternoon. I tried to ignore his raised voice, but the office was silent. He was in dispute with somebody called Alice, and from his tone, I doubted if she was a customer.

'I'm trying my best,' Luke said. 'I can't change my metabolism.'

Muffled complaining.

'Alice, please...'

More moaning.

'I can't talk about this at the moment.'

A long tirade, with the voice at the other end getting louder.

'I'll call you later.'

Shouting.

'Alice, I'll call you later.'

Silence at the other end now. Alice had obviously hung up, but Luke still held the phone to his ear. Where was his swagger now? I found it hilarious. He was even laughing, trying to maintain the illusion of an ongoing call.

'I'm sure we can sort this all out. Yes, miss you too. Speak soon,' he said, finally lowering the receiver. He was quiet for a moment.

'That's nice,' I said.

'What's nice?'

'Missing somebody like that.'

'It was a private conversation,' Luke said, haughtily. He sat at his desk in silence for a moment, and I tried to look as busy as I could, entering the last few customer details into the system. I

60

wondered if I had overstepped the mark, but if you dished it out, you should be able to take it, in my opinion.

Luke disappeared into the kitchen area shortly after. He had a nice bum, I noticed. A pity about everything else. When he returned, he was carrying two mugs on a tray, with a familiar paper bag beside them. He brought them to my desk, setting them down beside my laptop. He then pulled up a chair, and I pretended to jump as if I hadn't realised that he was there again. I was becoming a better actor than Dad.

'I just wanted to apologise, Evelyn. A pistachio and dark chocolate peace offering,' he said, handing me a Cosmic Cookies' bag. He must have bought them lunchtime.

'Oh, thank you. Apologise for what exactly? There's so much to choose from.'

He laughed. 'When I spoke about Brian earlier.'

'That was nothing,' I smiled, trying to sound as dismissive as I could manage, but still inwardly furious.

'I'm just protective of my dad.'

'Naturally.'

'I know that I have joked around with you a bit too, but you were the best person for this job.'

'Please don't compliment me. I won't know where I am. Plus, I was the only applicant, if I recall correctly.'

'True. Anyway, I hope that's how you like your coffee,' Luke said as he walked away. I just smiled.

Do you ever do things that you can't explain?

That mug of coffee was the polar opposite of my taste, and normally, I would say so immediately. I'm famous, notorious even, in my social circles for being blunt. Tea is my drink of choice, but *if* I can stomach coffee, I take it black, and this was an insipid shade of cream. Maybe I felt sorry for Luke. Maybe it *was* his flattery. More likely, it was because I couldn't remember the last time anybody had made me anything. Whatever the reason, I drank milky coffee for weeks afterwards at the Abacus and didn't say a word.

Brian looked frazzled when he bundled through the door, just before four. He smiled when he saw our expectant faces, lowering his laptop case onto the floor.

'How did it go?' Luke asked.

'Excellent... really, excellent. I think there's a strong chance of serious investment coming in. These things obviously take time, but the seeds were most certainly sown today.'

I had heard enough crap in my short life to know when somebody was spinning a yarn. As I glanced at Luke, it was difficult to imagine that he was fooled. Neither of us commented, and we settled down to our work. Brian seemed impressed with how I had handled my earlier appointments. I had also cleared a large part of the keying backlog, and in Brian's words, "had really hit the ground running".

Half an hour later, another customer came through the door. I was beginning to wind down to go home, but I rose from my chair with as much enthusiasm as I could muster. As often was the case, the customer was a man, probably a similar age to me, and he appeared nervous.

'It's okay, Evelyn,' Brian said, stepping towards him. 'I'll look after Toby.' It was a bad sign that the head of the next giant global tech corporation knew his customers by their first name, but I was just relieved that I didn't have to deal with Toby with the other two watching. Brian closed the consultation room door behind them.

As I settled back to my data entry, I realised that the

consultation room was not the haven of confidentiality I had presumed. I could hear every word being spoken through the partitioned wall.

'So, how can I help?' Brian said.

'It's not working out.'

'You can't rush these things. Finding the perfect person takes time. Did you try some of the things we suggested?'

'Yes, but I'm not meeting the right kind of women.'

'This is science. I'm a scientist, Toby. The Attraction Abacus algorithm has matched you. You are *absolutely* meeting the right kind of women. Why do you think that this isn't the case?'

A pause.

'They don't seem to like me much.'

There was another pause before Brian replied.

'I'm sure that isn't true. Look, you're one of our earliest customers. You were part of the trial. I shouldn't do this, but I want to help you out. Between you and me, we collect feedback from our dates. It's confidential, so I can't share everything, but I can give you some pointers.'

'I'd really appreciate it.'

'Okay,' said Brian. There was silence for a moment. I guessed that he was accessing the system. 'Right, here we go. One of your dates mentions that "he", that's you, Toby, "dropped the L-bomb two minutes after we took our seats at Wetherspoons."'

'I thought that she was perfect girlfriend material.'

'Okay, another date says you took her to meet your mother straight from your outing. You proposed to another date the first time you met her. Okay, okay, there's a recurring theme here,' Brian said, coughing. 'Let's forget the Attraction Abacus for a moment. I'm going to give you some man-to-man advice with

63

some sound reasoning behind it.'

'Appreciated, Brian.'

'You're trying too hard. Dating is not about effort. In fact, it's the complete opposite.'

'What do you mean?

'I'm a scientist, Toby. This is a simple mathematical equation. If a woman is into you, you can do no wrong. Conversely, if a woman is not into you, you can do no right. Therefore, Q.E.D., there is *never* any point in making an effort.'

Toby considered these pearls of wisdom in silence for a moment.

'What if a woman isn't sure if she's into you?'

A pause.

'We're talking about *love* here, Toby! What's wrong with you young guys? We're talking *Jack* and *Rose* on the *Titanic*. Nobody is giving up their floating debris if they aren't sure if they're into you.'

'Yeah, I guess.'

'Just cool it down a bit, and rein in the proposals. I'm sure things will start to work out.'

I was just packing up my things to leave when another figure loomed behind the glass door of the Attraction Abacus. The previous customer, Toby, had left ten minutes earlier, buoyed by Brian's "insightful" guidance. Brian had stayed in the consultation room to run through some figures. He had specifically asked not to be disturbed. Luke had left the office a few minutes after. He said that he would be back later, but there was little option other than to deal with this new visitor myself.

The young woman who walked through the door appeared irritated. She was probably mid-twenties, thin, and annoyingly attractive. She reminded me of a generic French actress — tall, dark, uniformly chic and aloof. The illusion was shattered when she opened her mouth, and a guttural South London accent filled the air.

'Where's Luke?'

'He just popped out for a while.'

'Where to?' she snapped.

'He didn't say.'

The woman huffed, slamming her designer handbag down on Luke's desk. She was keying at her mobile now, and while she waited for her call to be answered, she eyed me up and down. Her stare was ridiculously overt, and I didn't like the way she lingered on my shoes, finally sniffing dismissively.

'Perfect,' she moaned, giving up on the call. Her attention was drawn to the empty Cosmic Cookie bag on Luke's desk. 'For God's sake,' she said, picking it up between her thumb and finger in disgust, before dropping the bag in the bin. She fussed with her handbag for a moment before staring at me again. 'You must be the new girl.'

'Yes, I'm Evelyn. Pleased to…'

'Tell him I'll be back in five minutes.'

Before I could reply, the woman had turned on her heels and was strutting away to leave. As the door slammed behind her, I knew that it must have been Alice. It was all too easy to put a face to the whine at the end of the phone. I certainly didn't feel inclined to hang around to relay her message, so I scribbled a note on a piece of paper and propped it on Luke's laptop before leaving.

I've heard people say that we create our own monsters. It's easy to project a personality onto somebody else because of the way they make us feel, or the way we suppose them to be. Maybe

I *was* projecting, or I remember this introduction more negatively than it played out, but I don't think so. Alice spoke fluent bitch.

Chapter Six

I was settling into a nice groove at work. I enjoyed dealing with the singles when they came into the office and had developed my own little script for talking to them. I told the same jokes, about the same things, and received the same responses. It was incredible how similar human beings were when it really came down to it. Only the Abacus algorithm picked up on the differences.

Brian was often absent for large parts of the day in meetings. In the evenings, he mysteriously locked himself away in the consultation room. There seemed to be an awful lot of figures to look at. I had directed him to a few websites where he could brush up on his diversity language, and he did seem to be trying to learn more. He was very pleased with himself as he mastered new terminology, often dropping the odd word into our conversations. In fact, he was a little too pleased with himself, to the point of sanctimonious — the Abacus Renaissance man.

Luke asked to speak to me in the consultation room when he arrived. It was unusual behaviour, and he fidgeted in the chair opposite me when we took our places within it.

'This is a tad awkward,' he mumbled.

'Should I be worried?'

'Well, the Abacus is a little off target from our projections. The investment meetings to date haven't gained any traction as you know…'

'You mean the company is going bust?'

'The company is not going bust, Evelyn.'

'So, you're sacking me.'

'Nobody is being sacked.'

'Cutting my hours then.'

'No, but there is something.'

It was difficult to look at Luke, and I focused on the spider plant across the room. It was wilting again. Surely, I was indispensable just as a caretaker?

'What kind of something?'

'This is the awkward part,' he said, rubbing his chin. 'You may have noticed from your data entry that we're receiving a little bit of negative feedback from the guys about the number of dates that the Abacus is arranging for them.'

I nodded in silence. I *had* noticed there were more males on the books than females. I wasn't sure if this was a consequence of Brian's unconventional marketing techniques or something else, but this imbalance was a common complaint in a lot of the guy's feedback. Luke cleared his throat before continuing.

'It seems we have a... temporary ratio issue, with not enough women on our books.'

'So?'

'So, I wondered... well, we wondered if you had any friends who would consider going on a few dates? Perhaps... even... you might... consider it?'

'What!'

'Just dates,' he blurted, folding his fingers on the desk. 'Obviously, there is no obligation to become romantically involved with anybody.'

'That's a very generous concession, Luke!'

'This is difficult,' he said, fidgeting in his chair. 'We only need a little help to keep things on track until...'

'Until the investment arrives,' I interrupted. The sarcasm in my voice was barely masked.

'Yes, until the investment arrives. But even without the investment, we would be able to keep things running as they are a while longer.'

'Don't you think that this is horribly deceptive to our customers?'

'It's not ideal, I agree, but this is only a temporary... emergency solution.'

'And a lot of the guys might recognise me from the office.'

'We'd work out the ones who wouldn't.'

'Really, Luke?'

'You might even meet someone nice.'

I couldn't bring myself to reply. What a patronising dick this guy was! You may wonder why I didn't just refuse the request completely or even tell Luke where to stick the job. I'm not looking for sympathy, but when I analyse this conversation in hindsight, I reach a sad conclusion: I was accustomed to disappointment and being let down. It was ingrained in my DNA to adapt to crap situations without complaint, so I just went along with it.

'We need to add you to the Abacus,' Luke said a little later that day as we reconvened in the consultation room. 'If you're still in agreement?'

'I suppose so.'

'Great. You know the drill,' Luke said, smiling. 'Do you want a drink?'

'Can we just get this over with?' An anaemic coffee was not going to help.

'Of course,' he replied, jotting down my name at the top of

an application form. 'I'll try not to make this too painful.'

'Try your *very* best, please.'

He began to type before pausing. He was squinting at my face now. 'Your eyes are hazel?' he asked.

'Brown, actually.'

'Shall we say greeny-brown?'

'They're brown, Luke. This isn't a negotiation.'

'Fine,' he said, writing again. 'We also need your height and weight.'

'Don't even go there. I can do that myself.'

'I just thought it would be easier if…'

'I've done this before. If you just scan my face, I can manage the rest myself.'

'No problem,' he said, smiling guiltily. 'Whatever is best for you.'

The job was an upgrade on my previous role, but the financial fragility of the Attraction Abacus was already obvious. The dummy dates only highlighted that even more. Every job I started had some kind of jeopardy associated with it. Where were all the jobs for life that my parents' generation had enjoyed? Okay, my dad managed to create his own jeopardy, but I don't think the word redundancy was invented until I was born. It must have been the sixth Spice Girl.

Clinging to a room-share in a rented flat was the extent of my aspirations. I did have the best bedroom in the building. It was an old townhouse in the student quarter of town, as we liked to refer to it. I was entering a period of my life when leafy suburbs were probably more appropriate, and it should have been time to forsake the world of early-hour pizza deliveries, abandoned kerbside bottles and makeshift curtains, but my *double* bedroom was the envy of my peers.

My flatmates were okay, if a little bitter on this point, but I moved in first, so tough. Andy was a veteran stoner who worked in an electrical store in town. He had turned thirty but had the muscle mass of a twelve-year-old boy and the anaemic complexion of a prison lifer. He barely ate, but when he did, his diet made me feel like a health freak, just because I would heat up the occasional bowl of frozen vegetables in the microwave. Andy never got angry, but he did whine and moan about things a lot, like the washing up. I would rather have had a stand-up argument with him than listen to his whining sometimes, but he could have been worse, I guess. He stayed in his room gaming most of the time, occasionally crashing out with his music left on. I suspected he would burn the entire townhouse down at some point when he relaxed a little too much, so I always ensured my fire alarm was regularly tested.

Katey, my immediate room neighbour, was sweet but suffered from crippling anxiety. Katey worked in a local nursery but often took time off sick. Unfortunately, her safe place was the bathroom we shared. When I was working at the hotel, I accepted our bathroom's occasional unavailability as an occupational hazard to plan around, but since I had started at the Abacus, I was keener to assert my right to a regular timeslot in the mornings. Thinking about this now, I was making more of an effort with my appearance. It was entirely subconscious, but even so, *something* had changed.

I liked my bedroom. I had things set up exactly as I wanted them. There was a king-size bed in the corner of the room, with my daisy-patterned quilt covering it. A widescreen television sat to the left of my bed, with a desk taking pride of place in front of the window. The lighting in this spot was excellent for writing, surpassed only by the view's ability to distract me from writing — cats facing down foxes, deliveries, trees blowing in the wind. All the unmissable things. There was a bookshelf to the right of the desk, loaded with pretentious student reading that I had never even opened. The shelf also doubled as my treats stash, and though I kept most of my food labelled in the kitchen, the good stuff, like chocolate and biscuits, stayed here, wedged between *Ulysses* and *Crime and Punishment*. At some abstract level that seemed appropriate. I don't know how. Pride of place on my shelf was an ornament of Ganesha, the wise old elephant god. It sat on top of a metal box, where I stashed any spare cash for my India trip. My best friend, Olivia, had bought it for me when she first heard about my Goa dream.

I didn't have many friends locally. I had tried to forget my unhappy school years as best I could, and most of my university friends were still scattered around the Portsmouth area. I only came home to be closer to my mum after graduating and was reluctant to pick up the disastrous threads of my old life, so I largely did nothing exciting most of the week. My best friend, Olivia, occasionally visited, and we slept head to toe in my room when she did. Olivia said that I have excellent toes. She made me realise that my life wasn't doomed to follow the same trajectory as my parents'. There was a photograph beside my bed of a family holiday in Devon when I was five. My parents outwardly appear happy enough, but when I look at it now, I wonder just how far their marriage had already disintegrated by this point.

'The thing is, Evelyn,' Olivia said when I first showed the picture to her, 'you may be part of their photograph, but you're not part of their shit-show.'

It was obvious, really, but I had always felt somehow

72

responsible to a degree for what had happened between my mum and dad. A vague kind of childish guilt that Olivia had helped exorcise with lots of rum and Coke.

Trying to find excuses not to write, I checked my bank balance later that evening. The savings account for my India trip was growing nicely. I noticed it was accruing less than one per cent interest, so my trusted high street bank would only help me get to Goa a few seconds earlier. Still, my wages were higher now, and I settled down at my desk, finally focusing on the grand plan and feeling inspired. Things were on the up.

My first dummy date was a non-event. It's barely worth mentioning because it lasted no more than an hour. Fortunately, we had arranged to meet early evening, so there was plenty of time to get home again afterwards. The venue was an Italian restaurant chain on a retail park at the edge of town. Fortunately again, I did not accept the offer of a lift from my date, Aaron, even though it was a hassle to get there.

Aaron made it perfectly clear, within minutes of our arrival, that he wasn't in the market for commitment of any kind. He couldn't spit the words out fast enough. Further, the Abacus seemed to be some kind of sex finder tool in his eyes, where he could specify his exact physical requirements for a woman. When I explained that this wasn't the kind of relationship that I was looking for (even in a fake date), he left the restaurant shortly after. He didn't even finish his pizza, asking the server to box it up to take away, leaving me with the bill. Fake date or not, the encounter was a blow to my fragile ego. My solo bus journey home — all dressed up, but home by eight — felt particularly tragic.

'Would you mind if I collate some date feedback?' Luke asked the following morning in the office.

'Do you have to?'

'The data would be helpful.'

I reluctantly agreed. Having wasted an evening of my life, at least it would be an opportunity to exact some kind of revenge on Aaron.

'Any general comments?' Luke asked.

'I fully expect to see Aaron on Britain's most wanted list at some point,' I said. Luke paused, pen in hand. 'That's a joke. Kind of, anyway. He was very forward, shall we say. Don't write that down.'

'Anything I can write down?'

'He was mean.'

'Mean-spirited?'

'Mean with money.'

'Oh, so do you think that a guy should pay on a date?'

'Not necessarily, but I don't expect a date to dump a bill on me and run off without warning. Are you laughing, Luke?'

'No, that's bad. Of course, we'll reimburse you. Anything else?'

'He asked for pepperoni *and* anchovies on his pizza.'

'What!'

'I know…'

'That *is* going down on the feedback form,' Luke said, writing. 'I have a responsibility to other Abacus users. Were there any positives at all?'

'He had nice teeth.'

'Attractive in general?'

'I'd say so, objectively.'

'Objectively,' Luke said, laughing. 'Why is it that women

pretend that they're any different to men in that respect?'

'What do you mean?'

'You know, all that "it's what's on the inside that counts" stuff.'

'Maybe because it's true?'

'Really! Well, let me tell you that if a good-looking person walks into a room, men and women react in exactly the same way. Why pretend that's not the case? An ugly person has to work five times as hard to get anywhere with anyone.'

'This sounds like the voice of painful experience. Has it been tough, Luke?'

'Funny,' he said, smiling. 'I just find the whole pretence thing interesting.'

'Nobody is pretending anything. Where has this come from anyway?' I said, laughing. 'I can't speak for all of womankind. You want honest feedback for *yourself*, Luke? I'd spend less time in the gym trying to improve your physique and work on your charm instead.'

'Thanks for the tip, but this is the last place that I would come for advice.'

Brian returned from a meeting a little later and wandered over to my desk.

'Are you busy, Evelyn?'

'No,' I replied, wondering if that was the appropriate response to your boss under the circumstances.

'Did I mention the grand opening party?'

'I don't think so.'

'Sorry, there's so much going on,' Brian said, fiddling with a piece of paper in his hands. 'It's a little later than I had planned, but I've finally managed to sort something out. Here are the details. The party is Saturday week. It would be great if you could come. I've booked the rugby club near Lockwood. All our clients are invited, and I'm hoping to sign a few more singles up. You would mainly be a guest, but it would be great if you could help with a bit of schmoozing. Nothing too strenuous, and I'll pay you overtime.' He looked so pleased with himself that I couldn't possibly decline. It wasn't as if I had any other plans anyway.

'You don't have to pay me overtime for a party, Brian. I'd love to come,' I replied, raising my voice. 'I'm not a freeloader, after all.'

Luke either ignored me, or I wasn't quite loud enough.

'Great news,' Brian said, smiling. He checked his steps, turning back towards me again. 'Oh, I forgot to mention the best part. It's fancy dress, Evelyn. The party theme is *Star Wars*!'

'*Star Wars*?'

'Something wrong?'

'No… I guess you've done your market research.'

'What do you mean?'

'Well, I would have thought that those films would… pre-date the average Abacus customer, Brian?'

'Oh God, I hadn't thought of that,' he said, appearing simultaneously shocked and crushed.

'But they are iconic. I'm sure there are still some huge fans out there.'

'Yes… yes, of course,' he said, swallowing hard. I felt bad for even mentioning it, but the more I spoke to Brian, the more I realised just how much he was winging this entire enterprise. Had he taken advice from anybody at any point? It was becoming less surprising that finding investment was a challenge.

I sat at my desk staring at the flyer. I was aware that the *Star*

Wars films existed, but I had managed to navigate my entire life without watching any of them. The theme seemed pretty random to me for a new dating agency. It was obviously just Brian's idea of fun, and I was worried *for* him. Also, I had no idea what to wear. The idea of taking a taxi alone to Lockwood in any kind of fancy dress wasn't appealing. Maybe I could rope Olivia in to suffer with me?

Luke worked irregular hours in the office, studying for some kind of course at quiet times, so I frequently found myself sitting alone at my desk. At first, the responsibility had been a worry, but now I embraced the solitude when it arose. I could talk to customers in my own way, and I knew that there wasn't anyone listening through the thin walls of the consultation room. Brian was always around to open and lock up the office.

Once I had cleared the keying backlog, there were sometimes slow periods of the day. That afternoon, there were no scheduled office visits, and all the other applications were entered and up to date. Brian had popped out, but Luke was sitting at his desk, beavering away. He had just returned from the gym, and his hair was still wet. From what I could gather, Luke worked mainly on the promotional side of things, liaising with a much-maligned marketing company, First Impact. I'd already noticed that Luke gravitated towards the artistic side of the Abacus marketing. There was often an art package open on his screen, with intricate images at different stages of development. I was impressed with his work, though I could never tell him so. The Attraction Abacus algorithm was Brian's area, and that part of the system was completely locked down. (It's *extremely* valuable intellectual property, Evelyn.)

Luke was removing a wet towel from a red sports bag as I passed his desk on the way to the kitchen.

'You love that gym, don't you?'

'I hate that gym.'

'Nobody makes you go, Luke.'

'You'd think that would be true, wouldn't you?'

'I suppose it's just part of being the best you, then?'

'Yes… anyway…'

'Oh, I met Alice the other night,' I said, casually making the linkage.

'She said.'

'Alice seems nice.'

'Yes, she is nice,' Luke said, without looking up from his screen. He didn't elaborate, so I dropped the subject, turning my attention to the pile of textbooks stacked at the corner of his desk.

'What are you studying?'

'Accounts. I want to be an auditor.'

'Wow!'

'Yeah, it's pretty intense, but I'll get there eventually.'

'No, I mean, wow, that sounds incredibly boring. I can't believe any human being would *want* to be an auditor.'

'Now it's my turn to say wow.'

'I mean, *really* want to. Can we just say that you want to earn lots of money? That I could understand.'

He laughed. 'Oh, so *you* need to understand. What's so wrong with having a good career?'

'Nothing, but there must be lots of *great* careers that are a little less… dry.'

'In your opinion.'

'All I am saying is that we live in a world of beaches, waterfalls and sunsets. Why would anybody dream of checking accounts for a living?'

'Who said I dream of it, Evelyn? We can't all be sunset

watchers.'

'True, but I would have thought something artistic would suit you better.'

'There's no money in art. I'd wake up broke in a bedsit somewhere, eating cereal for Sunday lunch.'

'Nothing wrong with cereal.'

'Right. Anyway, what's your big plan?'

At this point, I froze. I was about to tell him about my writing and grand Goa trip when I felt giddy with déjà vu.

What's your big plan?

I was transported back to a refrigerator manufacturing company in the Eighties. I pictured my younger mum and dad, standing on the brink of their future lives, discussing my dad's big opportunity in Hollywood.

Do or die, Ange.

Luke was studying for something real and reliable. He would have letters beside his name and share a big house with Alice in the stockbroker belt someday. I was pinning my hopes on writing a novel on a trip that might never happen. Even if I succeeded, the chances were that nobody would ever read it anyway, just like most novels. In short, I had *become* my dad.

'Actually, nothing much, you're right,' I said, smiling. 'Anyway, I'd better get on.'

My creative writing class was held at the local college on Thursday evenings. Just being in the classroom invoked a sense of stunted personal progression within me. The plastic chairs, whiteboard and squeaky marker pens were overly familiar symbols of my very recent past. The class was too soon after university, which itself had felt too soon after secondary school. To add to this, I suspected that this particular course had been a poor choice of investment. The tutor, Kris Harper, had weak credentials to teach people to write. Only a single novel of his, *Lament of the Dragonfly*, had ever been published, and you had to dig deep on Amazon to find it. Boy, did he refer to it, though. This seminal work of fiction seemed at odds with its reviews. "A pretentious yawn-fest" was voted the most useful review. Another simply read, "Save your money".

Kris was also extremely lazy. All the reference material he distributed to the class was photocopied from other writing guides, and once he had handed out one of these ripped-off exercises, he sat at his desk working on his own projects. The course hadn't been cheap, and I no longer qualified for a student discount. I'd hoped that I would be able to develop a crush on Kris as some kind of compensation, but even that had proved impossible. He was just too irritating and looked like a permanently startled owl.

The class was largely split into two groups: those who sat in silence (like me), never sharing a single thing they wrote, and the others who would not shut up about every sentence they spat out. I understood that it was in my best interests to participate in our classroom discussions, but, confronted by weapons-grade neediness on all sides, it felt exhausting and pointless to even try.

Do you like it? You're just saying that. But is it any good, really?

I soon also realised that every piece of critique offered was only bait to get more feedback for the critic's *own* work. I made the mistake of reading another student's entire novel when I first joined the class, documenting three pages of detailed feedback for their consideration. In return, the same student said that he had "really enjoyed" my opening chapters that I had shared with him and "there was nothing more he could add". When pressed on the most basic of details, it was clear he hadn't read them at all.

The conversation with Luke earlier in the day had left a lasting impression on me, and after months of deluding myself that I had some kind of direction in life, I was beginning to look down and saw nothing but thin air beneath my feet. Dad had spent his entire life reaching for unattainable goals, and now I was doing the same. As I sat on the wobbly plastic chair in the stupid little classroom, I began to panic.

I waited back at the end of the session until the usual attention-seekers had shot off their mouths on the way out, before approaching Kris. He was packing up and appeared less than pleased at another interruption.

'I really need to go,' Kris said.

'I'll be quick.'

'Sorry, what's your name?' he sighed.

'Evelyn. You wouldn't know that because I never say anything.'

'I see.'

'To be honest, I'm totally wasting my time here.'

'Nobody is wasting their time here, Evelyn.'

'And my money.'

The comment wasn't intended as a complaint, but I could see the alarm bells ringing in his eyes. It had the desired effect either way.

'If you're quick then,' Kris said, pouring himself a new mug of tea from a Thermos. 'So, what are you writing?'

'Just a novel.'

'About what?'

'It's a romantic comedy.'

'Oh,' he said, raising the mug to his lips. 'Not my favourite genre, I can't lie. But there are genre conventions. You know about the genre conventions, I assume?'

'Well, this is kind of real life.'

'Oh no, big mistake, Evelyn. You *must* follow the genre conventions. Boy must meet girl, or boy must meet boy, or girl must meet girl, or…'

'I get it, Kris. Yes, that has happened.'

'And maybe they don't hit it off straight away.'

'This is all ringing true so far.'

'But at some point, they unexpectedly hook up.'

'That *does* seem unlikely.'

'It always does, Evelyn. It always does. Then things will be good, for a while at least, before something bad occurs and they are forced apart again,' he said, slurping his tea. 'But most importantly of all, at the end of your story, the main characters have to end up together forever.'

'I'm not certain it will play out that way.'

'In a romantic comedy, it *must* play out that way, Evelyn. In *literary* fiction, like I write, you might get away with a different ending. Something poignant or unforeseen, perhaps even tragic. I would refer you to *Lament of the Dragonfly*. The sense of lost love is unbearable, almost palpable,' he said, staring wistfully into space. 'But in a romantic comedy, love must simply conquer all. Trust me, nobody wants to read a romantic comedy without a happy ending.'

'Thanks for the advice. Maybe I need to switch genres.'

'Your call.'

'One last thing, Kris. If I manage to finish writing this damn thing, I was wondering how I should go about finding an agent?'

He laughed, almost choking on his tea. 'An agent! Are you a celebrity?'

'No.'

'Have you ever appeared on a reality TV show?'

'No.'

'Then forget it. Trust me, just forget it.'

Chapter Seven

I was beginning to realise just how much *Star Wars* fancy dress was going to cost me. As I paged through the umpteenth website, the same costumes were resurfacing, and there didn't appear to be a cheap option. Perhaps if I knew the characters, it would help. I stood from my desk, plodding across the creaking bedroom floor in my pyjamas to the television set beside my bed. I was horrified to see how many films there were in the series and immediately switched the television off again. I didn't have enough life left to watch them all, or even the remotest inclination to try.

I wasn't completely culturally deprived and had absorbed the names of a few of the headline acts, like *Darth Vader*, over the years, but most of the female fancy dress options were totally unfamiliar. I didn't like the look of the tight-fitting white outfits, and there was even some kind of belly-dancing get-up that was totally inappropriate for an early summer evening in Lockwood. I *was* tempted by an elaborate Geisha-looking costume, until I saw the price, so I switched my thinking to unisex options. Robots weren't tempting. I knew that an A.I. was going to take my job at some point, so maybe I should have grasped the opportunity to ingratiate myself, but all the robotic options just felt too impersonal for a party.

I was at the point of shutting down my laptop completely when I saw it. This was the costume for me. It had a furry head, something like a teddy bear, but there was a row of uniform white teeth that were more beaver-like. It was half cute, half ridiculous. Better still, you could buy the mask separately and improvise the rest of the costume yourself. I was going to be an *Ewok*. I only hoped that they hadn't done anything too offensive in the films.

My second dummy date was arranged a week after the first one. I had already decided beforehand that I would remain dispassionate and calculating this time. I managed this a little too successfully and felt sorry for my date, Rhys, who was a nice guy. He tried his best to connect with me during a game of ten-pin bowling, probably too hard, but I kept my emotional distance, and he realised that something was wrong by the tenth frame. I was itching to explain the deceptive situation but somehow managed to keep my counsel. The fake date thing felt shitty, but at least I could offer some positive feedback this time. Brian and Luke owed me for selling my soul like this.

I arrived early at the office the day after the date. I was wearing my smartest blouse and skirt. It was power dressing on a budget. The last few days had been a period of sober reflection for me, and I was determined to make the maximum effort with my job. Brian had already opened the office, but Luke was away studying in the morning (for a *real* career). I switched my laptop on and was about to get down to work when a text flashed up on my mobile. Olivia couldn't make the fancy dress party.

I quickly replied that it wasn't a problem, while the problem began to overwhelm me. I rarely contacted my other university friends, and it was highly unlikely that they would make the trip from Portsmouth just for a work party. My flatmates were non-starters. All my old school friends were gathering dust in my social media accounts somewhere. This was yet another failure on my part. I had allowed my social circle to shrink to the size of a doughnut. The punishment would be a solo taxi journey to Lockwood, dressed as a giant teddy bear.

A couple of customers came in that morning to complete their applications. I resolved to give them a slick, corporate experience. Brian had popped out, so there was nobody listening in on my meetings. It should have been the ideal opportunity to perfect my technique, but something was wrong. The more I tried to up my game, the more I failed. Previously, I had interacted with the singles naturally, but as I tried to inject extra professionalism into the proceedings, it made the appointments feel wooden and staged. I had under-estimated exactly what my earlier nonchalance had brought to the table, and every attempt to artificially reintroduce it just didn't work. I couldn't pretend not to care now that I did. I wanted this job to succeed.

Luke returned around midday. He had obviously been to the gym again, with the familiar red sports bag slung over his shoulder. His hair was still damp, or heavily gelled. He didn't smile at me as he usually did when he arrived. I knew that he hated the gym, but did he also know that the morning's appointments had gone badly? Perhaps one of the customers had complained? My paranoia grew and grew until, to my relief, Luke asked if I had a moment to talk through the dummy date feedback from the previous evening. Settling in the conference room, I opened a pad in front of me. Luke sat opposite.

'I made notes,' I said.

'Very organised.'

'I take this job seriously, despite what you might think.'

'Good to know, Evelyn. What do you have for me then?'

'Well, in summary, Rhys was a very nice guy,' I said, turning a page. 'He struck me as a kind, thoughtful human being.'

'Generous?'

'He paid for bowling, yes.'

'Attractive? Objectively, of course…'

'Objectively, yes,' I said, laughing.

'He sounds great. Any negatives?'

'To be honest… no,' I said, flicking through my notes.

'There must be something?'

'Not that I noticed.'

'Well, he doesn't have a 90-plus score. Okay, it says here that Rhys works as an outdoor activity instructor,' Luke said, reading an application form.

'Yes, he mentioned that. So?'

'Well, that's not going to be very well paid, is it?'

'I don't know what you mean.'

'I mean… his future prospects aren't that great.'

'Rhys was really passionate about his work, Luke. He likes helping kids. That's quite an appealing trait.'

'Really, Evelyn?'

'Yes, really. Do you feel threatened by that in some way?'

'Of course not,' he said, laughing. 'I've heard all this "follow your dream" stuff before from you. Poverty is not quite so appealing.'

'Well, he may not be taking some highfalutin course like you, but at least he is honest with himself.'

'What do you mean? I'm honest with myself.'

'Is that right? I haven't seen you look at that accountancy textbook for more than five minutes at a time before yawning and putting it down again.'

'Just because something is challenging, doesn't mean that it isn't worthwhile.'

'I know. You're just being the best you. Maybe you should try being the *real* you for once, like Rhys.'

'Maybe you should arrange to see Rhys again, as you're such a fan,' Luke said, somewhat childishly.

'Maybe I should. If I hadn't been stuck on one of these ridiculous *fake* dates, I might well have done that already.'

'Well, I won't ask you to do it again. Don't let me hold you back, Evelyn. Each to their own.'

'Yes, exactly. Each to their own.'

Chapter Eight

Luke knew that his relaxation was to be short-lived and tried to savour the last few moments lying on the bed. Alice was scrolling on her phone beside him, but he could sense that she was getting restless. He opened one cautious eye, squinting around her bedroom — impressively spacious and decorated in shades of pale green and cream. It was one of seven bedrooms in the house. Her father, George, had enjoyed a successful career at the bank, and the trappings were everywhere to be seen. It could have been that way for Brian, too, if things had panned out differently, he thought. Alice huffed and puffed a little more before finally slapping her phone on the duvet. All good things came to an end, he thought.

'We should do something,' she said.

'We *are* doing something.'

'No, this isn't *something*, Lukey,' she said, kissing his forehead. 'We're just slowly dying on this mattress.'

Alice stood, stretching beside the bed. Her lovingly toned torso was exposed by her rising blouse, and she pulled the bottom lower.

'I wanted to ask you something,' he said.

'Oh,' Alice replied, not listening to him. She scooped her phone from the bed, positioning it in front of her face to take a selfie. He realised that he was in the shot too. 'Smile,' she said, before freezing. 'Actually, can you do something with your hair?'

'Like what?'

'Maybe flatten it down a bit.'

Luke dipped his hand into the glass of water on the bedside table and blindly tried to plaster down his unruly locks, droplets running down his cheeks. She watched him in faint amusement.

'Better, I suppose,' Alice said, repositioning the phone. She paused again. 'Can you sit up? You look a bit… dumpy.'

'What?'

'It's just the position you're lying in.'

'Better?' he asked, wriggling up the pillow. He sucked his stomach in, too, for good measure. Alice glanced at him in disappointment before turning away.

'Don't worry,' she replied, moving the camera so that she was now the only subject in the frame. She pouted, taking the shot.

'Yeah, I wanted to talk to you about something,' he said.

'Do you fancy going to the gym?' Alice asked, still looking at her face in the phone camera and adjusting her hair.

'I absolutely do not fancy going to the gym again.'

'What *do* you want to do then?' she said, as if all possibilities had been exhausted.

'Like I say, I wanted to ask you something.'

'Ask what?' Alice said, slumping next to him on the bed. 'We've been talking for the last hour.'

'There's an art class on Thursday evenings. I know that we usually see each other that night, but I wondered if you wouldn't mind switching days so I can go along?'

'What? Why?'

'It's just a bit of fun. I used to enjoy it.'

'But if you have time to waste on art, you have time for extra study. You could qualify earlier as an auditor.'

'I know, but…'

'Dad has really stuck his neck out for you, Luke. That course is so competitive.'

'And I appreciate it. I'm not taking anything for granted at…'

'There's the strong possibility of a well-paid job at the bank when you complete it, too. Dad came up from nothing. He has worked hard all his life to get into this position. He's trying to help you, and there's not much that he asks in return. Just a bit of effort. Participate in life, Luke.'

'I am participating.'

'Barely. We must *all* try to be better. Every day is…'

'… a new opportunity to improve. I know. I haven't forgotten that.'

'Good. Then what's this art crap suddenly all about?'

'It's nothing. Forget that I said anything. It was just a stupid dream when I was younger.'

'That's sweet, but dreams are called dreams for a reason, Lukey,' Alice said, kissing his forehead again. 'They're not real by their very definition.'

Chapter Nine

The grand opening party came around before I felt ready.

I had managed to source a furry onesie online. It was cheap and matched the colour of my *Ewok* mask in the right light (near darkness). I made a spear from a length of bamboo, adding a tin foil point to the end. As I finally assembled the costume, it didn't look too bad in the bathroom mirror, but it was suffocatingly snug. The party had coincided with the hottest day of the year so far, and I only hoped that the temperature would drop by the evening. If I wore a T-shirt beneath the onesie, it would become a sauna suit. If I didn't wear a T-shirt, I would lose the option to lower the top half of the onesie later. I decided to bring a spare T-shirt with me in a bag.

'Evelyn,' Katey said, tapping at the bathroom door. I lowered the spear, which I had been prodding at my reflection. 'Do you mind if I get in there?'

'Sure,' I replied, opening the door. Katey walked straight past me without saying a word. I shuffled away, feeling slightly deflated.

Katey later joined me in the kitchen for a few glasses of Prosecco before the party. She said that it was like having a teddy bear picnic. We had finished the entire bottle by the time the taxi arrived, and I hurried out the front door, light-headed. It was still hot. The driver was scowling at me as I approached the passenger door.

'You can't bring weapons into the car,' he said, leaning

across the front passenger seat as I opened the door. I thought he was joking, but his expression didn't change.

'It's a bit of tin foil on the end of a stick,' I replied.

'It's a spear.'

'Can I put it in the boot?'

'I'd have to lock the boot.'

'Please, do what you have to do.'

The rest of the sticky journey was in silence.

Lockwood was the first place that people chose to go for grown-up dates. Once you had a car, Lockwood was finally accessible from town. Adult level one unlocked. It was the natural progression from swigging cider in the park. People referred to it as "going for a country drink". The countryside was pretty much flat, with a reservoir the only distinguishing feature, but it was the nearest countryside we had. The rugby club was just outside Lockwood. There were multiple sports pitches, and the clubhouse was quite a size. I had attended both a wedding and a 21st birthday party there before. It was a nice setting, particularly now, bathed in sunlight. Far too nice for a bunch of rugby players brutalising each other.

I arrived early as I had promised. There were only a couple of cars in the car park. The sign over the clubhouse door read, "The Attraction Abacus Grand Opening Party". To the left of the door, there was a life-size cut-out of the same scientist plastered to the office window, only he wore a cloak and held a lightsabre in his hand. Luke had designed the graphic, and I felt an odd sense of pride.

Brian had gone to town with the décor in the main function room. There was *Star Wars* paraphernalia everywhere, interspersed with Attraction Abacus branding, and the lighting was cool. It constantly changed the colour of the room. There was a good sound system rigged up, too. Brian entered the room, carrying a crate of bottles. He was dressed in a *Darth Vader* costume, with his mask pulled back over his head. Being tall, he cut quite an imposing figure, but the suit looked a little too tight around the middle. His face was flushed as he lowered the crate onto a table beside the entrance. I raised my mask too, and he smiled when he saw me.

'Great costume, Evelyn.'

'You too, Brian.'

'Thanks for coming early. I really need a hand.'

'No problem, what can I do?'

'Right,' he said, hands on hips, breathing heavily. 'It would be great if you could offer everyone a free drink as they arrive. Most importantly, ask our new arrivals if they have already signed up to the Abacus. If they haven't, give them one of these,' he said, passing me a stack of business cards. 'If they won't take the card, don't give them a drink,' he said, laughing, but I sensed that he wasn't joking.

'Is Luke here yet?' I asked.

'No, he's coming later,' Brian replied, a line of sweat trickling down his face. 'Alice,' he added, as if her name explained everything. It already did to me. 'There's also a pretty nice punch, if I say so myself,' he said, nodding towards a space-themed globe, full of a yellow liquid with fruit and ice bobbing at the surface. 'My own recipe.'

I began to unpack the drinks and prepare for the onslaught.

The party theme may have seemed odd to me, but I had underestimated the lure of a free bar. The room was filling fast. Surprisingly, nearly all the guests had opted for fancy dress. I may have been unfamiliar with the *Star Wars* films, but the costumes were like old friends to me. The free drinks were popular too, with a procession of taxis pulling up outside the clubhouse and disappearing. There were very few cars parked outside. Brian was topping up the punch thirty minutes after the first arrivals. It was going to get messy.

I felt less inhibited hidden inside my costume, and I clearly wasn't the only one. There were a few blossoming romances on the dance floor already. Well, bizarre alien couplings at least. Brian noticed me watching as he passed with another crate of bottles.

'This is how you throw a party, Evelyn. Take a room of confirmed singles and fill it with free alcohol.'

He wandered away a few moments later. I was feeling a little dizzy now but helped myself to another glass of Prosecco all the same. If I stuck to the same drink, I wouldn't get myself into too much trouble. Avoid the punch, I told myself. Whatever you do, avoid the punch.

The punch was surprisingly tasty.

The overriding flavour was mango, but this fruity veil belied a pokey aftertaste of spirits. I noticed that I had been spilling most of my glass without even realising it, anyway.

The sound system was pumped up now, and the function room was full, beyond capacity. The dance floor was also jammed. There were *Star Wars* characters grinding together and kissing everywhere I looked. Hands openly wandered inside costumes, and every concealed corner and cubby hole in the clubhouse was occupied by entwined bodies. If I were to describe the atmosphere at this point, it would be school disco meets Caligula, the orgy years. Bearing that in mind, it wasn't the best time for anybody to cut the music and try to make a speech, but that's exactly what Brian did next.

'Thank you all for coming,' Brian said. 'I'd like to welcome you to our grand opening party and...'

'Get the music back on,' somebody shouted.

'I'd also like to say a few...'

'Yeah, get the music back on, fat Vader,' another guy shouted.

Raucous laughter.

Brian tried to continue. I noticed he now held his arm protectively in front of his midriff as he spoke. The worst was yet to come for him, though. As Brian began to recount a potted history of the Attraction Abacus, the same heckler began to chant and clap. It wasn't long before everybody around him was doing the same.

'Fat Vader, go away! *Fat* Vader go away!' the crowd chanted, clapping in unison. Initially, Brian tried to talk over them, but that only encouraged his tormentors, and their voices grew louder. '*FAT* VADER, GO-A-WAY! *FAT* VADER, GO-A-WAY!'

'Have a great evening,' Brian said, returning the microphone to the stand and cutting his losses. He disappeared towards the bar amongst a chorus of cheers and jeers.

The room was beginning to spin.

I guzzled a glass of water, but it made little difference. I then grabbed a mozzarella and tomato sandwich from the buffet table, with some of it even reaching my mouth. That didn't help much either. As I tried to focus on the room ahead of me, I saw Alice. Moving through the crowd, rather parting the crowd entirely, she approached, wearing the inappropriate belly-dancing outfit that I had seen online. It looked totally amazing on her, and I was clearly not the only person to think so. I was too in awe to be jealous.

'Arish!' I slurred as she approached, instantly realising my communication limitations. She didn't recognise me anyway in my outfit. Instead, I just stared, with my eyes drawn to her perfect, flat, tanned stomach, with a gleaming jewel adorning her navel. I knew at that moment that no diet, exercise or even major surgery could ever offer me the same results. I think I mentioned that I graduated in Philosophy. As I stood there, swaying in my sweaty *Ewok* suit, Plato's world of forms sprang to mind. Plato was one of the Ancient Greek philosopher guys. In his world of forms, perfect versions of real-world objects timelessly existed in another abstract realm. Alice's stomach was the immaculate template for what all stomachs were meant to be in *our* world. My trembling hand reached out towards her.

'I want to touch it,' I tried to say, but the words barely left my mouth. I pulled the mask up over my face, smearing a line of drool over my cheek.

'Evelyn,' Alice said, finally recognising me. I jumped, retracting my hand, and I adjusted the sweaty strands of my hair. 'Thank God, it's you. What the hell is this place? No wonder all these creeps are single.'

'You look incredible.'

'I swear if another guy comes anywhere near me, I'll mace him.'

'Your stomach is amazing,' I beamed, still staring at her navel. Alice smiled awkwardly but then re-focused her abuse.

'Look at that pervert over there,' Alice said, scowling at a guy dressed in a hooded brown robe. 'Yes, *you*, loser. Put your eyes back in your head and get a life!'

'Alice, Alice, Alice,' I chuckled, shaking my head. Fortunately, I didn't elaborate — couldn't elaborate — or even remember what I had been thinking. 'Where's Luke?' I managed to slur.

'Oh, he's pissed somewhere. What a knight in shining armour he is! He decides to abandon me just when I've checked in to the world's premier creep convention.'

I made my excuses shortly after. My visit to the toilets was demoralising. The reflection that confronted me did not match my drunken mental self-image. Where was the cute inner teddy bear I was trying to channel? My eyes were bloodshot, my makeup was ruined, and my hair was plastered to my head. Worse still, I had managed to lose the carrier bag containing my spare T-shirt somewhere, so I would have to sweat it out in my *Ewok* suit through the rest of the evening. The only consolation was that I was too wasted to really care.

I grabbed another drink of water. The rehydration programme didn't seem to be helping, and what I really needed was some fresh air. I remembered that there was a balcony overlooking the pitches at the rear of the clubhouse. That did mean navigating the entire length of the dance floor on very wobbly legs.

A few steps into my epic quest, I forgot the plan and started to dance with a group of *Stormtroopers* to "Mr Brightside". My attempt to spin out of an improvised dance move left me flat on my backside. By the time I had clambered to my feet, my new friends were gone. I scanned the dance floor, trying to remember what I had been doing. The pulsing lights turned red, through blue to green. It was disorienting and difficult to see anything, but there, at the extremity of the dance floor, was a familiar shape.

'It's another *Ewok*!' I squealed to nobody.

I was pushing through the crowd now, with the abandon only

a drunk on a pointless mission truly knows. I had been looking for another *Ewok* the entire party, and this was the only one I had seen. By the time I had wriggled through the mass of sweating bodies on the dance floor, the *Ewok* had gone, but I had made it to the rear door of the hall. I could feel a cooling breeze as I opened it, staggering out into the fading summer sun.

I swayed at the edge of the balcony, disoriented. A few steps beneath me, the balcony was filled with couples. Could Brian's party have backfired altogether? There didn't seem to be another single left in town.

'See, it doesn't matter what your score is, Brian!' I shouted into the sky, stumbling forward down the steps. A woman below me screamed, bracing herself for the impact of my falling body, but I regained my balance like a ballerina, at least in my own mind. Beyond the balcony, the sky was alight, bathing the rugby pitch before me in shifting shades of orange. It was beautiful, epic even, and I felt central to the spectacle somehow, swaying in the evening air, spear at my side. I was no longer just Evelyn. I was Evelyn the Holy.

'Is that you, Evelyn?' somebody shouted to my left.

As I shaded my eyes from the sun, the other *Ewok* I had been stalking was scurrying towards me. I hurried down the steps to greet them. Instinctively, we touched raised spears as we met on the balcony. I noticed that their spear was proper merchandise, not a home-made bamboo job like mine. As the *Ewok* raised its mask, the face beneath was a surprise.

'Luke! You're the other *Ewok*!'

'No, you're the other *Ewok*!' Luke slurred. He was grinning stupidly. Alice had been correct on the pissed point. His normally floppy fringe was flat on his head, and his blue eyes were glassy and pink.

'We're great, aren't we?'

'We're the best,' he agreed, raising his spear to touch mine again. 'I'm trying to hide from Alice. She's *furious*,' Luke said, dissolving into giggles.

'Yes, I spoke to her. She did seem a little unhappy.'

'A little unhappy!' he said, giggling. 'Alice is always a little unhappy.'

It amused him so much that he doubled over with laughter at that point, gasping for air. I waited until he was only semi-hysterical before replying.

'You should really go and talk to her,' I said, trying to keep a straight face.

'No, she can't see me like this,' he said, laughing. 'She'll lose her shit. No, best that I stay out of her way.'

'Why would she even care?'

'Oh, Alice would care alright,' Luke slurred, 'Extra gym sessions all next week,' he said, giggling. 'But I'm not a trophy, am I, Evelyn?'

'Nobody would *ever* consider you a trophy, Luke.'

He laughed. 'Anyway, I need to talk to *you*.'

'Why?'

'I've got some punch. You should have some.'

'What? I don't think that's a good idea.'

'That's the whole point. It's a very *bad* idea.'

I took one of the cups from his hand, like Luke, beyond the point of seriously considering consequences or even rational thinking.

'So, what did you want to talk about?' I asked.

'Our conversation the other day,' he slurred, swaying. 'I just wanted to say that you were right. Why would I want to be an auditor?'

'No, you were right. It's a great career.'

'No, *you* were right,' he said, prodding my shoulder with his index finger. 'We only get one life. I should be true to myself. I want to live in the moment,' he added, spinning on the spot with his arms extended. 'I want to feel the wind blowing through my hairy *Ewok* chest.'

'Ah, but after that moment comes another moment,' I said, laughing. 'If you screw up the first moment, the second moment is guaranteed to be crap. I've seen it with my own eyes before.'

'Moments, moments, moments,' he slurred. 'Let's drink to moments,' he added, raising his plastic cup in the air. The punch splashed down his arm and all over the balcony floorboards, creating a yellow puddle beneath our feet.

'To carefully considered moments,' I corrected, raising my cup.

He didn't reply immediately, distracted by something over my left shoulder.

'Evelyn!' he said, pulling my arm. The cup was still at my lips in the other hand, and I spilt half my drink down my onesie as I jerked forwards. I was giggling to myself as I tried to follow him through the crowd, bundling into bodies with my head down. I didn't dare look up, hearing the complaints of the people we passed. Finally, we reached the boundary of the balcony, resting against a waist-high wooden fence. Luke was staring madly into the distance, finger pointing. 'Look, a sunset, Evelyn!'

'No, I don't want you to see it,' I said, blocking his eyes with my outstretched hand. 'Think of your career.'

'Too late,' he said, pulling my hand away.

We were both laughing as he wrestled my hand away from his eyes a second time, again nearly falling over. After a moment, we finally stood still, looking beyond the balcony. He sighed deeply at the same point that I did, and that seemed hilarious, too. The sky was so vast, with only the playing fields and the reservoir, a distant pool of orange, to anchor the vista. There were lazy patches of purple cloud inching across the sky, spectacularly backlit by the sinking crimson sun. It was the most amazing sunset I could remember. Neither of us were laughing now as we watched in revered silence.

'The people need to know about this,' I said eventually.

'Evelyn, we will tell *everybody* about this.'

'It's magical.'

'Other worldly,' Luke said, and then turned to face me. 'I like you, Evelyn.'

His words were strangely blunt, yet strangely perfect. His *Ewok* mask was pulled up onto his forehead, as was mine. He was staring at me for a few seconds too long, and then his head moved towards me.

He was going to kiss me.

I did not move away.

As his lips were inches from mine, our raised masks collided, blocking the contact. Luke turned his head to the other side, moving towards me again, but the beaver teeth of our masks collided for the second time. He crouched slightly, manoeuvring into a lower position, but as he advanced for a third attempt, there was a voice behind us.

'What are you doing?'

I turned to see Alice.

She was standing amongst a group of assorted aliens and robots, and I jumped, nearly falling backwards. They were all staring towards us in silence. The scene was so surreal that for that split second, I thought that I was *in* a film.

Luke was frozen beside me.

I waited for him to say something, but he just stood there with a horrified expression on his face. I struggled to think of some kind of explanation myself, but my mind was completely blank. Instead, I turned to face Luke again, who wasn't laughing any longer. We both swayed in silence for a moment, just staring into each other's eyes.

I gagged and threw up all over his hairy *Ewok* legs.

Chapter Ten

I woke up at the flat, half on the couch and half on the floor.

My cheek was pressed against a heart-shaped cushion (Katey's) on the couch, damp with drool, and my legs trailed over the carpet. I was still partly wearing my *Ewok* suit, though I had wriggled out of the left shoulder at some point in the night. The manoeuvre had left me trapped in an arm-lock that had been effective enough to stop me from undressing further. To the left of the couch was the washing-up bowl from the kitchen sink, which I could smell was not empty. I tried not to look at it or inhale too deeply again.

How had I got back to the flat? The end of the party was a montage of troubling images, but I couldn't put them in any order. I think the taxi driver had refused to take me home. Brian was involved at some point, and then I recalled climbing into the back of a car with a carrier bag between my knees. Had I argued with Alice? It was a possibility, but that recollection was thankfully even hazier. I was too wounded to worry. Instead, I pulled myself up onto the couch completely, curled into the foetal position, and willed for the blessed release of sleep.

When I finally awoke again a few hours later, head pounding, my flatmate, Katey, was able to fill in some of the gaps. The concern, bordering horror, on her face was advance warning of what was to follow. She sat in the armchair opposite me, arms folded and distant, as if my condition might be contagious. Katey had been awoken by repeated knocking at the door in the middle of the night and had helped a couple of *Jedi Knights* drag me into the lounge. The stairs had been too daunting to transport me any further, and I "had not been at my most cooperative". Katey had brought me the washing-up bowl, and a glass of water with some paracetamol. These were untouched on the table beside me. I gratefully guzzled them now.

It was difficult to concentrate on her words as she recounted the sorry events. I felt horribly guilty, and I was also terrified by the potential repercussions. There was something else, though. As I reached for what was *really* bothering me, the realisation came as a shock: I wanted to know what Luke was doing. I was worried about what had happened to him after I had left.

Who would care about a non-kiss? We lived in a world of casual relationships and non-commitment. A world of *Tinder* and hook-ups. A non-kiss was nothing at all. It wasn't worth even talking about. The problem was that *I* cared about it. I lowered my head back onto the couch, mortified by the realisation.

I spent the rest of that Sunday in my room in bed. It was a day spent full of self-pity, regret and total confusion. The biggest question I posed myself was simply, why?

I had almost kissed Luke. Luke was a dickhead. Luke had a girlfriend. What the hell!

The girlfriend part was a problem for him, surely? It couldn't be an *us* problem. There was no us. Luke almost certainly didn't give a shit about me. My own emotions were trickier to navigate, particularly as I had to face him at work. Why *had* I wanted to kiss him at all? The punch wasn't entirely to blame. My one functioning brain cell was on board with the idea at the time, but nobody irritated my conscious mind more than Luke. It had been some form of alcohol-induced insanity.

I needed to analyse my feelings objectively, imagining the scientist in the Attraction Abacus window prodding my emotions around in a Petri dish. How was anybody supposed to know if they liked someone? You must need some point of reference, which I didn't have.

My cynicism about relationships ran deep. Relationships were just like exchanging feedback on my writing course. Give a bit of something to get something else back, whatever you might be after. It might be affection, companionship, sex, money, lifestyle, or support. Everybody wanted different things, but they all wanted something. Relationships were nothing more than a series of emotional transactions, with one party often getting the better side of the deal.

I considered the basis for most of the relationships I knew about. From the outside, there seemed to be lots of people who were simply happy to find anybody. Basically, they were relieved not to be alone. Maybe it was insecurity or even just low expectations at the heart of that. Perhaps, just indifference. These people would hop in the first cab off the rank if it transported them away from single town.

I suspected there were others who paired up for more practical reasons, like combining their salaries to become a mortgage-busting super-couple, or to develop their own child-processing mini-plant. Other matches were made for cultural fits of different varieties, such as religious or ethnic compatibility. Something that wouldn't rock the boat too much on the home front. There were solid reasons for hooking up with somebody with similar interests. At least you could waste your life doing the same things together. Perhaps finding somebody who fitted in your social circle was another approach, so the nights out and holidays would be great at least. Even the relationships based entirely on physicality had something, where the thinking didn't extend any further into the future than hopping into bed that night.

Yes, relationships were confusing. I had always found the process of moving from one relationship to another even worse. It wasn't just another partner you needed to get to know. It was an entire family. Just so much effort, always ultimately wasted, as the whole cycle repeated itself when you moved on. The overbearing mothers, always judging and testing to see if you were good enough for their little Johnny. Washing up a family roast for ten, just to prove that you were domestically subservient enough to pick up where she had left off. Trying to cook a meal for ten, just to show that you were a Michelin chef in waiting. I'd lost track of the crap I had pretended to be interested in to please Mummy, because I knew that if I didn't, it was the surest route out the door. I had tried to knit, watched the inanest soaps imaginable, and even briefly learnt to tap dance to please one of these over-maternal psychopaths. The trendy fathers were no better, kidding themselves that they still had it. Or the broken fathers that didn't say a word, with your very presence alone being an irritation to them. Siblings who wanted to be your friend, when I wasn't even certain that I wanted to be there at all. Jealous siblings who wanted to be your enemy. And then there were grandparents, uncles, aunts and cousins. A cast of thousands that I had to pretend to be interested in, remembering birthdays and sending cards, because obviously my boyfriend didn't. Somehow, even though I had just shown up, it was my job.

The party wasn't even worth worrying about. The little I knew about Luke was disenchanting, to put it nicely. He was probably full of remorse, trying to make things up to Alice, even as I thought about it. It had just been a stupid, drunken mistake, I concluded. There was nothing more to it. If I hadn't needed the job so much, I would have resigned to avoid the embarrassment of ever seeing him again.

All the same, the encounter had piqued my interest in relationships, and I decided to seek some advice. Just at an abstract level, for my novel research, of course. Meanwhile, I had to face Luke at work. That wasn't a pleasant thought.

When I skulked through the door on Monday morning, Luke was not at his desk. I was relieved and then disappointed in the space of a few seconds. It only prolonged the agony of clearing the air. Brian greeted me with a smile, as he always did. He then started to discuss some application details, without any mention of the party at all. In some ways, it was a relief, but it didn't feel healthy to ignore the situation completely either. The apocalypse I had envisaged over the weekend did not materialise at all. The morning was surprisingly normal, and I even began to forget about the party entirely as I ploughed through the application details on my desk. The afternoon was equally uneventful, too.

Brian was still crunching numbers in the consultation room as I was leaving that evening. He deserved investment just for sacrificing every evening of his life. When he saw me standing at my desk, he popped his head around the door.

'Evelyn, I just wanted to apologise before you leave.'

'Apologise?'

'Yes, I've been trying to pluck up the courage all day. I'm not good at stuff like this.'

'Apologise for what?'

'The punch,' he said, rubbing his forehead. 'Luke told me that you were drinking it. I got a bit carried away with my

108

measures. If you have any dry-cleaning bills or anything like that, just let me know. It was completely my fault. I feel so bad about it.'

'It's fine, Brian.

'Are you sure?'

'Certain,' I said, smiling. 'Have a nice evening.'

That was an unexpected and pleasant end to the day. As I crossed the road from the office, I was still dwelling on relationship dynamics and wanted to talk to somebody about it. The strange thing was that I decided that I would visit my dad for that discussion. On the face of it, he could be seen as a logical choice. Dad was dying, so potentially I had less time to talk to him than everybody else. He also had less time left to judge me about the conversation afterwards. I'd like to pretend that these were the reasons, but part of me suspected, rather feared, that we were very alike, as he often said. If I'm honest, it felt like my best shot at understanding myself. I grabbed some chocolate from the supermarket and headed straight for the bus stop.

There were blue curtains pulled around Dad's bed as I entered the Kipling ward an hour later. I loitered behind them, fiddling awkwardly with my phone. A nurse emerged a couple of minutes later, managing a tired smile, as she pulled the curtain back. She pushed a trolley of equipment away with her. Dad didn't even notice I was there at first. He looked thinner, and his eyes were darkly shadowed. I swallowed hard, feeling guilty that I had visited him for my own selfish reasons. His face lit up when he noticed me.

'Ah, the prodigal daughter returns! I'd slaughter a fatted calf, only there's a tube stuck up my arse.'

'Too much detail, Dad.'

'I can't sugar-coat things.'

'Still, you're looking better,' I smiled, moving closer.

'Bravo! Acting is in your genes.'

He wasn't stupid, and it had been a stupid thing to say. Dad's voice was weaker, to the point that I thought it might be another performance for my benefit, but perhaps not this time. It was uncomfortably warm in the ward, and I removed my jacket. When I pulled the chocolate that I had bought him from my bag, he was watching me.

'This is for you,' I said, ignoring his stare.

'Thank God it isn't more grapes! Vitamins don't seem relevant at this point,' he said, edging up his pillow. 'I didn't expect to see you again.'

'It was a slow week in my diary.'

Dad tried to laugh but then winced as he shifted on the bed. He looked awful. It hadn't been *that* long since I had seen him, but he had deteriorated significantly. It freaked me out to see him that way, and I started to read through the cards on the cupboard beside his bed to avoid getting upset.

'Nice cards.'

'Yes, five of them,' he croaked. 'It's not much of a haul for a lifetime, is it?'

'Not everyone sends cards.'

'Your mother certainly doesn't. She doesn't visit either.'

'Did you really expect her to, Dad?'

He winced again as he moved. I helped him sit higher in bed, and I could feel how weak he had become. His arms trembled beneath his body. The small movement was enough to tire him out, and I waited for him to catch his breath.

'It seems a little late in the day to hold grudges,' he said at last.

'Mum is just trying to move on with her life, that's all.'

'She's fortunate that she can.'

I wasn't certain what he meant by the remark. Was it self-pity about his health situation, or was he claiming still to harbour feelings for Mum after all this time? Perhaps he had romanticised their marriage, stuck here in bed for so long. It certainly hadn't been great as I remembered things. All the same, an opportunity had already presented itself, though it felt awful, like stealing from a shopkeeper's cash register when their back was turned.

'You must have really liked each other once,' I said.

'Indeed, we did, Evie.'

'So, how did you know?'

'Know what?'

'That you liked each other.'

'A generation truly lost,' he said, laughing. The laughter triggered a coughing fit, and I waited for him to be still again.

'I'm serious, Dad.'

'What? You're honestly asking me how you know if you like somebody?'

'I guess.'

'God, Evie, you can't come here with real problems,' he said, shifting on the pillow. 'You know that I was always just the relief parent.'

'Your opinion is all I want.'

He closed his eyes, licking his dry lips. This was a sure sign that he was ill. Dad never hesitated to talk about his life, and he was hesitating now. I didn't think he was going to reply at all until he opened his eyes again.

'I'm an actor, Evie.

'Yes, I know,' I said, smiling. Well, he was briefly, amongst other things. It was kind of true.

'No, I'm an *actor*,' he repeated, grasping my wrist, as if I

111

didn't understand.

'Are you saying that you pretended to like Mum?'

'No, no, I'm not saying that at all,' he replied, visibly frustrated. 'An actor is what I actually *am*. I was an actor long before I ever tried acting. Whenever I'm doing something, anything, I feel like I'm just acting out a role. I have always done. The moment invariably escapes me. Even right now, I feel like I'm an actor lying in a hospital bed pretending that I'm dying. It's like it isn't *me* doing it. Even as I say things, it's like they aren't my own words. It's as if I'm playing out the script of a film. Even back then with you and Mum, it was like I wasn't really there at all.'

'Well, you weren't there after I was ten.'

'Evie, please, I'm trying to explain. When I first met your mum, she made me feel like I was exciting. Her belief that I was exciting made me believe that I *could* be exciting. It was empowering. I began to play the role of what I thought an exciting person should be. So, I wasn't pretending to like her. I did like her. I loved her, and I'm sure she loved me, for a while at least, until I cocked everything up.'

'So, it was how she made *you* feel.'

'No, it was more than just that,' he croaked, looking disappointedly at me. 'I sensed that she needed that excitement in her life, in the same way that I wanted to be exciting. It was a two-way street. She was seeing that pen pusher at the time. I can't remember his name.'

'Martin.'

'That's right, Martin. My God, that guy was dull. I couldn't talk to him for more than five minutes without switching off. I know that your mum doesn't believe it now, but I swear that if she had stayed with him, it would be *her* in this hospital bed, dying of terminal boredom.'

That was debatable. 'But you took the exciting-guy role a little too far.'

'The role changed, I'm afraid, Evie. At every single point, I thought that things were about to improve, but my mistakes piled up into one humongous shit-berg. Before I knew it, I was no longer playing exciting guy, but I had somehow become typecast as a perennial loser. Your mum didn't look at me in the same way, and I didn't like playing that new role. I left for all your sakes. The situation wasn't good for anybody.'

I looked away. That point was more than debatable. It was a complete liberty to claim he had left for our collective benefit, but it felt too late in the day to pull him up on that now. I just nodded, staring out the window. He carried on talking for another five minutes, but most of that time was filled with self-pity. It was my fault. I had asked for his opinion, but I had only wanted to hear what I wanted to hear.

There wasn't much concrete advice to take away from our discussion, but some of what Dad had said struck a chord with me. For too long, *I* had felt like a passive observer of life, with the scenery of the world racing past me, existing rather than actively participating. I was an actor of a kind like him, more of an extra in my own life, and I had to take control if things were ever going to improve. A frank discussion with Luke would be the starting point.

Chapter Eleven

It was incredible how quickly my courage deserted me. After firing myself up for action during the walk to work, I felt all strength leave my body as I turned the handle of the Attraction Abacus door. I could see Luke sitting at his desk through the glass, and I nearly turned back. In fact, I was turning away as I opened the door and stumbled through it.

Luke glanced up and smiled sheepishly.

I smiled sheepishly back.

It was a sheep-off.

Fortunately, Brian emerged from the consultation room at that exact moment to diffuse the awkwardness. He was wearing his trademark investment-hunting suit, briefcase in hand.

'I'll be back around one, Evelyn. There aren't too many details to enter, but have a word with Luke if you run out of things to do. There's... err... something else he needs to talk to you about.'

'Sure,' I replied, heading for the sanctuary of my desk. I was curious about the conversation to come, but I was in no state to face it immediately.

Brian was right. My data entry only lasted about an hour, and frustratingly, there were no visitors to the office. I pretended to work for another hour, tapping at my keyboard and squinting at the screen as if I was trying to crack the Enigma code. I eventually stopped bothering to maintain the ridiculous illusion. Boredom was an unfailing antidote to anxiety for me. I swear, if they kept me hanging around long enough on Death Row, I'd leap on Old Smokey and tell them to fire it up.

So be it. I would initiate the conversation.

Luke sensed that I was standing next to his desk, I'm certain of it, but he continued to stare at the open book in front of him. I could see that it was some kind of accountancy textbook.

'So, you're going to be an auditor again?' I said, smiling.

'Oh... yes,' he replied, pretending to jump. He closed the textbook on his hand, cynically keeping the page place for later reference, I noticed.

'Funny the things we say when we drink too much,' I replied, before he could continue.

'Yeah, I'm...'

'And the things we do.'

Straight for the jugular. I wasn't messing about. He was squirming now.

'Look, Evelyn, I need to apologise for...'

'It's fine.'

'No, it really isn't.'

'It's Alice you need to apologise to,' I said, staring into his eyes. 'I hope she managed to forgive you.'

I don't know what I expected, or even hoped for, but he just nodded. I could tell that he wanted to look away, but I wasn't about to let him off the hook that easily.

'Just like that?'

'She wasn't happy,' he eventually mumbled.

'You said that Alice is never happy.'

'I said a lot of things that I shouldn't have. My relationship with Alice is complicated. I need to explain sometime.'

'Spare me,' I said, finally looking away. 'Brian said that there was something that you wanted to talk about.'

115

'Ah, yes. That's a little awkward.'

'Well, we might as well get all the awkward stuff out of the way, don't you think?'

'Maybe we should go in there,' he said, nodding to the consultation room.

It was difficult not to think back to the party as Luke sat opposite me at the desk. I wondered if I could ever look at him in the same way again. He was silently wrestling with his words, and my own thoughts were racing while he did.

Had I really wanted to kiss this guy?

Luke was quite good-looking, but not exactly my type. He had already proved himself to be unreliable and a cowardly philanderer who bad-mouthed his girlfriend. I tried to imagine him thirty years older, fat and balding, having just pissed all over my toilet seat after a night down the pub with his dull auditor workmates. His art materials would be gathering dust in the loft, while he pawed over the latest tax regulations. I imagined him forgetting birthdays and anniversaries, with his head stuck in a copy of *The Financial Times*, boring me shitless about the stock market. There would be no writing excursions to Goa with this guy (You can't trust the water, Evelyn. Not even the ice cubes!) We'd take our holidays with Luke's boss and his wife in a villa in Portugal, close to a golf course, where Luke could spend every day pretending to miss shots and kissing his boss's backside. I must have been temporarily insane to even consider kissing him. As for a relationship, forget it! Had I learnt nothing from my parents' marriage? It would just be easier to fast-forward to a time when we were indifferent, possibly hateful, towards each other and save all the effort of the ride.

'So?' I said, unable to wait for Luke to gather his thoughts any longer.

'Well, I know that I said that I wouldn't ask you again, but I wondered if you are available for… another dummy date?'

'What!'

'It's a bit of an emergency. Our numbers are really down for the guys.'

I don't know why I was so shocked. It was nothing new, but Luke was glossing over the party entirely. At least he had the decency to be ashamed this time. Of all the scenarios I had envisaged that day, this was not one. A tearful tumbling into each other's arms was a long shot, but a request for me to date yet another guy was way off my radar.

On the day of the third dummy date, I considered pulling out, but a surge of anger convinced me to go ahead. I should be looking at the date as an opportunity. I was benefiting from a service for free that other people paid for. I really had liked Rhys on my previous date. Maybe date three would be even better. I should take it more seriously. Screw Luke!

Dating had been a minefield for me. I felt like a salesperson if I didn't date exclusively, so my previous dating process had been inefficient, timewise. Also, setting the emotional thermostat correctly for a date had always proved an issue for me. In the spirit of a mutually enjoyable experience, I had to be nice on a date. If I were too nice, I could convey a level of enthusiasm that I wasn't feeling. This made any declination of a subsequent date unexpected for the other person and awkward for me. If I wasn't nice enough, I jeopardised a future date for myself, and this was the way most dates had gone. I could never quite gauge the correct niceness level.

Dating apps had never really worked for me either. I found

the general concept of rejecting someone or being rejected difficult without even meeting in person. Apps didn't work for me in general. Some of my friends avoided social media apps for their mental well-being, but I can't claim the same was true for me. I just wasn't nice enough to use them. I was rarely pleased for anybody else when they posted something exciting, like holidays or trips away. I silently stewed in jealousy instead, wondering why I couldn't afford to do nice things. I couldn't be bothered to "like" things or respond with supportive comments when confronted with blatant attention seeking. Life felt too short. Most of all, I had a low tolerance for what I considered dumb or offensive views, especially from people I thought I knew well, so the rest of the time was spent scrolling in fury. Okay, I recognise that these aren't attractive traits, but I am being honest.

Sex was also at the back of my mind whenever I dated. I don't mind sex. I probably like it less than some people and more than others, but I dread the first encounters every time. You leave your private parts alone in a room together and hope that they get on, like children from different marriages forced to socialise with each other (for the record, I know all about that too, and trust me, it doesn't usually work out like the film, *Stepbrothers*.) In summary, it was just a relief to get the first time over with.

My date, Josh, had scored okay on the Abacus. He was a reasonable catch, according to the algorithm. Luke wished me luck as I left the office that evening. I thought I detected sadness in his voice, though I was almost certainly projecting emotion that didn't exist. I ignored him anyway.

It was Friday. My sister had invited me to a party, and I kept the option open. Normally, the Abacus suggested a compatible date activity, but on this occasion, Brian had left the choice to

Josh. This was the first bad sign: Josh's date suggestion lacked imagination. Checkers was a very popular bar in town. It was the epicentre of pre-club drinking, often frequented by underage clubbers bluffing their way past disinterested doormen. I had been one of those underage clubbers once, and it felt like my Checkers' days should be over.

Josh was early. He had said that he would grab a table near the window, and he delivered on his promise. My initial impression was that Josh was quite good-looking, but he seemed totally out of place in Checkers. We were a similar age, but he dressed older, wearing jeans and a shirt that I was sure my dad possessed. He tapped his fingers on the table to the R&B/Hip-Hop blaring around the bar, as if he had never heard music before in his life.

Facially, Josh reminded me of an elongated Daniel Radcliffe, but his glasses didn't suit him. They made him look like a Seventies porn star. The thing is, I'm quite partial to a nerd, but I don't like a nerd pretending that they aren't a nerd. A warm summer evening in Checkers is far from ideal for getting to know somebody, and he had made a poor choice of venue. He should have been true to himself.

We shouted and signed to each other as best we could above the music, but it was tiring. Josh was working for an insurance company, but he had opted for a degree as pointless as mine, graduating in Film Studies. He seemed a little ashamed of this, but it was the first enticing thing that he had said to me. The second was that he was estranged from his dad. I side-stepped the question about my own job, luckily remembering not to blow my cover, before blabbing on about my writing. I was mildly interested now, waving to get his attention above the music.

'Do you want to go to a party?' I shouted.

'Sure.'

It was a warm summer night. We stopped to buy some drinks from Tesco Express on the way. Josh insisted on paying, picking up a bottle of rum and a litre of Coke. I felt deceptive accepting it, but the discussion became embarrassing at the checkout. Even the joker of a cashier offered to pay for it. Thankfully, my sister, Abby, opened the door to the party, hosted at the flat she shared with her boyfriend. It was only a five-minute stroll from the Abacus office. Abby was wearing a short purple velvet dress with a psychedelic pattern that made my eyes hurt. She no longer dyed her hair, now favouring her natural auburn shade, like mine, but the style still felt like a natural evolution of her teenage indie cut.

'Evie, so pleased you could make it,' she said, throwing her arms around me. She never showed signs of affection, so I knew that she was pissed. Fortunately, I was a little bit pissed too and hugged her back. 'And who's this?' she added, glancing over my shoulder. For a horrible few seconds, I couldn't recall my date's name.

'This is Josh,' I said, remembering just before he had to prompt me.

'Welcome, Josh,' Abby said, shaking his hand stiffly. 'Evie, how long have you been dating? You never tell me anything!'

'It's early days,' I said, smiling.

Abby stumbled down the doorstep onto the concrete path, bright red lipstick smeared over her front teeth. I wondered what she was doing until she placed one hand on my shoulder and the other on Josh's, wobbling slightly. She closed her eyes.

'I'm picking up very good energy from you two. Very good energy indeed,' she slurred. We followed her inside without comment.

The party soon felt like a mistake. My original intention was to disappear in the crowd if I wanted to bail out. My revised intention was to talk to Josh, but the party was inappropriate for either purpose. It was more what I would call a "gathering". There were around twenty people sitting and standing in an approximate circle in the lounge, drinking. There was music playing, too low for us to become anonymous. I lowered myself onto the floor, sitting cross-legged on the carpet at the edge of the room. Josh looked reluctant to join me but eventually slid down the wall by my side. I had grabbed a couple of glasses from the kitchen as we passed it, and poured us both a rum and Coke, holding the glasses between my knees.

I felt like our arrival had interrupted something, and it became clear what that was. A conspiracy theory conversation re-started in earnest, and it didn't stop. Trust me, they went through the whole card. State-planned assassinations, secret organisations ruling the world, vaccinations, alien cover-ups, fake science, fake news, fake everything. It was exhausting.

Josh looked bored. I continued to pour us both rum and Coke, drinking most of it myself without pausing. I *did* drink too much in social situations. I don't think I had a drink problem. I was quite happy not to touch a drop all week, but I did like to line up my weekly units in one hit to overcome the awkwardness of social interaction. This was all Luke's fault. We wouldn't be here at all if it weren't for him. I was pissed now, and I could take no more of this bullshit.

'Well, you're ignoring the big one,' I said to a guy squatting near me. 'You must have heard about the gravity cover-up, right?' He shook his head. His girlfriend was listening too. Maybe she thought that I was trying to hit on him. 'You won't read about this one in the mainstream media, that's for sure.

They're putting gravity in our food. It's all they talk about at Davos these days. You've heard of M.S.G.?' He nodded. 'M.S.G. really stands for monosodium *gravity*. It mixes best with salad. N.A.S.A. developed the stuff, in between faking moon landings. This is lockdown in plain sight, guys. They're pumping us full of it, so the elites can keep us on the ground where they can control us. You've got to stay one step ahead,' I said, tapping the side of my temple.

The guy looked at me in disgust, and even my sister was scowling at me further across the room. 'Nobody likes a piss-taker, Evelyn,' she said.

'I think we should leave,' I said to Josh.

I could barely walk in a straight line. I think Josh was already done with the evening, but I was insistent on one more stop. Even as I fumbled with my key to the Attraction Abacus office, I knew that I was making a big mistake. I was carrying the remains of the rum and Coke in a carrier bag, and I inadvertently clattered the bottle against the glass panel. Too hard.

'Where are you going, Evelyn?'

'Don't worry, I know the owner,' I said, crouching to check the glass for cracks. Nothing. Vertigo forced me upright again. Once inside, I switched the light on. The office was silent and alien at night, and I quickly disabled the alarm before it belted out.

'I don't think we should be in here.'

I wobbled on my feet, looking at Josh. Finally, I felt the sense of guilt that I should have experienced from the start. Josh was a nice guy. He didn't deserve all this crap, just because of Luke. I couldn't tell him the truth about our date, but he had suffered enough tonight.

'I'm sorry, Josh. You're a great guy, but I don't think we're really suited to each other. I'm just too... spiky,' I slurred.

'Well, I was thinking that I should be going.'

'Yes, you go ahead. I'll be fine here. I said that I'd help my friend with a few things.'

Josh looked at me with suspicion. I don't think that he was buying the story at all, but he now had the excuse that he needed.

'It was nice to meet you, Evelyn.'

'Yeah, you too, Joshy.'

The door closed behind him. He couldn't get away fast enough.

I was alone in the darkened Attraction Abacus office now, sitting in Brian's executive chair with my feet on the desk, finishing my rum and Coke. Luke's accountancy textbook was open on his desk, and I grabbed it, taking a marker pen from his drawer.

I was disturbed from my developing artwork by my phone vibrating on Brian's desk. It was an angry message from my sister. I ignored it but noticed that there were two missed calls earlier from another number that I didn't recognise. It looked like a regular mobile number rather than a scam. On every other occasion, I would have ignored these too, but, unfortunately, I was pissed and called back. It was late, and it took a while for the call to be picked up.

'Evelyn?' a groggy voice answered.

'*Luke*?'

'Yeah, it's me.'

'Luke... how did... why did you call?'

'I got your number from the Abacus. I hope you don't mind. I just wanted to see if the date was okay.'

'I... couldn't you just wait for the feedback form?' I

snapped.

A pause.

'I mean, I called to see if *you* were okay.'

'So, you phoned twice, and when I didn't answer, you went to bed? Thank God, you're looking out for me, Luke!'

Another pause.

'I'm sorry, I thought I might be intruding. I wasn't sure what to do. Look, I feel bad about this whole fake dating thing. I definitely won't ask you to do it again. It's not something that should *ever* have happened.'

'Don't feel bad. I had an amazing evening.'

'That's great. Even so, it wasn't fair to you. I know this isn't a normal... boss/employee arrangement.'

'Oh, I don't know. It feels exactly like a pimp/prostitute thing we have going on, from my perspective, Luke.'

A longer pause.

'Like I say, I'm sorry. I was only checking in to see if you were okay. I can see that it was a mistake calling.'

'No, not at all. You can pass a message to Brian from me.'

'What's that?'

'Well, I was thinking that the algorithm doesn't really factor in sex appeal. I mean, my date, Josh, is hot. Really hot. I think he was undersold,' I slurred.

'Okay, I'll pass on your feedback.'

'In fact, I'm heading back to his place right now. I might shag his brains out. Warn Brian that I could be late Monday,' I said, hiccupping.

'I'll warn him. Goodnight, Evelyn.'

'Goodnight, Luke.'

Chapter Twelve

'What must never happen again?' shouted my flatmate, Katey, from somewhere outside the kitchen. It took me a few seconds to realise that I had been speaking aloud as I sat slumped at the table.

'Nothing,' I shouted back, turning my attention to the large mug of tea, untouched before me. Even tea was undrinkable, though I desperately needed to rehydrate. I'd managed to eat half a slice of buttered toast, but it wasn't sitting well on my stomach, and all I really wanted was sleep.

I won't bore you with this latest bout of self-loathing. I'm only mentioning this at all because of what happened as I sat there moping. My phone vibrated on the table, making toast crumbs dance on my plate, like body-popping ants. I was more intrigued by the spectacle than the call but finally checked my phone. It was my sister. She had tried to contact me three times and had finally left a message. The last thing I needed was another lecture about my behaviour, so I pushed the phone out of view. I would apologise properly when the dust had settled.

The washing-up water was cooling rapidly in the sink, and I really needed to tackle the mess before my other flatmate, Andy, discovered it. He would throw his toys of out the pram for sure. The phone vibrated on the table again. This time it sounded like a text, and I grabbed the handset, like a sulky teenager. The text was from my sister.

'Where are you? I've been trying to call. It's about Dad xx.'

I stared at the message, motionless. I knew something must be wrong but still couldn't face calling Abby. I began texting back instead.

'Bad news? xx.'

There was a long pause before her reply finally arrived.

'The worst xx.'

Everybody dies.

It's a fact that we accept at the back of our minds, but most of us avoid examining the thought too frequently in the foreground. It felt implausible that my dad could die. Somehow, his unique brand of self-delusion and naivety seemed like it would protect him forever. How could all of that just *go*?

My world suddenly felt small and vulnerable. I know that sounds self-centred, and, yes, I was sad *for* Dad, but that wasn't even nearly all that I felt. There was a sentimental sense of loss for the life we had never shared together, mixed with distant nostalgia for the good times that we *had* enjoyed, but the overriding emotion I felt was anger. Anger that Dad had left me for a second time in my life. Anger that the genes he had passed me could not cheat death. Anger that I now had to face the fact that *my* generation was the next to drop off the great conveyor belt of life. Ridiculous, selfish — yes, I called myself all these things and more, as I cried myself to sleep that night. I know that this is a romantic comedy, and I don't want to bring anybody down at this point, but Dad's death was a shock.

The next few days were a bit of a blur. I didn't feel ready to see Mum or Abby, so I stayed at the flat, mostly locked in my bedroom. Katey was sweet and brought me the occasional cup of tea. Andy repeatedly said that he didn't know what to say to me, until I snapped on the third occasion and suggested that he should try something different. I took some time out from work. Brian was really understanding, to the point that I felt a great warmth towards him. I hadn't been working at the Attraction Abacus that long, but it made me realise that I was already part of another family of sorts. I received flowers from the office. They were the first flowers that I had *ever* received, and a few days later, Luke called. This time I recognised his number.

'Evelyn, I'm just checking in. I'm so sorry for your loss.'

'It's okay,' I replied. It was that universally stupid response we trot out as instinctive pacifiers.

'Dad… Brian said that there is absolutely no rush to return to work.'

'I appreciate that, and the flowers you sent.'

'That was the least we could do. How are you bearing up?'

'Okay, thank you,' I replied, with heroic stoicism in my voice. I worked on the basis that nobody was really interested in bad news, but there was a balancing act to strike if I wanted to stay off work a little longer.

'Just let me know if there is anything I can do.'

'I will,' I replied. We had worked through the standard consolation template, and I owed it to Dad's creative juices to step things up. 'The funeral will be shit, though. It's the first time that I've been to one.'

Silence for a moment.

'I could come with you?'

'What do you mean?'

'Well, you know… if you don't want to go on your own. Only if Josh doesn't mind, of course.'

'I don't think it will work out with Josh,' I replied, cringing at the thought of our previous call. 'I guess Alice might think it's weird, though?' I asked, trying to get back on the front foot.

'She'll be fine. It's not like a date.'

'No, of course.'

'Just a bit of support.'

'Absolutely.'

The line was silent again as I considered this.

'Yes, that would be nice,' I replied.

I didn't think that the offer was odd at the time. The funeral arrangements had already been fraught, with our dysfunctional family life spilling over into dysfunctional family death, and I was glad of *any* support.

Mum was unsure whether she should attend the funeral at all until we convinced her that it was okay. Dad's later relationships had been sporadic, and he had been single at the time of his passing, so why shouldn't she? It felt like Abby and I were the only true constants in Dad's life, so we should be the ones to put a tribute together. The problem was that we had very different ideas of how things should go. Abby was keen on a woodland burial with a "spiritual" edge. Dad had lived his life in a spiritual vacuum as far as I was concerned, and I didn't want the occasion to unwittingly become his last great acting performance. However, Abby was older and considerably pushier, so I found myself conceding ground at every turn. If I could just prevent his funeral from degenerating into a pagan horror film scene, it would be the best that I could hope for.

We decided that a family limo following the hearse was inappropriate, and Dad had not left enough money to pay for one anyway. The funeral would be his last act of financial irresponsibility towards us all. It was this lack of funding that thwarted most of Abby's grand plans, and faced with a choice of financing her ideas or accepting a standard cremation, she agreed to keep it simple.

We struggled to decide on the photograph that would be displayed on the screen at the service. Abby preferred a still from *The Country Dentist*, taken during Dad's favourite episode, *Easter*. Dad plays a rookie locum dentist, called into action when the head of the practice is hospitalised with appendicitis. A crisis predictably soon arises, with the village vicar breaking his molar on a walnut cake, baked by a spurned love interest. This suspicious injury jeopardises the vicar's much-anticipated Easter sermon.

'What are you going to do?' the dental technician asks Dad, as the hapless vicar groans in the surgery chair next to him.

'He needs emergency root canal,' Dad replies, pulling on a pair of latex gloves and staring moodily into the camera. 'I'm going to save the tooth... and I'm going to save Easter.'

The closing credits roll.

It was a nice photograph, and I appreciated the sentiment. Dad at the pinnacle of his career and all that. But we had taken the piss out of that scene so many times after he had left that it felt disrespectful to use the photo at his funeral. I preferred a blurry headshot of Dad as a young teenager, playing *Danny Zuko* in *Grease*. The yellowing school programme had been lovingly stored with Dad's important paperwork, and this photograph truly epitomised him, to my mind at least. Abby disagreed.

'He died an older man. You can't use the photo of a kid, Evelyn.'

I daydreamed on that point for a while. If there was life after this one, surely, we wouldn't roll up to heaven with arthritis on a mobility scooter? I preferred to picture Dad as an eternal teenager, belting out *Greased Lightnin'* to a garage full of slick-haired cherubs. By the time I re-focused on the conversation, Mum and Abby had already settled on another old family photograph, and it was too late.

Everybody thought it odd that I wanted to walk alone to the service. I had the offer of multiple lifts, and even Luke offered to walk with me, but I wanted the time to get my head around the day. What I didn't consider was the size of the wreath I had ordered, with chrysanthemums poking up my nostrils as I tottered along the street. This was more stubbornness on my part: I wanted to bring my *own* flowers with my own private message, but these could have easily travelled by car without me. So be it, this would be some kind of weird pilgrimage for Dad.

I was often late, but I was determined to be early that day. I finally selected a bottle green dress to wear. The shoes I chose had a slightly higher heel than I normally preferred. Not high by most standards, but high enough for me to feel like I was in danger. Coupled with the flowers right in front of my face, it felt inevitable that I would stumble in front of a bus before I arrived. Two family deaths for the price of one.

It was September now, and the crematorium grounds were flooded with autumnal sun. There were crane flies hovering about everywhere, freaking me out as they bumbled into my bare legs below my dress. I had arrived a full hour early and found a bench where I could sit and gather my thoughts.

It occurred to me that this might be the closest thing to a "big day" I might ever experience. I had never pictured myself as a bride. It was difficult to believe that other women still did, given the carnage of most marriages. Fairytale weddings must surely be off the menu, and even a marriage of convenience was beyond my imagination. But the daughter of a deceased father? Nobody could take that away from me. This was a starring role, even if I had to share it with my sister.

130

I needed to distract myself from my growing sadness, and I also needed to do something with the flowers. There was still time to kill. It had been an error of judgement to come to my first funeral alone without knowing the form. I wandered down the side of the crematorium. It was a Seventies building, feeling even more dystopian in its dated attempt to appear modern. I continued towards the garden of remembrance at the rear. After depressing myself further by reading a few of the plaques, I decided to complete the circuit around the building, back to where I had started. There were tears building up in my eyes.

I stopped in my tracks.

At the far side of the crematorium, there was a crowd of mourners laying flowers in a segregated area of the garden.

How had I got the time wrong?

Now, I could not stop the tears from falling; I had even messed this up for Dad! I hurried towards the group, hiding my weeping face behind my flowers. I could not look at anyone, gently laying the wreath on the grass in front of me. I was sobbing uncontrollably now, and I felt an arm rest around my shoulder.

'It's okay,' an older woman said beside me.

'I'm not usually a crier,' I sniffed.

'You're allowed to cry today.'

'It's crap, isn't it?' I sobbed before dissolving into tears again. The woman just rubbed my shoulder. I had no idea who she was, but her voice was warm and comforting, and I snuggled next to her.

'I know. Just let it all out,' she said.

I did, and after a few minutes of serious bawling, my heaving shoulders began to calm. The only comforting thought was that if Dad could see me now, he would know that I really did care. I'd left it too late to tell him, but my red eyes and snotty nose would be all the evidence he would need from his celestial perch.

I finally looked up again, sniffing. In the distance, I could see a man in a suit, waving towards me. It took me a few seconds to realise that it was Luke. He was frantically gesturing for me to join him.

'That's better,' said the woman beside me, who hadn't noticed Luke. 'She had a full life. Just remember the good times you shared with her.'

I froze, glancing towards the other floral tributes on the grass. The nearest spelt the word "Gran" in lilies.

Oh!

I didn't want to abandon my flowers, but I couldn't pick them up again either. I waved at Luke, pointing towards my wreath and then gesticulating for him to approach. He eventually understood and began to step across the grass. The woman was still talking to me as he arrived.

'We've spoken about this before,' Luke sighed, looking at me in pity. 'I'm so sorry about this,' he said to the woman beside me. 'She gets a little confused. It's getting better, though. She'll be allowed around children again soon,' he added, making silent gestures behind my back. 'Supervised, of course,' he whispered.

He scooped up my flowers from the grass before the woman could reply and led me away.

Maybe I *should* tell you about the service, but I don't really want to. I was numb most of the time anyway, unable to look at the photograph of Dad on the screen, let alone his coffin. I had written him a poem, which I partly read aloud at the lectern, in between floods of tears.

I don't remember much at all. Just blurred ovals of pink staring back at me. Tuneless singing. Meaningless words. My sister doing some weird thing with a moon symbol. The only thing I vividly remember was Luke holding my hand. We didn't discuss it, but he held my hand the whole time that I wasn't speaking, and I remember not wanting to let go at the end of the service. I squeezed hard. He may have incurred ligament damage. At the very least, Luke stopped me from tipping Dad's coffin over, something I had convinced myself that I might do, during an intense spell of doom-dreaming.

I have Dad's stiff arm draped around my shoulder, and we are kicking out together in a chorus line funeral finale. Relatives are aghast. Children are crying. Dad's face is frozen in a rigid smile. Come on, sing along! New York, Newww Yorkkkk da da da dada…

The rest of the service just passed me by. It was as if I had passed into a tunnel, and I only recall truly re-emerging at the wake, with Mum smiling at me.

'He's nice,' Mum said.

'Who?'

'Luke. I think he likes you.'

'Oh, I just work with him,' I replied, looking towards Luke, who was grabbing us a couple of drinks in the distance. I also noticed that he helped himself to a cream cake while Alice wasn't about to witness.

'Is that so?'

'You look great,' I said, ignoring Mum's smirk. It was the first time I had taken in her appearance, and I was pleased that she had tried hard for Dad, wearing a navy dress that was a good look for her. Her hair had almost returned to its natural auburn colour, but it was still cut short in a bob. 'I had some nice conversations with Dad at the hospital, near the end.'

'I didn't think I should go.'

'I know.'

'It's not that I don't… didn't care. There just didn't seem to be anything left to say,' she said, raising a glass of white wine to her lips. She left a smudge of lipstick on the rim.

'I understand,' I replied. Neither of us spoke for a moment, both of us, I suspected, emotionally drained. Mum was miles away, and a thought crossed my mind. 'Can you remember what first attracted you to Dad?'

Mum laughed. 'That was a long time ago.'

'You must remember.' I wanted to know if Dad's version of events even remotely coincided with reality. He was a fantasist after all.

'Why do you want to know?'

'It's just interesting. I guess it must have been difficult for you to know if you *really* liked him at the time. Enough to spend your life with him.'

'Oh,' Mum said, looking knowingly over my shoulder towards Luke. I was as transparent as my empty glass, and I suddenly felt ten years old again. 'Well, your dad was a bit of a character. He made me laugh a lot.'

'I can imagine.'

'He was generous, although he was hopeless with money. Thoughtful too, at the start at least.'

'And all of that was enough for you?'

'I looked forward to seeing him. I really liked him. What more do you want, Evelyn?' Mum said, laughing.

'You loved him?'

'Yes, I think I did, whatever that means.'

I felt a sense of secondary pride for Dad at that moment. I

swear his creative juices pumped faster through my veins as Mum said those words.

'That's nice to know. For the record, Dad said that he loved you too.'

'He said that?'

I nodded. Mum was tearing up now, and I moved quickly to lighten the mood.

'Dad also said that Martin bored you shitless and that you needed the sense of danger he brought to your life.'

'Maybe he was right,' Mum said, smiling. She dabbed her eyes with a tissue. 'The problem was the danger was real.'

Chapter Thirteen

The conversations with Mum and Dad had proved cathartic, and I looked at my life through new eyes. Perhaps their marriage had broken down, but they had loved each other once. There must be lots of couples who stay together all their lives without ever loving each other at all. I don't know why that knowledge was so important to me, but it gave me hope.

I felt a definite sense of purpose when I returned to work, and more significantly, I was determined to clear the air with Luke. I didn't appreciate the mixed messages I was receiving from him. It was unfair to Alice too. Brian was out for the day at an investment meeting, and the morning was busy. The data entry tray was piled high, and I suspected that nobody had even looked at it in my absence. Predictably, the plant in the consultation room was a withered stump.

There were three visitors that morning. The last of them was a woman who was the same age as me but with considerably longer eyelashes. I couldn't build up much of a rapport with her; I felt like she looked down at me and acted as if she had no place in a dating agency. I knew that every woman on the books was worth three guys to Brian, so I bit my tongue. To counteract the negativity of that appointment, the Abacus received some nice email feedback from an adrenaline-junkie gay couple who had thrown themselves out of a plane on the algorithm's advice. Fortunately, their parachutes had opened. I remembered how elated Brian had been, successfully dealing with their office appointment. He had perhaps overused his diversity lexicon, but the couple were very forgiving all the same. I felt like a proud teacher.

"Awesome job, Attraction Abacus. Thanks for finding our forever-afters," the message read.

It was uplifting, and I worked harder to clear the keying backlog. This was the kind of loyalty that Frank had vainly strived for at the hotel, but here, I lived it. There was so much going on that I didn't get a chance to speak to Luke at all until early in the afternoon.

'Wow, what a morning!' Luke said, leaning back in his chair. 'Sorry it was such a full-on day to come back to, Evelyn.'

'I prefer to be busy,' I smiled.

'I hope you're okay.'

'Yes, thanks for coming to Dad's funeral with me.'

'It was great… in a tragic way, of course.'

'Of course.'

'Really sad.'

'Yes.'

This was my opportunity. I had carefully rehearsed a little speech, but at that precise moment I froze.

'Oh, I nearly forgot,' Luke said, saving me. 'I think we might have had a break-in at the Abacus.'

'That's terrible.'

'Yes, nothing seems to have been stolen, thank God. There was an empty bottle of rum in Brian's bin, though. Someone drew a penis on my accountancy textbook, too. It appears that I was specifically targeted, as the intruder wrote, "Boring. Boring. Boring. Luke is a dickhead." above the drawing. The strange thing is that no windows or locks were broken, and only three of us have keys. All very weird,' he added.

'That is weird.'

'Yes, and Brian left an extra job for today. I need to get away early for college, so I wondered if you could pick it up for me?'

'Sure.'

'You'll need these administrator credentials to log in,' he said, passing me a piece of paper. 'A few of the Abacus scores were corrupted by an update. We just need to manually correct them.'

'No problem.'

'Maybe we can catch up later?' Luke said.

I just nodded, inwardly furious with myself for not saying my piece when I had the chance.

I hadn't really absorbed the significance of what I had been asked to do. Luke had surely missed the implications, too, or perhaps he had just forgotten. Normally, I only dealt with raw data for the singles' applications. The algorithm would process these applications overnight and generate the Abacus score. Our singles never saw their Abacus scores, and neither did I. The administrator credentials that Luke had given me allowed me to view these sacred, hidden numbers. All of them! Within seconds of logging in, I searched for my own name.

Evelyn Foster. Abacus score: 67.

I sat back in my chair, staring at the number.

67.

Was the score a percentage? Equating that percentage to an exam grade would make me a C+. Was I just a C+?

At some level, that score validated what I had always felt about myself, but it was now ruthlessly confirmed in writing. I tried to think of the *precise* ways I could have been marked down. I was still on the right side of thirty. I'd flown through the aptitude test, so I couldn't have lost points for stupidity. It must be my appearance.

I calmly strolled to the bathroom, where there was a mirror mounted above the basin and studied my reflection objectively. My face was *fairly* symmetrical; there was a slight bump on the bridge of my nose, where I had face-planted while learning to roller-skate. My mouth was perhaps on the large size, but by no means a comedic feature. My eyes were okay. Yes, it would be harsh to label my appearance unattractive, though I could accept that I wasn't stunning. Perhaps my BMI had let me down? I had been comfort-eating since the news of Dad's death and may have gained a few extra pounds, but surely everyone was overweight according to those BMI jokers? I lifted my top, sucking my stomach in. There couldn't be enough around my middle to downgrade my score. I needed some context.

Back at my desk, I immediately checked for Alice's profile. I know this was masochistic, but I needed the worst-case scenario as a starting point for comparison, expecting to unearth an Abacus merit distinction for abdominal muscle excellence. After a few minutes of frantic searching, I finally accepted that Alice didn't have a profile in the system. My second thought was Luke.

Luke Asquith. Abacus score: 73.

I cross-referenced Luke's mobile number to confirm that it was him. Sure enough, it was. According to my exam grade calculations, that made Luke a straight B. What the hell! How had Luke scored higher than me?

As if summoned from a bottle, the Abacus genie approached my desk at that exact moment. Keep calm, I told myself.

'Everything okay?' Luke asked.

'Fine,' I replied, staring at my screen.

'Why does that sound like "not fine"?'

I looked up at this point. My well-rehearsed speech was about to fly out the window.

'See, there you go again, talking as if you know me.'

'What do you mean?'

'What do *I* mean? Well, maybe I'm a little bit confused, Luke. One minute, you're trying to stick your tongue down my throat at a party. The next, you're holding my hand at my dad's funeral, and yet, you have a girlfriend. Her name is Alice, if I recall correctly.'

'Why are you saying all this now?'

'It seems as good a time as any, doesn't it? I was wondering if you feel like you can do whatever you like, just because I'm a half-orphan now.'

'I would never do that.'

'Perhaps it's because you're a few points higher on the Abacus scoring than me then.'

'Oh, you're not meant to…'

'Too late, I've seen it! Would you say that you're better looking than me, Luke?'

'Absolutely not.'

'Though you might think that you're smarter than me, I guess, because you're taking your fancy auditor qualifications. I'm sure I could do the same if I were prepared to bore myself to death.'

'I don't think I'm smarter than you, Evelyn.'

'Maybe there is some kind of *guy* premium added on?'

'I don't think it works that way.'

'So, what is it? We're roughly the same age. I don't have ten dependent children.'

'I don't know exactly how the scores are calc…'

'You'd better be considerably richer than me.'

'Evelyn, I honestly don't know how the algorithm works. Only Brian deals with that.'

I paused for a moment to compose myself. Luke was staring at me now, and the time was right.

'So, what *is* going on... between you and me?' I asked.

Luke sighed, slumping into a chair beside me. He covered his face with his hands.

'I told you it was complicated,' he said.

'It's not normal for your boss to hold your hand at a funeral.'

'I know.'

'So, what *is* this?'

Luke rubbed his face now, and I wondered if he was even going to reply, hiding behind his fingers.

'I really like you, Evelyn.'

'But?'

'But I have certain obligations to Alice.'

'Obligations?'

'Well, obligations to Brian, really.'

'You're not making any sense.'

'Okay,' he sighed, lowering his hands. 'I think I mentioned that there is a third-party investor backing the Abacus. The investor is a friend of Brian's called George. They worked together at a merchant bank in London a few years ago. Brian made a bad call when he worked at the bank and lost the company a lot of money. He also lost his job in the process. Brian struggled to find another job, and George helped him out financially, so that he could start the Abacus.'

'So?'

'I'm getting there. You need to see the full picture to understand this. That period out of work was particularly hard

141

for Dad. He really wasn't himself at all, and Mum and Dad temporarily separated. It was a mess. Anyway, Brian now sees success at the Abacus as his chance to win Mum back. The problem is that George isn't doing quite so well financially these days, either. The invested money has become a bit of an issue between them, and George is Alice's dad.'

'Oh, that's awkward,' I replied.

'It's more than awkward,' Luke said, slumping in his chair. 'It's a disaster. It's all I ever hear about.'

'Even so, that's no reason for you to be with someone if you don't want to be.'

'Don't get me wrong, there's a lot I like about Alice. We're not amazingly compatible, but it would be the wrong time to break up with her, even if I wanted to, given the situation.'

'That's not your problem. Or Alice's.'

'Maybe, but some things might seem easier from the outside.'

'I'm sure Brian wouldn't want you to…'

'He wouldn't, but I don't want to see *him* in a worse mess,' Luke interrupted. He was sitting with his arms crossed now, like a belligerent child. I considered pushing him off the chair, but he looked way too grouchy to laugh about it. When he continued to sulk in silence, I lost sympathy.

'It sounds like something you need to sort out between yourselves,' I sighed, standing up, 'but I would prefer it if you were less familiar with me. You're *using* Alice through misguided loyalty to keep Brian and George happy, and you're also using *me* in the process.'

'I'm sorry, it really isn't like that. I wouldn't…'

'I need to clear the data entry backlog. Would you like a coffee?'

'No, thank you.'

I walked away to the kitchen, leaving Luke wallowing in self-pity. I felt a lot better. Standing up for myself was satisfying, and things also made a whole lot more sense now.

We didn't speak further that afternoon, and Luke disappeared to college around three. I corrected the Abacus scores as Brian had requested (resisting the temptation to upgrade my own), and I locked the office up just after six, working extra to catch up with the application entry. The earlier conversation still played on my mind. In hindsight, this was a low point in my relationship with Luke. I decided that he was either weak or deceptive, and neither was an attractive personality trait to me.

I remembered my pre-planned grocery shopping trip too late, and I couldn't face visiting the supermarket with the prospect of cooking dinner late afterwards. For the first time since I had joined the Abacus, I decided to eat out straight from work, justifying the expense on a difficult day.

Sometimes, I wonder if there are strange forces at play in the universe. Normally, I would have headed straight to an anonymous fast-food joint, where I could stare at my phone in a secluded corner and be in and out within thirty minutes. For some reason, I was drawn to the Wetherspoon's pub in the High Street, The Five Bells. The all-day drinkers were starting to leave as I arrived (before they were thrown out), making way for the evening clientele.

Grabbing an orange juice at the bar, I managed to find a quiet table at the rear of the pub, with only one other suited guy working at a laptop at a table opposite. As I glanced up from my menu, my mind filled with gourmet burger options, I realised too late that it was Brian. There was a pint glass in front of his laptop, which could have been his first, but his tie was loosened around his neck, and his cheeks were flushed. So much for investment meetings!

Brian hadn't noticed me arrive, and there was still a chance to switch tables before he did, for both of our sakes. I silently rose from my chair, side-stepping the table and picking up my drink. As I slid my handbag over my shoulder, Brian looked up.

'Evelyn!'

'Oh, I didn't see you there, Brian,' I said, laughing. 'I thought you were more of a Thirsty Donkey guy.'

His puzzled expression suggested that he had forgotten the name of the gastropub we had visited on my first day at work, and I must have sounded plain weird.

'The meeting ended earlier than expected,' he replied, in a reciprocal non-explanation to my nonsense.

'Did it go okay?'

'Actually, it didn't start at all,' he slurred. It was *not* his first drink of the day. 'I took a train to London, only to be told that they couldn't see me this afternoon.'

'That's a bit off,' I replied, still loitering beside his table, orange juice in hand. I didn't want to hear this brutal honesty from my boss while I still hoped to have a successful career at the Abacus.

'It was *off* indeed, Evelyn. Do you want a drink?'

'I was just finishing this one before heading home.'

'I wondered if we could have a quick chat?'

It wasn't really a question, and complete rudeness aside, there didn't seem to be any option other than to agree.

'Sure,' I replied. Brian nearly toppled a chair, trying to pull it out for me. I steadied it quickly, perching beside him before he fell sideways too.

144

I can't recall exactly what Brian wanted to chat about. I suspected he just wanted somebody to talk to, but after five minutes of work waffle, the conversation unexpectedly became more interesting.

'I'd appreciate it if you didn't tell Luke that you saw me here. He worries,' Brian said.

'Yes, of course. Luke explained the situation.'

I instantly realised that I had said too much, and tipsy as he was, I could see that Brian had picked up on it.

'What did he explain?'

'Oh, you know.'

Awkward pause.

'All of it?'

'Yeah, I think so.'

There didn't seem to be any point in lying, and Brian just nodded before finishing his pint in one gulp.

'I could tell you my side of the story, if you have time?'

'Sure' I replied. My stomach was rumbling, but it was a day for discovering the truth, and I was interested as much as hungry.

'You can ruin your entire life just like this, Evelyn,' Brian slurred, tapping his middle three fingers on the table. 'Tippety-tap. Think about our ancestors, the cavemen... the cavepeople, sorry. They ruined their lives by not running fast enough and getting eaten. But now, a little tippety-tap on a mouse... just the tiniest twitch of your pinkies... and everything is gone. Your house, your car... your marriage.'

'I'm sure they haven't *gone*, Brian.'

'No, no, they haven't *gone* gone. But they could go... just like that. Just a little twitch,' he slurred, repeating the drumming motion on the table. 'It's crazy, isn't it?'

'Well, yes.'

'I had a good marriage, Evelyn. I know Sarah always wanted stuff. She was far more into stuff than I was, but it was a good marriage. I think there are two kinds of people. Predators and prey. Luke and I, well, we're prey. That's not a bad thing. I think being prey is great in its own right,' he slurred, losing his train of thought for a moment. 'But Sarah and Alice? They're predators. Alice's dad, George? A definite predator too. Are you a predator, Evelyn?'

'I don't really understand what you mean.'

'Do you know why I wanted to start a dating agency? I could have started any kind of business I liked. It's because I believe in love. I'm a romantic. The first time I ever met Sarah was at Victoria Falls. We were both travelling at the time, and we met there, just like that. This was before the internet. This was before someone had written a thousand blogs on the best places to stay on a budget in Bali. Back then, travelling almost felt like exploring. To meet someone like Sarah there... well, it was almost impossible. I knew instantly that I was crazy about her. I even said to her, on that very first day I met her, that I would love her for as long as the Victoria Falls kept on falling. That's a nice thing to say, isn't it?'

'It is, Brian.'

'I meant it,' he slurred, disappearing in thought again. 'Someone told me that they switched Victoria Falls off at night, and I believed it. That's not analogous to my love for Sarah, by the way, but how stupid was I back then? Anyway, after the troubles at the bank, Sarah and I separated. Not divorced but separated, you understand. I missed her *so* much,' he sighed, staring right through me. 'Anyway, I had a great idea to win Sarah back. I proposed that we return to Victoria Falls on the 8th of August. It was the exact day and place that we met travelling all those years before, and I suggested that we start from the beginning, all over again.'

'What happened?'

'What happened?' he said, shaking his head. 'Well, Sarah had stopped answering my calls by this point. I emailed her the plan, sorted out my jabs, and then flew out to Zimbabwe a few months later. I waited there eight hours that day, no shade, almost dead on my feet. Eight hours, Evelyn! But she didn't show up.'

'Wait, you travelled all the way to the Victoria Falls without *agreeing* that Sarah would meet you there?'

'Yes.'

'That's hilarious, Brian.'

Silence for a moment.

'What? Don't you think that is even tragically romantic?'

'Borderline creepy.'

'I see,' he replied, slumping in his chair. 'I appreciate your honesty.'

I imagined that Brian had not encountered this exact female perspective before, certainly not on any romantic rendezvous since, at the local Harvester perhaps, where his dewy-eyed date would push aside her breaded mushroom starter as Brian recounted this tragic tale (hoping to secure a tumble around her bedroom later, on the back of a mid-week special and his heartbreak woes. Maybe I was just cynical.)

'There's still the Abacus. Luke said that this is the way you plan to win Sarah back now.'

'Which makes days like today all the harder to take,' Brian sighed. 'George wants his money back, and I need to find alternative investment soon.'

'Maybe you need a new approach?'

'What do you mean?'

147

'Well, you're trying to sell a fresh, dynamic dating service, aren't you?'

'Correct.'

'But, without being rude, you're not fresh and dynamic, Brian. I mean, you're a nice guy and all that, but when you turn up to these investment meetings with your tatty old laptop case, maybe it isn't the right… image.' Brian was silent for a moment, and I wondered if I had gone too far.

'My God, you're right, but what can I do about it?'

'Perhaps Luke and I could accompany you to the meetings?'

'I don't know if…'

'You're a scientist, Brian. This is simple mathematics. To date, your attempts to secure new investment have yielded a zero per cent success rate. Any new approach can only be an improvement on zero, or equally bad at worst.'

'It could work, I guess.'

'It will work,' I replied, with a conviction I didn't feel. Work or not, though, this seemed a good solution to multiple problems.

Chapter Fourteen

Ganesha, the wise old elephant god, eyed me suspiciously from the bookshelf. My wishes had been clear and precise to this point. Save money, fly to Goa and finish my book. I sensed he didn't appreciate the evolving new rescue mission with the Abacus. Financially, I was inching closer and closer to my dream, but at the same time, the dream was transforming before his elephant eyes.

As I stared at my laptop screen that night, the words didn't come easily to me. It was difficult to write a romantic comedy when the main character was so conflicted. Although Luke's explanation had made some kind of sense, I didn't appreciate his methods. There was a worrying additional layer to my feelings, though, itching beneath my skin. Despite knowing that Luke was wrong, something still drew me towards him. I was hugely conflicted. He had been so kind to me at Dad's funeral, but his relationship with Alice was ongoing. I was in danger of being played by a player. Still, I told myself that Luke wasn't a player. He was just naive and trying to help Brian. My suspicious mind immediately countered the thought. Nobody ever believes that they're being played by a player. That's how players roll. Either way, I still found him extremely frustrating, and it was good that he had promised to avoid any further overfamiliarity.

I needed to tidy my room. My wardrobe's contents were scattered all over the carpet, and if I didn't wash some of the clothes soon, I would be in mad outfit territory.

Thinking was just too exhausting.

There was a lull at the Abacus the following morning. Both Brian and Luke were back, and I think we all needed time to adjust to the original office dynamic again. It was a bit like the reality TV shows when the size of the camp suddenly changes, and everyone loses their shit. There was another factor at play, of course. It was uncertain exactly what had been said to each of us, though we all knew that different conversations had taken place. It felt like the setting of a John le Carré novel.

Given this uneasiness, I was particularly self-conscious when a customer arrived just after ten. The walls of the consultation room felt paper-thin, with an invisible audience once again listening in beyond them. I whispered my way through the appointment, without my usual patter and swagger. It was a relief to be back at the sanctuary of my desk, mindlessly keying application details again. Luke smiled as he passed. He was wearing a navy shirt and black jeans. They suited him. In another life, I might have even told him so. Brian, on the other hand, was visibly suffering from the previous evening. His face needed a good iron today.

We were all cheered by the news from First Impact, the marketing agency, that the Abacus website traffic had increased by twenty per cent in the last month. Although there was an inherent mistrust of First Impact, this increase was borne out by the number of singles' applications we were processing. I had noticed more footfall in the office, too. It was approaching midday when Brian made his big announcement. A customer had just left the office, and Brian asked Luke and me to join him at his desk. We each pulled up a chair, waiting expectantly.

'My meeting was unfortunately postponed yesterday,' Brian

said, avoiding my eye. 'However, the investors were back in touch this morning, apologising for the non-show, and they have restated their interest in our venture.'

'Sounds promising,' Luke said.

'It *is* promising,' Brian agreed, grinning. 'Their email today got me thinking. Why go all the way to London to try to explain what we're doing? What if our investors came here and saw for themselves? We have a dynamic team and great premises. What better way to get the flavour of the Abacus?' Luke noticed that I was trying not to smile, though it wasn't for any reason he suspected. Miraculously, the investors agreed to the idea by return, with only a week before the meeting was rescheduled at the Abacus office.

This agreement instigated a frantic period of activity. Brian, who worked late every evening anyway, seemed to live in the office that week, often wearing the same clothes the following day. He said that he was working on the business plan, but it was difficult to understand why this involved so much time and effort. The office was crazily busy in the daytime too, with singles arriving through the door in a regular procession. It hadn't been *that* long since the Abacus had opened, but Brian felt that we needed to "spruce up" the office, in his words. The first new feature to arrive was a water-cooling machine on the next Tuesday morning, which was purely cosmetic, judging by the lack of interest shown in it. Our trusty Lidl mugs were out, replaced by a bone China tea/coffee set that I was too frightened to touch. Even the plant in the consultation room was replaced. I stopped Luke from throwing the old, withering stump out, offering to adopt it. I felt a connection with this valiant survivor and had little time for the verdant new pretenders taking its place.

'This is their future without water, Luke,' I said, waving the dying plant under his nose.

The final addition arrived on Thursday, when Luke bundled through the door with what looked like a surfboard under his arm. As he set it upright, next to the consultation room, all became clear. It was a cardboard cut-out of the scientist in the Abacus window. "Step this way to find your forever-after," the speech bubble read above the scientist's head.

'I love it,' I said, knowing that Luke had designed the graphic. 'You should do this for a living.'

'It's okay. The colour has bled a bit here,' he said, picking at a minute blemish at the edges.

'Guess it's all over for the Abacus,' I replied, squinting at the defect.

I appreciated that Luke was trying to keep his distance that afternoon. He had obviously taken on board what I had said, although he was now approaching Victorian levels of politeness towards me. We had always taken turns to make each other drinks in the office, but when Luke approached my desk with a China teacup and saucer in his hand, it was a step too far.

'Thank you, my good man,' I said.

'Tea, which I have noticed is your preferred beverage these days.'

'Very observant.'

'Not *too* observant, though, I hope?'

'It's fine,' I replied, ignoring his smirk.

The air had been cleared. It felt as though we were all working towards a common aim, and I remember being particularly happy that afternoon. I should have known that things were about to change, and they did five minutes before I was due to leave. The door opened, and I sensed movement beyond my desk. I looked up to see Alice standing in the

152

doorway. It was our first encounter since the party, and I immediately panicked. Our eyes met, and she paced slowly towards my desk in an outfit that I knew I couldn't afford. There was nowhere to run or hide.

'How are you doing, Evelyn?'

'Fine, thanks. You?

'Good,' Alice replied, frowning at me now. 'Have you done something different with your hair?'

'Not really.'

I hadn't had time to wash my hair that day, and it looked like shit. I knew it, and Alice knew it. I instantly felt like the awkward teenager I had once been at school, with my clothes and make-up never quite making the grade with the cool kids.

'Oh,' Alice replied, walking away in satisfaction. She smiled at Luke as she passed him, stopping in the centre of the office, in view of Brian's desk.

'It looks so different in here. All these new things,' Alice said, standing hand on hips, surveying the office. 'You love spending other people's money, don't you, Brian?' she said, laughing.

'We have to speculate to accumulate,' Brian said.

'I would have thought you would have learnt not to speculate quite so much by now.'

'I guess I should have,' Brian replied, staring at his screen. No quips, or witty replies. It was a low blow, but Alice wasn't finished.

'Dad says he'll be calling soon. He said that he wanted to chat with you about a few things.'

'That will be nice. Send him my regards.'

'I will do,' Alice said, turning her attention to Luke. I noticed that Brian had taken the opportunity to slip away to the

153

consultation room while he could.

'I'm nearly done here,' Luke said, tapping at his keyboard.

'That's fine. I just called in with some good news,' Alice said, smiling. 'The Dorset cottage is going to be free this weekend. My parents said that it's okay for us to stay there. Just the two of us. The hot tub will be on. Remember the fun we had in there last May?'

Alice was staring at me as she spoke, and I knew her voice was raised for my benefit. I didn't look at Luke, but he replied after a few seconds.

'That sounds great.'

'We could book a meal at The King's Head. It's just down the road. They have an amazing salad bar, remember?'

'Sure.'

'It gets busy, though. You should book it now.'

'Yeah, I will,' Luke said, smiling. Alice just watched him for a moment.

'I mean right now.'

'Oh, yes. Will do,' he said, tapping at his screen.

'Perfect. It will be a chance for us to spend some quality alone time,' Alice said, smiling flirtatiously. 'Too many things have got in our way recently,' she added, looking directly at me again. She leaned across the desk and kissed Luke.

I quickly looked away, my cheeks burning.

Luke and Alice were in a relationship. Witnessing their intimacy shouldn't have hit me so hard, but here in the Abacus office, a place I had always associated with Luke, it was too much. All the little jokes we had shared that day suddenly felt ridiculous. What had I been thinking?

I wanted to leave my desk, but I couldn't move or even look up. I tapped at my keyboard, without focusing on the screen, praying that they would both hurry up and leave. When they finally did, a few minutes later, I didn't take my eyes from my laptop, grinning madly at the screen as I shouted my goodbyes. The door closed behind them, leaving me sitting in empty silence.

When Saturday arrived, all enthusiasm for the upcoming meeting had gone. My plan had been to research the investment company that morning, but there felt little point in trying to shine at the meeting now. When I half-heartedly opened the laptop in my bedroom, I already knew that I wouldn't write anything either. After a few minutes of staring out the window, I realised what I was really there for.

My first Google search was "best things to do in Dorset". Within half an hour, I had convinced myself that Dorset was the romantic centre of the universe. Durdle Door, Lulworth Cove and Chesil Beach looked idyllic in the photographs. My mind was running amok, and even a picnic at Monkey World seemed romantically perfect, conjuring a *Mary Poppins*-esque mental scene, complete with dancing chimpanzees. My mood darkened completely when I remembered the hot tub. Luke and Alice would be spending the weekend there (and in the bedroom) without even considering monkeys for a second. I needed some fresh air.

My local park was hardly a wildlife sanctuary itself, but there were a few grey squirrels and ducks kicking about as I wandered aimlessly through the trees. Autumn was most certainly in the air now, with reddening leaves gusting around my feet. Even the weather felt like it had reached the conclusion of something good, and everything was about to change. My phone beeped from my jacket pocket. I fumbled for the handset.

Ridiculously, I thought that it might be Luke, but it was a message from my best friend, Olivia. The mere sight of her name was enough to jolt me back to reality. Why was I moping about? This wasn't me. Somehow, I had allowed myself to become the very kind of person that Liv and I would ridicule on a night out. It was pathetic.

I stomped through the swirling leaves to a bench, positioned in front of a small pond, glistening at the centre of the park. The bench was shaded by thinning branches above me, and I wriggled out of the sun entirely. No longer in the glare, I could read the message. Olivia had a new job. She wanted to talk to me about it at some point.

I didn't feel like calling her back. I wasn't in the right mindset to discuss jobs or anything really. Any conversation about Liv's situation would inevitably lead to a conversation about my own. I liked to be positive and optimistic when I spoke to my friends. Nobody really wanted to hear anybody else unloading their troubles. Best friend or not, I preferred to deal with problems myself. I instinctively knew what I *should* do, and even if a friend pointed out the obvious, it was a totally different thing to go through with it. I should leave the Abacus and forget Luke.

A squirrel fell from the tree right beside me, hitting the ground with a dull thud. Dazed, but amazingly unhurt, it instantly scurried away up a neighbouring tree trunk. The interruption scrambled my rational thoughts.

Luke was with Alice right now.

I felt physically sick when I pictured him in a hot tub, cavorting with his model girlfriend. They cracked open a bottle of bubbly, surveying the sprawling country estate that they would one day inherit. Yes, Luke was having the time of his life, while

I was sitting here dodging kamikaze squirrels.

That was when it hit me like an oncoming truck.

I had ignored all the little warning signs and had sleepwalked right into this. I stood from the bench, covering my mouth with my hand in shock. I had been so stupid.

I liked Luke. I *really* liked Luke, despite everything!

How this had happened, I did not know. All my previous analysing and pontificating had only served to throw me off my own trail. The truth had always been right in front of me. This should have been a beautiful moment of realisation and self-awareness, but instead I felt totally helpless and lost.

Chapter Fifteen

Luke's opportunities to speak up were decreasing by the hour. If he didn't act soon, things were going to get messy. Just a few words to spit out, and he could carry on with his life, God willing. But it was her face! Every time Alice looked at him, he squirmed. Alice "did" angry well, and even if he became angry too, she would become angrier still. He could never find a top gear to match hers.

His first failure to act had been just prior to their early morning run. It was also his greatest failure, because if he had said something then, she could have just cranked up the music on her phone and run off her fury. Also, there would have been more of the weekend left to recover. However, it had felt too early in the morning for the challenging discussion.

He tried to catch Alice's eye multiple times when they returned, but this made him realise how little she looked at him. Things were destined to get progressively worse unless he spoke up soon. Alice packed her overnight bag without a murmur from him. She hated packing, and he stood stewing in the corner of her bedroom, watching her sort through her extensive selection of toiletries on the carpet, before trying to cram them into a travel bag. The angrier she became trying to fit them all in, the more he retreated into his shell.

Even financial hardship failed to stir him into action. He knew that his credit card was almost maxed out, but when Alice "suggested" that he fill the car with petrol while she finished packing, he was just glad of the temporary reprieve to leave the house and regroup his thoughts. A full tank of petrol, which he had no intention of using to drive to Dorset, was a small price to pay for a mental reset. Once the tank was full, he delayed his return, sitting at the edge of the garage forecourt, munching a chocolate doughnut. The car rocked repeatedly as traffic passed beside him in the road, but he barely noticed. This was pure comfort eating, and, yes, he was very aware of the empty calories that he was stuffing down his throat, but didn't they taste good? Alice wasn't there to witness it. All the same, he was careful to dispose of the wrapper.

It would be time to head back soon, but a last few minutes to think things through alone was what he needed. He knew that he wasn't weak, as such. His first wasp sting was soon laughed off as an infant without fuss. When he broke his leg as a child, he barely cried. But this stuff? Well, he was no good at this stuff. He just went along with things. He was easy-going. How much more of his life would he have spent just going along with things if he hadn't met Evelyn? Probably the rest of it. She was the wake-up call he needed. Evelyn gave him a new sense of direction and a reason to face a situation that he would donate his left testicle to avoid.

It was difficult to define exactly how he felt about Evelyn. Avoiding overused greeting card language, he liked it when she was around. Everything felt *less* when she wasn't. It was an odd, unfamiliar sensation. They were very different people, though, so a future together was difficult to visualise. However, their current relationship, whatever that might be, made it clear that his present one was all wrong.

That wasn't the whole story, though. If *he* was going along with things, then surely Alice was too? His existence alone

159

seemed an irritation to her most of the time. He obviously didn't match up to her expectations as a physical specimen either. She encouraged him with his career, though he sensed that was more to please her father, George, or perhaps simply to ensure that she would maintain the lifestyle to which she had become accustomed. There were plenty of fully formed career guys in their circle of friends. Why did she waste time trying to train a dumb puppy who peed all over the carpet when he should have been sitting? There needn't be blame in relationship break-ups. They could both be right, yet simply wrong for each other. Yes, he would say all of this when he returned, he thought, turning the car ignition.

George opened the door when Luke arrived back at the house. He seemed peeved that he had answered it for the second time that morning. Things were about to get so much worse, Luke thought. Would George partake in the forthcoming hostilities? Neutral ground would have been far smarter. He also cringed when he returned to Alice's room. She was sitting at her dressing table, applying her makeup in anticipation of their trip. This always took significant time and effort. The stakes were rising by the minute, and he had to say something right now.

'Alice…'

'You're finally back then,' she said, widening her left eye to apply mascara in the mirror.

'Yes, I was…'

'Can you grab my case from the spare room?'

'Well, there is…'

'Luke, can you just do it now?' she said, giving him a death stare. 'We don't have much time.'

He found himself fetching the case, which in turn meant that he was still going to Dorset with Alice. This was getting

160

ridiculous. It wasn't until he had dragged the case downstairs, setting it beside his own holdall, that he managed to spit his words out as Alice joined him. The spacious hall of her parents' house, moments before they were about to leave for a weekend away, could not have been a worse place or time to do this.

'Alice, I'm not going.'

'What?' she replied, freezing with one arm in her jacket.

'I'm not going to Dorset,' he said, clearing his throat. 'I think we should... take a break.'

'Take a break?'

'You know... split up for a while.'

'Are you crazy!'

'Is everything okay?' Alice's mother, Yvette, called from the lounge.

'Everything's fine,' Alice shouted back, still staring at him. 'Let's talk outside. My parents don't need to think any less of you than they already do, Luke.'

Alice's family home was impressive, and the front garden was larger than most back gardens. They stood beside his unwashed car, parked at the edge of the crescent-shaped gravel drive, beneath a Poplar tree. It looked spectacularly out of place. Alice was staring at him now.

'What is going on? I thought you wanted to go to Dorset?'

'I did... but I don't think...we're right for each other.'

'You woke up this morning and suddenly thought this?'

'I guess that I've been feeling like this for a while.'

'You guess?'

'I *have* thought like this for a while. I think it would be better if we stopped seeing each other.'

Alice just stared at him and didn't speak for a moment. The silence was awkward.

'No,' she said, finally.

'No?'

'No, you're not splitting up with me, Luke. Just get in the car and stop being so ridiculous.'

Oh shit, she had called his bluff! What was he going to do now? Quick, remember all those things that he had thought about at the garage.

'Don't you think that it would be better for you too? You haven't seemed particularly happy recently.'

'I see,' Alice said, her expression hardening. 'You're setting me free. That's what's really happening here. Any more glib break-up shit you want to throw in?'

'Alice…'

'Before you say it, I know that it's you, not me. That much is fucking obvious to anyone, isn't it?'

'I just thought…'

'No, *you* don't break up with *me*. That's not how this works. I mean, look at us. That would just be ridiculous.'

Silence for a moment. Even before he spoke, he knew that his words were about to be a mistake, but he couldn't stop himself.

'Well, maybe… *you* could break up with *me* then? I mean, we might both be happier?'

A horrible pause.

'There's no need for blame in a break-up,' he added, quickly. 'We can both be right, just wrong for each other.'

Alice didn't need to reply for him to understand. Her eyes said everything. He had failed to adequately convey his chocolate doughnut musings and had royally screwed this up.

Chapter Sixteen

Brian asked us to start early on Monday morning. The investors were due to arrive at midday, but he wanted a dry run of the meeting beforehand. Luke showed up a few minutes after I did, and I avoided his eyes as we greeted each other. Part of me didn't want to know a single thing about his wonderful weekend in Dorset. Another part of me wanted to know everything. There was no chance of avoiding him in the consultation room, where four chairs were strategically arranged around the table. Everyone had dressed up smartly, with Luke and Brian wearing suits, while I belatedly realised that I was wearing the same green dress as I had worn at Dad's funeral. Did my outfit forewarn the death of the Abacus? I should have chosen more carefully.

There was a nervous tremor in Brian's voice as he handed out an agenda to us both. It was great to be prepared, but after a wobbly introduction, it was clear that Brian's preparations had gone too far. He was trying to choreograph our every word and movement, with each of us taking turns to deliver our own little soundbites in an unnatural collective script. The net result felt like an amateur dramatics night at the local theatre (and Dad had dragged me along to enough of those for me to be an authority on the subject). Brian even rehearsed his jokes and quips, which would prove difficult to laugh at again later. I wondered if it would have been better just to take our chances in the real thing. The whole time, I avoided Luke's eyes, staring at Brian's agenda whenever he asked me a question.

It was approaching one o'clock when the investor finally showed. Brian had been pacing the office for the previous two hours, but raced back to his desk, feigning surprise as the man entered. Brian's chair was still rocking as the door closed. I missed my cue to show the man in as rehearsed, and he marched straight into the office. Our planning had failed in seconds.

The man was in his forties, wearing a designer coat that was at least a decade too young for him in style. I could instantly tell that he fancied himself. His silvering hair was sharply cut, and his physique was clearly honed. He flashed me a smile before turning his attention to Brian.

'Marcus Storer,' the man said, extending his hand across Brian's desk.

'Rupert Fotherington,' Brian replied, shaking it. 'I mean, I'm Brian Asquith, but I was expecting Rupert Fotherington.'

'Rupe couldn't make it today. I'm deputising.'

'Oh, I see,' Brian replied, clearly disappointed. 'Great that you could come in his place,' he added, quickly recovering.

'Not a problem. Look, I don't mean to sound rude, but I must be away by two,' Storer said, glancing at his watch. 'Do you mind if we get straight down to it?'

'Of course.'

This really wasn't the start that Brian had planned, and we quickly convened in the consultation room. Storer hesitated by the door, reading the speech bubble above the cardboard scientist's head.

'Cute,' he said dismissively. I felt a spiteful sense of pleasure at Luke's big effort falling short, and we wandered inside.

It was all a bit awkward, and we continued to deviate from the rehearsal once seated. Storer declined a drink, and the China tea set remained untouched in the kitchen, with four different varieties of milk silently turning to butter on the tray. Brian handed out the agenda, but Storer pushed his copy aside.

'To be open, I'd like to save us all some time here,' Storer said, leaning back in his chair. 'We've read the Abacus blurb. We like aspects of what we see, and I've come here with a few exploratory ideas of how we could potentially work together.'

'Sure,' Brian replied.

'Okay,' Storer sighed, sitting forward again. An expensive-looking watch poked from the end of his shirt sleeve, clanking on the desk. 'Let's talk about the River Nile, Brian. The longest river in the world. If the River Nile were an investment, you'd be happy to have a piece of it, right?'

'I guess,' Brian said, visibly trying to anticipate where this was heading.

'Yeah, who wouldn't? The thing is, we call it the Nile, but what does that mean? It's a river consisting of many lakes and reservoirs. It's a river that has multiple branches and channels, all feeding the main body of water. We call this river the Nile, but it consists of many separate parts. The question I've come here to ask is, would you be happy to be a channel of the biggest river in the world?'

'I'm not really sure what you mean,' Brian said.

For the first time, I caught Luke's eye. He looked skyward and smiled. I smiled back, despite myself.

'Okay,' Storer said, sniffing loudly. 'Full disclosure time. We have another little project on the boil, and that's the real reason that I wanted to come here today. I think there could be a great opportunity for us to work together if you can think flexibly. I believe that there's huge synergy between the ideas.'

'In what way?' Brian asked.

'Elite dating is the big thing right now,' Storer said, sniffing.

'There can be serious challenges to meet the *right* people if you're successful. Studies have indicated that elites struggle more to find meaningful relationships. Eighty per cent of our most successful people are also our most lonely. Their time is precious, and it's difficult to reach compatible singles with their busy lifestyles. I'm championing this initiative from painful personal experience, believe me. That's why we will be launching this baby in the next eighteen months,' Storer added, passing around a handful of gold embossed business cards from his pocket. It's a new dating service called *Giltie!* The name is a play on words and a subtle reference to investments and gold. My idea. Flirty, yet classy, right?' he added, grinning.

'This sounds more like competition than synergy,' Brian said, studying the card.

'That all depends on you. Like I said, there are aspects we love about the Abacus. We admire the purity of how you distil every individual customer down to a single score, taking all their attributes into account. We are specifically interested in your high-scoring individuals.'

'In what way?'

'Okay, full disclosure, I mean *only* interested. Your scoring system allows us to syphon off the elites from the dating pool. You can bring us your beauties and your brainiacs. Your rich kids and your sugar daddies.'

'That's against the principle of what we're doing here. The Attraction Abacus is about dating for everybody,' Luke said, startling me that he had made a sound. 'The concept of scoring isn't to exclude. It's to find an ideal match.'

'And that's nice. I know that you guys are coming from the right place with that. We all like to believe that there's someone for everybody. But the truth is, nobody really wants to see what's going on at the bottom of the Abacus scale. It's tragic, right? Let's stay in the light and keep our breakfasts down,' Storer said, laughing. 'The Abacus could sort the wheat from the chaff for the *Giltie!* service. With the collaboration I'm proposing, we could be confident that anyone accepted to *Giltie!* had attained a minimum Abacus score. At a *Giltie!* event, we would be certain that the *right* kind of people are attending.'

'So, what kind of Abacus score are you thinking?' Brian asked.

'I'm thinking 70 plus to start with.'

'Isn't that a little high?' I blurted, surprising myself this time.

'High?' Storer laughed. 'That number is just to get us started. It will be heading way north of that once we're established. This is elite dating. It's not charity work, Veronica.'

'Evelyn.'

'Sorry, Evelyn. You just remind me of a Veronica,' Storer said, smiling creepily at me.

'I still think this conflicts with what we're doing here at the Abacus,' Brian said, looking puzzled.

'Okay, let me spell this out for you,' Storer said, fiddling with his watch strap. 'It all goes back to the River Nile, Brian. If my proposal were to be accepted, there would be *no* Abacus as such. Your algorithm would become a feed to *Giltie!* But, like the Nile, this feed would make you part of something so much bigger and more lucrative. You would be a very rich man.'

'I see,' Brian said, clearing his throat.

Collective silence for a moment.

'Okay, I know that I've hit you with a whole load of information in one go,' Storer said, standing. 'There's no need to rush into any decisions today. This is just the beginning. There are no guarantees that I can get it past the guys at my end anyway. I like what you're doing here. I really believe that the Abacus has legs, so sleep on it, and let me know your thoughts later in the week.'

'Wait, Evelyn and Luke have prepared a quick demonstration for you,' Brian said, also standing. 'They were going to show you how our Abacus applications are processed.'

'Detail,' said Storer, moving towards the door. 'I'm a bigger picture guy, but their time will come,' he added, winking at me. 'Sorry, but I really need to shoot. It was amazing to meet you all.'

He closed the door, leaving us all looking at each other in bewilderment.

'What a prick!' Luke said as the sound of the exterior door closing in the distance reverberated around the consultation room.

'He certainly was,' said Brian, looking through the consultation room glass panel to check that Storer had gone before continuing. 'I'm sorry for wasting your time, Evelyn.'

'No, it was… interesting,' I said, smiling at them both.

Perhaps I should have been worried about the implications for my future as I sat there, but that wasn't the thought occupying my mind at all. I had previously been horrified to consider that I was a C+ in the Abacus scoring. In a week when I really needed a boost to my ego, I now visualised myself as nothing more than wheat chaff.

I could hear frantic footsteps behind me. I turned to see Luke hurrying along the street, tie blowing over the shoulder of his jacket, his fringe standing on end.

'Evelyn.'

'Everything okay?'

'Yes, I just wanted a quick word,' Luke said, breathing heavily.

'Don't worry about the meeting.'

'No, it's more of a personal thing.'

I studied his face for a moment, trying to work out what was coming next.

'You said that you would cut that stuff out.'

'I know. I'm sorry. It's just that… I've kind of broken up with Alice.'

'Kind of?'

'Well, she isn't really accepting it.'

'I'm sorry, Luke, but I don't know how I can help.'

'We were meant to drive to Dorset this weekend, but I just couldn't go,' he said, looking into my eyes. 'I hope you might know why.'

A million inappropriate replies sprang to my doom-dreaming mind, but I managed to keep my mouth shut. I can't deny that I was pleased to hear the news, but I was wary, especially of what I thought he was implying. A safety valve activated in my brain. Remember your doomed relationship genes!

'Like I said, I'm sorry, but that's something you need to sort out with Alice.'

'I know. I just wondered if you would come for a walk with me at the weekend to talk things through?'

'I don't think that's a good idea.'

'Just a walk. As friends.'

Luke had helped me through Dad's funeral, and I didn't like to let him down when he played the friendship card, but alarm bells were still ringing.

'Why don't you have a walk with Alice and talk through it

with her?'

'She's not very receptive to ideas like that at the moment.'

He was smiling at me now, and I found myself smiling back.

'I don't know, Luke.'

'Maybe I could call Saturday to see how you feel about it?'

'Maybe. Look, I really need to head back now.'

I turned before he could reply, leaving him standing in the street.

What is wrong with human beings? I have read accounts from several successful people claiming that the moments following their greatest triumphs were the emptiest of their lives. It seems that happiness lies within the pursuit of our dreams, and the worst thing that can happen is that we fulfil them. That's what I said to myself as I lay in bed that night, unable to sleep. It was the essence of my humanity that was the problem, not me.

Staring at the darkened bedroom ceiling, I felt agitated when I should have felt elated. Luke and Alice were, potentially, no longer an item. There could well be a few more twists in the tale, but this was excellent news. I *was* pleased, but as I tried to examine my own thoughts more closely, I realised that I was actually plain scared.

The idea that I liked somebody and that they might like me back was terrifying. I recalled my last conversation with Dad, when I had realised that I was just a bit player in my own life. Presented with the opportunity to be a leading lady, I was now anxious. There was something at stake. I was emotionally invested in the Abacus. I was emotionally invested in Luke. Maybe being single and working a zero-hour job at a hotel had suited me. I had nothing to lose, and I had simply existed in a constant, semi-disgruntled state, which in hindsight was quite relaxing. My main issue with being single was that everybody else had a problem with it. Personally, I had been happily unhappy with the situation. Now, all I really wanted was to be left alone in peace.

There was something else that bothered me in the darkness, though. What was I doing to Luke? It was clear that Alice pressured him into doing things that he didn't really want to do, but these things were also positive. Going to the gym was healthy. Alice might be a little obsessed with appearances, but it was beneficial to his well-being. It could even be Alice steering Luke towards his auditor career, while I was encouraging him to follow his passion. What kind of advice was that? I had no real plan. Was I a self-deluded shepherd, leading my flock of one lemming over the side of a cliff?

I don't know how many times I checked my phone that night, rolling onto my side, with a pale light illuminating my face from the carpet. No messages appeared, time after time. What was I even looking for? If Luke had tried to contact me, I would have deliberately ignored him. I flipped over in frustration, patting down my pillow.

Luke called me early on the following Saturday to arrange the walk "we had agreed". We both knew that we hadn't agreed on a thing, but I didn't protest, feeling curious and confused in equal measures. He picked me up mid-morning. It was the first time I had been inside his car. It was an old Toyota Yaris, with a *Homer Simpson* air freshener dangling from the rear-view mirror. There was an exotic, slightly unpleasant, cocktail of smells clinging to the air when I closed the door.

'Not what I expected,' I said, as I took my seat, avoiding the takeaway cartons and assorted rubbish scattered around my feet.

'It's just a first car. I'm upgrading when I get through my exams.'

'Not the car. I mean this,' I said, kicking at a burger box beside my toe.

'Oh, yeah. I take my chances when I can, sorry.'

'And I had you down as a health freak,' I said, laughing.

'Yeah, right…'

'Please tell me that isn't a gherkin on my shoe.'

'Absolutely not. I would have one hundred per cent eaten that. I'd still eat it now.'

I knew that Luke was grinning without looking, and I didn't acknowledge him. We pulled away into the sunshine, dazzling through the windscreen. I'm not really a countryside walker. My mum used to drag me out at weekends sometimes, but it never ended well. I'm not a huge fan of farm animals, mud or being wet and cold. Most significantly, I can never see the point in just walking for the sake of it. I don't know what to think about when I'm wandering aimlessly around. There's too much opportunity to reflect on things, and that is never a good idea for me. I clasped my hands behind my back, faking the classic country squire pose, and tried my best to appear engaged, while wishing it would all be over as soon as possible.

It wasn't the best start as we pulled into the deserted National Trust car park. Rain-filled craters shimmered from the sandy mud all around us. They hinted at the ground conditions we would face on the walk. Luke read my mind, looking down at my white trainers.

'Are you wearing those?'

'They're very comfortable,' I replied, dismissing his smirk.

We set off, following a path winding upwards through woodland from the car park. Luke was wearing a pair of walking

172

boots, of course. I had plenty of time to reflect on my poor decisions as he fastidiously tied the laces. My trainers were already caked with mud after the first short climb, but I pretended not to notice the hideous clumps clinging below my ankles. I was curious to know what had happened that week and was becoming frustrated by the small talk as we walked. We had skated around recent events on the car journey, and it felt as though it was time to address the obvious. Following the path for another five slippery minutes, we emerged into a clearing. I squinted across the dewy field ahead of us and could wait no longer.

'So, how are things with you and Alice?'

Luke was standing, hand on hips, staring into the distance. The sun was shining through his floppy quiff. The view was bang average, and I sensed that he was avoiding the question.

'I'd rather not talk about it,' he said at last.

'I thought that was the whole point of coming for this walk?'

'Yeah, I know. It has been a tough week, though. Do you mind if we forget all that, just for now?'

'Fine, but remember I'm only here as a friend.'

'I remember,' he said.

We continued across an overgrown field, leading to a metal gate at the periphery. Luke unhooked a loop of blue rope, dragging the gate through the long grass sprouting beneath. I slipped on the mud as we passed through the gap, regaining my balance quickly. Luke thankfully didn't notice, and we continued into the grassy-hilled valley beyond it. There were sheep precariously perched on the sloping bank to our left, and the bank to our right dropped away into woodland beneath. The sun was directly before us, and I shielded my eyes with my hand. Luke was lost in thought, staring at the ground in front of his feet as he walked. I was trying to be understanding, but I had come for a reason.

'So, what *do* you want to talk about?' I said, breaking the silence. He looked up, surprised.

'Sorry, I know that I'm distracted. This is unfair to you.'

'That's why I'm here. As your friend. You might find that talking about something else helps?'

'Okay, tell me something that I don't know about you.'

'Like what?'

'Well, I've met your mum and sister. Any other family?'

'You've met my sister?'

'Yes, she was trying to guess my star sign at your dad's funeral.'

'Oh, you *have* met her. I guess I was a bit out of it at the time. No other family. How about you?'

'You know my parents' situation. I'm an only child.'

'Yeah, that figures.'

'Excuse me?' he said, stopping. I ignored his mock indignation.

'You deserve it, dragging me out here. I'm still uncomfortable going for this walk behind Alice's back.'

'Technically, I'm single.'

'Realistically, you're not single enough. It's called being on the rebound, Luke.'

'Maybe, but this could be a good chance to get to know each other.'

'That sounds like date talk to me.'

'Maybe we could think of it as pre-date talk? You know, like an Abacus assessment. It could save us some time and heartache. We could reveal our innermost flaws right from the start. A lifetime of insight in one walk,' he said, laughing.

'We'd pick attractive flaws. You know, like you do at

174

interviews. I work too hard. I care too much about my job.'

He laughed. 'Not if we're honest.'

'There are different levels of honesty.'

'What level would you want?'

'Brutal honesty. The kind they keep on high shelves away from kids.'

'I'm not sure I'd want to hear that.'

'You'd have nothing to fear from the truth.'

'You're right,' he said, 'and we should be able to laugh at anything too. That's important.'

'Okay, in the spirit of this honesty, there is something I need to get off my chest first. I've been worrying about my influence on you.'

'Your influence?'

'Yes. I just want to say that you should be true to yourself. You shouldn't listen to Alice *or* me about anything.'

He laughed. 'I can think for myself. I know that you feel guilty about the Abacus situation with Brian, but it might never come to…'

'It's not just that.'

'Whatever you're worried about, don't be. I'm weighing everything up in my own mind. My decisions have nothing to do with you.'

'That's good,' I said, as we continued to walk. 'That's really good. Anyway, let's lighten things up a bit. What's your favourite book?'

'I don't read much.'

'Ignoramus. Favourite song?'

'Mm-hmm, it would have to be something by Coldplay.'

'Really, Luke?'

'What's wrong with Coldplay?'

'Nothing at all,' I said, smiling at his reaction. 'They're very well loved. I'll go for "Someone Like You" by Adele as an all-time favourite.'

'That's a break-up song. Are you trying to mess with my mind?'

'It's just a beautiful thing,' I said, laughing. 'Tragically romantic. Aren't you romantic?'

'Well, I have to say, yes, don't I?'

'Not if you don't mean it. This is meant to be honesty time.'

'I think I am. Are you?'

'Not in the conventional sense, no,' I said. 'I can live without flowers from a garage forecourt, thanks. Not that I have ever received any. What would impress me more is a unique romantic experience, tailored just to me.'

'Like what?'

'I don't know. I haven't experienced it yet. I would rely on the love of my life to show me that one day.'

'No pressure on them.'

'Absolutely none. How about favourite film?'

'Tricky again,' he said, lost in thought for a moment. 'I think I'd have to go with *The Shawshank Redemption*.'

'I could have guessed.'

'Oh?'

'A safe, popular choice. Too popular, some might say. The title sounds kind of smart, too, which makes you feel smart for liking it. No way it would be in anybody's top ten if it were called *Jail Break*. A real auditor's choice, Luke.'

'Wow, I see where this brutal honesty thing is going. I don't suppose I'll recognise your favourite film. That's the whole point.'

'What do you mean?'

176

'Some pretentious art house classic, I'm guessing?'

'No, actually, I'll go for *Toy Story*.'

'Predictable in its own right.'

'How so?'

'Choosing a kid's film. "Look at me, I just don't care what other people think. I have my own mind". It's a self-righteous selection.'

'Are you saying that I'm self-righteous?'

'Are you saying that I'm insecure?'

'Okay, the gloves are off,' I said, laughing. 'How many children do you want?'

'Two… or is zero an option?'

'Three. You really are a walking cliché.'

'But not quirky for the sake of it.'

I laughed. 'Three words to describe yourself at school?'

'Scared. Quiet. Studious.'

'I'll summarise that as nerd.'

'Fine,' he said, laughing. 'And you?'

'Troubled. Lonely. Insecure.'

'I'll summarise that as loser.'

'Wow,' I said, laughing too. 'Something more abstract before we fight. Ski or surf?'

'What?'

'No context.'

'Ski,' he replied.

'Awful choice. Up or down?'

'Up all the way.'

'Lacking imagination.'

'I'm speechless.'

'Smashed avocado or bacon?' I said, ignoring him.

'That's a trap!'

'Make your choice.'

'Avoc…'

'Such privilege! Bacon would have been selfish, by the way.'

'So, I can't win?'

'None of us ever can. Haven't you seen all the arguments on social media?'

'So deep!'

'I'm a philosophy graduate. What do you expect?'

We were both laughing now, and I forgot where I was standing. The motion of my laughter was enough to dislodge my footing, and I began to slowly slide down the muddy slope before me. My mud-caked trainers offered zero resistance, and all I could do was windmill my arms to stay upright, squealing, as I slid. Somehow, I glided to a graceful halt, turning sideways a few metres away.

'Ta-dah!' I said, spreading my arms.

'See, you *do* like skiing!'

Luke scrambled down the slope after me but lost his footing. A despairing flailing arm failed to prevent him from landing hard on his backside. His startled expression was simply perfect. I had forgotten what it felt like to laugh properly. I was laughing so hard that I doubled over, gasping for air. Eventually, when I could finally breathe, I helped Luke to his feet. It took us both a few minutes to compose ourselves.

I remember feeling incredibly happy at that moment. After all the overthinking of the previous week, this was the perfect antidote. I sensed that Luke was on the same page, and it seemed as though a weight had been lifted from both of us. For a fleeting moment, I understood walking in the countryside. Dozy sheep watched us from the sun-lit hillside opposite. A blackbird sang from the glistening hedgerow beside me. I felt like a poor man's *Snow White*.

Luke was standing a little too close now, his face silhouetted by the sun. His blue eyes were studying me. His dark fringe was moist with dew. I shifted backwards, but I didn't want to move away completely. He was still holding my hand from where I had helped him to his feet.

'Are we doing well with the honesty thing?' Luke asked.

'I think we're all set for a divorce.'

'Saves time. A marriage in one hour.'

'The Attraction Abacus would have rejected us right from the start.'

'Yes, it's incredible,' Luke said. 'We have absolutely nothing in common.'

'You'd think there would be *something*, statistically.'

'And yet,' he said, moving closer to me.

'And yet.'

He kissed me.

This time it was a real kiss.

I know.

I had made a big thing about Alice. I had also made a big thing about Luke being on the rebound. Maybe I'm just a bad person. I have little to say in my defence except that, technically, Luke *was* single.

Chapter Seventeen

Things were complicated now. I could no longer pretend that it was possible to continue as normal. Luke drove me home after the walk, and I insisted that we discuss the morning's events another time. He needed to completely resolve the situation with Alice first before we could even begin to think about a relationship. Nevertheless, I felt great. My flatmate, Katey, asked if I was okay when we met in the kitchen.

'Don't I seem okay?' I asked, passing her a mug of tea.

'Just different.'

'I'm good,' I said, surprising myself with my own choice of words. I don't know if I appeared manically heightened, but Katey watched me with suspicion over the rim of her mug.

That evening, I settled at my writing desk, feeling inspired. I was midway through a new chapter when my phone vibrated on the desk. I was half expecting the call to be from Luke, even though I had asked him not to contact me. I was shamefully disappointed to see that it was Olivia.

'Liv!'

'Evie! How's it going?'

'Good. Where are you? You sound like you're down a well.'

'I'm in India. It's manic here.'

'What are you doing in India?'

'I'm working here. I've just started a new job.'

'Wow, so jealous,' I said, cringing that I hadn't called her back since she left the message.

'Ah, that's exactly what I wanted to talk about. I've been waiting until everything was agreed before I spoke to you.'

'Very mysterious.'

She laughed. 'Not that mysterious. The company I work for is setting up a new facility out here. I'm managing the rollout.'

'Sounds interesting.'

'It sounds incredibly boring, Evie, but there *is* an interesting angle. I will be based here for another twelve months. I'm going to have my own place. It's massive! Just south of Gokarna, right near the beach. It's not Goa, but it isn't that far away.'

'Wow, that will be great.'

'And maybe not just for me.'

'Oh?'

'There are two bedrooms in the apartment. I only need one. I've checked with my boss, and he's open to me sharing with a friend. I immediately mentioned you, of course. I was thinking that you could write that book you've always spoken about. I'd be working during the day anyway, and we could have fun together in the evenings.'

'That sounds amazing, Liv.'

'Amazing, but?'

'I'm not sure if I have enough cash saved and…'

'You'd only have to pay for the flights. You can live here, rent-free. The company pay for everything. I even have a grocery allowance. I can't possibly eat my way through it alone.'

'But I wouldn't be able to stay for long?'

'My boss can arrange a work visa for you. You'd be documented as working for the company. He would be bending the rules a little, but nobody will check or even care. This is a big project. Most people are coming with partners anyway, and your visa is small fry to them. My boss knows that I'm more likely to see the project through if I'm settled here with a friend.'

'Wow!'

'Wow, indeed. It's what you always wanted. You'd have your big chance to write your bestseller, and I'd have my best buddy here to party with.'

'I don't know what to say.'

'Yes, springs to mind,' Olivia said, laughing. 'I'd just need all your details, passport number, etc., for the property insurance and visa if you're coming. My boss wants to sort it all out as soon as possible. And you need to get some jabs arranged.'

'Of course... yes, sorry to sound so hesitant.'

'I know, it's a shock. But a nice shock?'

'It couldn't be better.'

'Look, I must go. I have no idea how much the call is costing me. I'll message more details, but I just wanted to hear your voice when I told you.'

'It's amazing!' I squealed, trying to deliver the enthusiasm Olivia expected and deserved.

'Speak soon, Evie.'

'Love you, Liv.'

The phone was dead.

I sat back in my chair, trying to process what had just occurred. The news *was* exciting but also confusing. After years of stagnation, everything was moving forward at the same time. I stared across the room, and Ganesha, the wise old elephant god, looked back at me from the shelf.

'This was you, wasn't it?'

He was guilty by his silence, and I closed the lid of my laptop. There wasn't a chance I would be able to concentrate any more that evening. My head was full of images of exotic Indian beaches, and entire days spent writing my book. Even as I imagined all these wonderful, colourful scenes, my mind was drawn back to a muddy hillside, where Luke's face grinned back at me beneath the sun.

It *was* all my dreams come true, but why now?

I had missed so many weeks of my writing class that I didn't expect the tutor, Kris, to recognise me when I returned that evening. I decided to attend for two reasons. Firstly, I was devastated by how much money I had wasted on the course, and secondly, if I were to spend twelve months writing in India, it would be useful to have some expert direction before I left. In the absence of that, there was only Kris.

Kris was particularly hopeless that lesson, tossing out a photocopied extract about characterisation to the class. The name of the writing guide source was still visible on the front of the handout. He wasn't even bothering to hide his laziness any longer. His instructions were for us to read the extract and write something relevant, while he worked on his own new novel at his desk. It would have been better to stay home and work in my room.

After enduring some toe-curling efforts read aloud (one guy reduced himself to tears with his own words), I mentally checked out and spent the rest of the session daydreaming. Even so, I was determined to speak to Kris at the end of the lesson, and to my surprise, there wasn't the usual procession of neediness shuffling away beside his desk. Kris had broken everybody's spirits.

'Evelyn,' he said, rubbing his pointed chin with his bony fingers.

'I didn't expect you to remember my name.'

'I noticed that you haven't been attending recently,' he said, eyeing me suspiciously. 'I hope you're not going to ask for your money back. No course refunds.'

'It's fine, Kris, I'm not looking for a refund.'

'Oh,' he replied, relaxing his posture. 'How can I help?'

'Well, I've come to a crossroads with the novel that I'm writing.'

'It's a psychological thriller, isn't it?'

'A romantic comedy, actually.'

'Oh yes, not my favourite genre.'

'You mentioned that before.'

'But there are the genre conventions.'

'You mentioned those too.'

'So, what's the issue?' he asked, having clearly exhausted all helpful possibilities in his mind.

'Okay, my main characters are kind of together, so it feels like it should be the end of the story, but…'

'But?'

'I can see that there will still be problems.'

'Ah, I assume there is some other kind of conflict thwarting their happiness? Conflict comes in many guises. In *Lament of the Dragonfly*, the protagonist faces internal, social and political barriers that must be overcome before she is able to reach her goals. It could be an opportune time to re-read the novel.'

'I'm not sure if…'

'It might have gone right over your head on first reading. Like the eponymous dragonfly itself,' he chuckled smugly.

'Thanks, Kris, but…'

'Have another read and refer to the novel to see where you are going wrong. I know that you're capable of learning from your mistakes with a strong reference text for guidance. I believe in you.'

'That's very kind, but…'

184

'Think nothing of it, Evelyn. I really must be leaving now,' he said, closing his laptop. His beady eyes fixed on mine for a second. 'Just remember the crucial point about conflict as your novel reaches its conclusion. In a romantic comedy, our young lovers must find a way to overcome all the obstacles thrust in their way and live happily ever after.'

A year spent separately on different continents didn't sit well with any romantic comedy conventions that I was aware of. As I approached the door of the Attraction Abacus, I felt incredibly guilty. This was the best job I had ever had, not to mention how I felt about Luke, but Olivia needed me to act quickly. Also, Brian should know my plans as soon as possible. It was awkward, but I might never have another opportunity like this. More to the point, what if I didn't go to India at all? I pictured bitter ancestors, screaming at me from the branches of my ghostly family tree.

Don't be a sucker like I was, Evelyn! Be true to your dreams. Remember our doomed relationship genetics. You'll be ditched by Christmas.

A failed relationship *was* a possibility, but then I had never felt this way about anybody before. Surely, that was reason enough for staying. As I pushed the office door open, I still had no idea what I was going to do. There were raised voices booming from the consultation room as I entered, and Luke jumped to his feet when he saw me.

'Fancy a drink over the road?' he said, sliding his jacket from the back of the chair. It didn't seem like a question, and I turned on my heels and followed him.

We sat in the window of the café opposite the office, where I had once waited for my interview. It felt almost nostalgic, gazing across the road to see the cartoon scientist plastered on the Abacus window. *Looking for love? Science can help!* How alien that had seemed at the time.

Luke returned from the counter with a coffee for himself and a strong tea for me. Would I ever meet another guy who would remember my strong tea preference if I went to India? It had taken Luke weeks to retain the information. As he sat beside me, it was difficult to believe that this was the same man who had canvassed me in the street at the start of the summer. I noticed so much more about him now. The way the bridge of his nose creased when he smiled. His almond-shaped eyes. God, I was pathetic.

'So, what's happening? I said, stirring my tea.

'George turned up this morning.'

'George who?'

'Alice's dad, George.'

'Oh,' I said, stirring faster. 'Sounded like it was going well in there.'

He laughed. 'Their beautiful friendship might well be over. I could hear every word.'

'Was it bad?'

'The worst. George wants to pull his entire investment from the Abacus.'

'Surely, he can't do that?'

'It's his money.'

'So, what will Brian do?'

'I really don't know,' Luke said, staring at his coffee. 'He didn't believe that this would actually happen.'

'There's still the other investor who came to the office?'

'You met him, Evelyn.'

'Yes, I did,' I replied, reaching for some words of optimism.

They didn't come. Luke smiled.

'I'm sure it will work out okay,' he said, eventually. 'It's just a tough time.'

It was a very unsure-sounding sure, and we drank in silence, staring at the office opposite. George didn't emerge for another twenty minutes, looking red-faced and ruffled. Facially, he reminded me of a stern old Dickensian magistrate, dressed in contemporary clothes. George huffed away along the street in a cloud of resentment. Luke didn't comment. His eyes glazed over, staring out the window, lost in thought. I tried to drink my tea, but I gradually felt worse and worse, until I had to say something.

'I feel kind of responsible,' I said.

'It's not your fault.'

'But maybe if…'

'It's not your fault, Evelyn.'

'Perhaps if I… left for a while, it might take some financial pressure away from Brian?'

'What do you mean?'

'You know, take some time out from work. Give Brian some breathing space on the wage bill.'

'That's the worst thing that could happen. Brian needs you right now.'

'I *am* taking an extra salary.'

'We couldn't operate with just the two of us. That would be the final nail in the Abacus coffin.'

'Not even for a few months?'

'It's a thoughtful idea, but the whole thing would collapse. There's too much to do. Brian has invested a lot of time training you. The best way that you can help him is by carrying on the way you are. He is working all the hours he can already.'

'Yes, of course.'

187

We were silent for a moment. I drummed my teaspoon on the table, trying to think of something to say, but Luke beat me to it.

'Look, I completely respect your feelings about the Alice situation, but things will be very different soon. It's not all about the Abacus. Selfishly, I would hate it if you weren't around.'

'We can think about that when the dust has settled,' I said, smiling.

'I know.'

'You need to look after Brian for now.'

'I will,' he said, gazing into space again. 'It's difficult, though. Sometimes life is so baffling. Three words to describe how you feel right now?'

'Mm-hmm, I would have to go for confused, excited and conflicted.'

He laughed. 'I think we're on the same page. I can't argue with any of those.'

I smiled, knowing that he was wrong, of course. If I was going to leave the Abacus, things were going to be very messy.

I stared at Olivia's email for the fourth time that night. All the necessary arrangements were in place. I had the green light to join her in India. All I needed to do was send my details.

Brian has invested a lot of time training you. The best way that you can help him is by carrying on the way you are.

Every time I began to reply, I found something else to distract myself. I hadn't sorted my sock drawer for years, but tonight, it felt like an immediate priority. The clock on my bedroom wall hadn't shown the correct time since January, but I changed the batteries and carefully reset the hands. I didn't fool myself with the distractions, of course, but it felt like my head was going to pop every time I tried to contemplate the decision I needed to make.

This might seem strange to you. Finally, I had met a guy I liked who miraculously seemed to like me too. This should be an easy decision to make. To fully appreciate my dilemma, you'd need to understand what writing meant to me. This wasn't just a passing fad. Without being too melodramatic, writing had saved my sanity at school.

I wasn't a particularly academic child. I think, given a more stable home life, I could have achieved more. Maybe not a lot more, but the general chaos of my upbringing was a definite handicap, emotionally. Not that I was a disruptive child in class. The only trouble I caused was through my lack of understanding of what the hell was going on. This, in turn, was down to a failure to concentrate or engage with anything that was happening around me as I wallowed in sadness and insecurity. It's easy to blame other people for our shortcomings, but my parents were distracted with their own problems, and I probably didn't receive the support that I needed. My sister certainly made things worse, taking out her own issues on me. To be balanced, I wasn't very cooperative either, so any effort anybody did make, I pushed away with a snarl of misguided adolescent rage.

English had a purpose that felt relevant to me at school. I could read books for pleasure and escape from reality. I could write about things to work problems through in my mind. There wasn't a single definitive moment that inspired me. I recall more of a warm glow of comfort from the encouragement I received in a subject where I showed some capability. I avoided homework in general, but found myself spending hours reading, locked in my bedroom (when my sister was out, of course.) I wrote terrible, self-pitying poems, but the process helped me

189

make sense of my situation. Most of all, I planned my own grand novel, recording pages and pages of notes in brightly coloured felt pens, ready for the time when I felt emotionally mature enough to put it all together. When that time never arrived, I started to write anyway. Now, I had a chance to complete it.

There was no more time to think, and I needed to reply to Olivia, slumping in front of the laptop screen again. After several drafts, where I honestly explained my situation, before deleting the entire thing, I finally took the coward's way out and lied. It would buy me some time at least.

'I'm embarrassed to say that I can't find my passport, Liv,' I typed. 'I haven't been abroad for a few years, so I must have packed it away somewhere. I've asked my mum to look at her place, and I'll keep searching here. I hope a bit of a delay won't cause you or your boss any problems. Love Evie xx.'

I couldn't bear to think about it all for a second longer and quickly hit the send button. India was five or six hours ahead, so Olivia would be safely in bed. There would be a whole night's sleep before the problem needed to be confronted again. I switched off my laptop and literally buried my head in the pillow.

Chapter Eighteen

The following day started positively. Olivia emailed me to say that the passport delay wasn't an immediate issue (but it would be great to sort things out as soon as I could). It bought me a little more thinking time, at least. Brian was surprisingly buoyant when I arrived at the office. I thought it was just a brave front until I spoke to him in the kitchen.

'Some good news,' he said, grabbing a carton of milk from the refrigerator. 'Our investor friends have been back in touch. They want to host a trial collaboration event in London. At a hotel in Mayfair, no less.'

'Very upmarket.'

'I know. They're paying for everything.'

'That's great. So, how will it work?'

'Well, we may have a few more applications than normal to process in the next few weeks. Marcus Storer, that guy who came to the office, is going to send through some of the *Giltie!* applications that they have received. We need to process them in the Abacus and score them. We'll supplement these with the singles in our own database and send on all the details.'

'Sounds simple. Nothing else needed our end?'

'No, we're just a channel of the River Nile, remember?' he said, laughing. 'This is going to be a *Giltie!* event. They'll send out the invites and deal with everything else. Marcus told us to sit back and enjoy the ride.'

There were certainly more applications to process in those

weeks. Although Brian aspired to the Attraction Abacus becoming a global dating agency, it had been very much a local affair to date. The *Giltie!* applications we received from Storer came from much further afield. This presented us with a few logistical problems, given that most of these singles would not be able to come to our office.

We tried to use our face scanning software on photographs that were often blurry or, in many cases, clearly not recent. Success was limited at best. Height and weight details were taken on trust, though I had seen firsthand how often these numbers were tweaked by the singles. The various personality and aptitude tests were completed sporadically without a task master standing over the applicant, so I couldn't claim to have huge confidence in the data we were collecting for the Abacus algorithm.

As the week progressed, Storer was disappointed at the number of elites we were identifying. I was copied in on these emails, as if I could do anything about the situation, and ignored them all. Storer was hoping for four to five hundred singles to attend the event, and when it appeared that we could not identify that many elites, he told us to forward all our scores in bulk. He would invite the highest scoring seven hundred singles, in the hope that at least four hundred would accept. Mysteriously, he had a plan to handle the situation on the day.

I worked hard to process all the details, but Brian worked even harder. On some occasions, I suspected that he had slept in the office. I often felt like saying something as I left in the evenings, but I wasn't sure if it was appropriate. Brian was always so engrossed in his work that he barely noticed me leave, boxed away in the consultation room, his face glowing from the screen in front of him. It was difficult to understand why he needed to be working quite so much. I did wonder if he had been evicted from his home, but Luke assured me that this wasn't the case.

Luke had a few college commitments but helped as best he could. There was an unspoken understanding between us now, and our relationship would remain on hold until things were calmer. I felt so conflicted whenever I saw him. I wondered if he was regretting his choices, despite his assurances to the contrary.

Olivia didn't chase me for my passport details, though I was aware that the clock was ticking on my deception. I still had no idea what I was going to do long-term, but the *Giltie!* event was a chance to think about something else for a short while.

I had never ridden in a limo before. Storer arranged for us to be collected from our homes, and I was the last pick-up. It was a nice gesture, avoiding the awkwardness of taking a train to London in our best outfits, but there was no avoiding the walk from my flat to the car. I had borrowed a dress from my sister; the Paris dress, as we referred to it. According to family legend, the dress was outrageously valuable and had been designed by an obscure French fashion house. The dress was passed between us for all formal social events with hushed reverence. However, something felt different when I squeezed into it that day. Either the Paris dress had shrunk, or I had expanded, with the wine-coloured halter neck satin garment feeling more like a straitjacket. It was cut just below the knee, and my stride was reduced to a ridiculous little shuffle. I would clock up my daily recommended ten thousand steps by the time I reached the front garden gate from the stairs.

Brian and Luke were grinning like fools through the open window as I approached the car door, adding to my self-consciousness. The limo was already drawing enough attention along my road as the red-faced driver tried to negotiate the speed bumps and double-parked cars. My neighbours didn't seem to be buying into the full limo experience, given their tooting horns, colourful language and gestures. I pretended not to notice them, folding myself backwards into the car like a penknife to escape their attention. I just hoped that my arse would not split out of the dress as it greeted Luke.

'You look amazing,' said Luke.

'You're not looking so bad yourself,' I replied, turning to the suited guys to my right. 'You too, Brian.'

'Very kind, Evelyn.'

'The party should be great. I've heard they make a mean punch,' said Luke, grinning at me as I wriggled beside him.

'Funny,' I replied. It would have been a less demure response if Brian weren't sitting there.

It was getting dark as we stepped from the limo outside the hotel. Luke and Brian each looped an arm into mine as we approached the entrance, and I felt quite touched. These were my guys. Even as that thought crossed my mind, an instant sadness swept over me. My dad would never loop his arm inside mine again. Not that he ever had; he would have already been inside the hotel by now, hitting the free bar, but that wasn't the point. He was gone forever. I felt tears welling up and cursed my stupidity for getting upset at that precise moment.

'Are you okay?' said Luke, looking at me in concern.

'I just need a minute.'

'Are you sure?'

'Yes, you two go ahead. I'll catch you up.'

They eventually left me, and I breathed deeply, standing motionless in the street. I was annoyed for acting a diva as much

194

as feeling upset, but all my emotions were just too raw to ignore. The hotel looming above me would have been impressive to somebody else. The back-lit facade glowed arrogantly in the darkening London sky, and there was a flag fluttering from every continent on the planet. Some of them, I'm certain, were made up just to boost the numbers. With a final deep breath, I shuffled towards the vast revolving door, feeling like an overweight chicken with a sock pulled over its body in my dress.

My hand had barely connected with the glass panel when I realised that there was a second entrance to my left — perhaps the only true entrance — where a uniformed concierge was holding the door open for me in anticipation. It was too late. I half-waved an apology, but the door was already shifting under my weight, and I moved with it. Once completely entombed in my personal glass sector, I realised how heavy the revolving door was, and my ridiculous little steps couldn't shift it effectively in the tight dress. Instead, I pushed only with my arms. The glass panel behind me now moved faster than I could shuffle away from it, hitting my backside with an inelegant slap. I had bumped forward, but not nearly enough. There was no option other than to repeat the ridiculous motion, like a car shunting another down the street, until I emerged into reception, almost tumbling forward. Luke, ever my rock, was pissing himself laughing as he waited for me, a few feet away. Fortunately, Brian had already disappeared, but I noticed a few other people smirking.

'What an entrance!' Luke said as I approached him.

'Hilarious. You could have helped me.'

'You were doing so well on your own.'

'Can we just get a drink?'

I was in no mood for Luke's crap. By the time we had reached the function room, I was already regretting my abruptness and found myself over-compensating. Annoyingly, I don't think Luke even noticed, and when we caught sight of Brian, almost hyper-ventilating at the periphery of the room, everything was immediately forgotten.

'Are you okay?' Luke asked Brian.

'It's very grand, isn't it?' Brian muttered, loosening his collar. 'I hope everything runs smoothly.'

We were about to enter the function room when a young guy in a tuxedo intercepted us.

'Can I see your invites, please?'

Brian was carrying all three, and the tuxedo guy peeled a bar code from our respective invitations, attaching them each to a gold-coloured lanyard that we were asked to wear around our necks. We obliged and wandered in.

The function suite *was* impressive. It felt as if I had stepped back into the Roaring Twenties. The art deco room, predominantly decked out in white and gold, was certainly striking, but there were too many mirrors for my liking, and the carpet was disorientating, with a bold geometric pattern of navy and white that made me feel as if I was being sucked into a giant puzzle. The sound of flirting has a particular tone, and it filled the room like an amorous birdsong, rising above the nondescript background music. The *Giltie!* branding throughout the room was subtle and blended perfectly with the décor. It blended too well, in fact, with the gold logo barely distinguishable from the other gold fittings. The party was destined to be there.

The function suite was already full of people. All the guests had dressed up, to the point that I didn't recognise anybody. I was accustomed to greeting the singles in their casual clothes at the office. Tonight, it was formal dresses and suits all the way. Even the Paris dress did not feel nearly Parisian enough. I had planned to drink mineral water, but then I noticed waiters carrying trays of champagne. The canapés looked amazing too; exotic enough to be unrecognisable to my uneducated eye. I felt a greed rising within me, as if I had wandered into an adult Disneyland, and I suddenly wanted to go on *all* the rides. Plus, I was socially terrified and needed a drink. Just don't overdo it, I told myself, not for the first time. I took a glass of champagne from a passing waitress. Storer was walking towards us through the crowd. I noticed him checking his reflection in a mirror before he reached us, placing his hand on Brian's shoulder.

'A big night for the Abacus, Brian,' said Storer, grinning. His words carried menace beyond the superficial smile. I didn't know what Storer had done to his hair or face, but it looked as though both had been moulded from plastic tonight.

'Looking forward to it,' Brian replied, swallowing hard. Equally unconvincing from him, too.

'Have you downloaded the *Giltie!* app yet?'

'Oh, not yet, sorry.'

'You should try it,' Storer said, pulling his phone from his jacket pocket. 'Your Abacus rating is stored on the barcode of your necklace. If you scan it with the *Giltie!* app like this,' he said, focusing the phone camera onto Brian's lanyard, 'you can check out your compatibility with another guest. Nice, huh?' There was a beep, and Storer squinted at the phone screen. 'A twenty per cent compatibility rating. Looks like it wouldn't work out between us, Brian, sorry,' said Storer, laughing too hard at his own joke. He wandered away before Brian could reply.

Chapter Nineteen

An hour later, we were still chatting awkwardly in our little huddle. I wasn't sure exactly what I should be doing at the party. I don't think Luke or Brian knew either. We watched from the periphery of the room, hijacking a drinks tray whenever one passed. None of us had downloaded the *Giltie!* app, though I was approached a few times — on the last occasion, by a guy who scanned my badge in silence, before turning away without comment. I felt like an out-of-date sandwich.

It was awkward. We all repeatedly commented on how well the evening was going, while I suspect, all thinking how awful it *actually* was. The atmosphere was odd. I couldn't define the exact problem until I heard a few murmurings of discontent beside me. A man pointed to the far end of the function room, where a group of people were congregating. Storer pushed through the crowd at that moment, looking ruffled.

'We have a problem, Brian.'

'What's the issue?'

'Best if you see for yourself.'

Brian spilt his drink in his haste to follow Storer, while Luke and I just stared at each other.

'Do you think we should go too?' I asked.

'I guess,' Luke replied, shrugging. At least we had some purpose now as we eased through the crowd after them. An area at the rear of the function room was the focus of everybody's attention. The floor was raised, perhaps where a band might play, but as I craned to see further, I noticed that there was a door leading to an adjoining room. There were two guys in tuxedos standing in front of it, with a length of white rope separating the room from the rest of the party. There was a sign above the door that read, "*Giltie!* Lounge", in gold neon lights.

'Good luck getting in there,' said a woman in a blue dress beside me. It could have been paranoia, but I swear that she looked me up and down as she said it.

'Wait here, and I'll see what is going on,' Luke said. I smiled awkwardly at the woman and gripped my glass tightly — my only social prop in a room full of strangers. It was difficult to see through all the bodies, but eventually I spotted Luke emerging from the crowd. He stopped short of the white rope, where, after a brief conversation with one of the tuxedo guys, he was allowed to pass into the segregated room. He didn't return.

I waited alone for another ten minutes before finally losing patience, and I decided to join him. The mood of the crowd seemed to worsen the closer I edged towards the lounge. By the time I reached the rope barrier, it was plain ugly.

'Pass please,' said the stockier of the two guys in tuxedos as I approached. I did not anticipate a problem as he scanned my pass, but it was clear that he wasn't going to let me through, silently shaking his head. I had to say something.

'I work here,' I said. 'Well, not directly, but…'

'Sorry, this is a private area.'

'You just let my colleague through.'

He was looking over my shoulder now, disinterested.

'Your score isn't high enough,' said a woman beside me. 'That was what I was told by the other dickhead. Charming, isn't it?'

So, this was Storer's big plan for the day. Invite enough

people to fill the function room but only let the high scorers through to the lounge, where the real *Giltie!* party was being held. It figured. I would have been more offended, but there had been plenty of time for me to dwell on my inadequate Abacus rating. I was a 67-scoring also-ran. There was nothing I could do to help if I couldn't even access the lounge.

A few minutes later, there was a disturbance nearby. Two bloodied faces burst from the lounge entrance, guided by a ruffled-looking security guard with a hand on each of their shoulders. I recognised one of the men; he was one of the brainiacs, as we referred to them, who had scored highly on the Abacus scale with their aptitude test results. He didn't strike me as the fighting type, and the studious-looking guy beside him appeared harmless enough, too. Luke, Brian and Storer emerged behind them, with Storer in a heated discussion with Brian as they walked. Luke spotted me, smiling sheepishly, and headed in my direction.

'Everything okay?' I asked.

'Could be better,' Luke said.

'Were those guys fighting?'

'Yes, apparently they disagreed over the greatest romantic poets of the nineteenth century.'

'Maybe not the ambience Storer was reaching for in the lounge,' I said, smiling.

'Yeah, he isn't happy.'

I stopped speaking then as I noticed Brian and Storer approaching, still deep in discussion. I could see from their expressions that this wasn't just a cosy chat, and neither man acknowledged us as they reached us.

'But it's the *general* quality, Brian,' Storer said, face flushed. 'This is meant to be elite dating.'

'Well, we gave you details of the best candidates. They each must have scored highly on some criteria.'

'Some criteria! We are meant to be shopping at Harrods here, Brian, not Poundland! Don't you get it?'

I didn't like to see Brian getting a hard time and turned away, hoping Luke would follow me so he didn't have to witness the discussion either. Thankfully, he did, appearing as dejected as I felt. A woman who had been refused entrance was arguing with the security guard at the barrier now.

'I'm beautiful!' she screamed. 'Let me in.'

'She *is* beautiful!' shouted a guy nearby, and the crowd applauded and cheered as they embraced and began to kiss.

We grabbed a glass of champagne from a passing waiter at the same time, smiling together at our mutual eagerness to drown our sorrows.

'This is going well,' I said as we drained our glasses.

'Yes, I think we should make it a regular thing.'

'Three words to describe how you feel?'

'Floor, swallow me.'

'Kill me quickly.'

'Let's just pretend we're not here,' Luke said. Our pretence was short-lived as Brian approached, resting a hand on each of our shoulders.

'I'm sorry, there has been a mix-up on the ride back. I can't re-book anything until nine tomorrow morning. The good news is that Storer is arranging some hotel rooms for you tonight. Just ask for the Abacus staff rooms. There's no point in you both hanging around at the party any longer than you want to. I'll be working through the night to sort this mess out,' he added, glancing skyward. 'We can catch up on the ride home together.'

'One room?' Luke repeated, as we stood, glassy-eyed, at the reception desk, a few hours later.

The echoing silence of the reception area was in stark contrast to the bustling function room we had just left, with a solitary concierge standing behind the long marble-fronted desk, back-lit in white and gold light. Definite shades of *The Shining*. For a fleeting moment, I convinced myself that he *was* a ghost. The grey-haired man, immaculately dressed in a suit, eyed us suspiciously as he typed at the screen. We were both pissed. I was mindful that I was swaying slightly and that Luke was slurring. After racing through a little too much complimentary champagne, we had finally decided to cut our losses and leave the party around one.

'The Abacus, you say, sir?' the concierge said, his keystrokes clattering in the silence.

'That's right.'

A pause.

'Yes, just one room booked,' the concierge said, studying the screen. 'The last room we had available, in fact. A certain Mr Storer only took this recently.'

'I see.'

'The hotel is very busy for the party tonight, sir. There is nothing else I can offer you,' the concierge said, looking from Luke to me. 'It *is* a double room, though.'

There was silence for a moment as we processed the implications.

'I can sleep on the floor,' Luke blurted.

'Yes, sure. We'll work it out,' I agreed, quickly. 'Anything is better than staying at the party.'

'True.'

'Let's do it.'

202

'There are complimentary vanity kits in the room,' the concierge said, smiling at us now. 'They should contain everything that you need. Mr Storer requested them for you earlier. Your room is on the third floor. Turn left out of the lift, sir.'

'That's perfect, thank you,' Luke said, dropping the room key card as the concierge passed it to him. He then collapsed onto his face as he tried to pick it up again.

We were giggling like schoolchildren as we wandered the empty corridors of the grand hotel, seemingly taking every possible wrong turn. When our laughter became too loud, we took turns to silence each other, revelling in the silliness of the situation. Somehow, *I* found our room, much to Luke's disgust. Luke noticeably wobbled as he tried to operate the lock with the key card, before almost falling through the door. He flicked on the light switch within, standing hands on hips as he surveyed the room before him.

'Impressive,' he said.

'I'm glad we're not paying for it,' I said, manoeuvring next to him.

It *was* a nice room. Certainly, larger than most I had stayed in, particularly in a city. There was a bold, contemporary feel to the décor, unlike the traditionally styled communal areas of the hotel. A bright colour scheme of yellow and plum prevailed, but did not overpower the room, with neutral walls and carpet softening the combination. The furniture was modern and sleek, with a huge, plump bed as the centrepiece of the room.

'And there it is,' I said. 'The bed. The magnificent, humungous double bed.'

'The room is all bed, isn't it?'

'Do you think the room is trying to tell us something?' I said, not intending for the words to sound quite as flirtatious as they did. Luke was suddenly coy, and I found his mood change sweet. He hesitated for a moment, and we were both silent.

'Perhaps I should get us a drink from the minibar?'

'You know you can't afford to even look at that minibar.'

'Storer is paying.'

'I'm not sure our credit will extend that far after tonight,' I said, perching at the edge of the mattress. It was difficult to recline any further in the Paris dress, and my legs poked out in front of me as if rigor mortis had set into them.

'Screw Storer,' Luke said, theatrically yanking the small refrigerator door open. 'He can bill me.'

'You're so masterful!'

'Nobody keeps *me* from a packet of dry roasted peanuts.'

'You're not going to eat them in here, are you?'

'Why not?'

'Well… it's the wrong vibe.'

'The wrong vibe?' he said, rising from the mini bar. 'What's the *right* vibe then?' he added, plonking himself beside me on the bed. He was calling *my* bluff now, and it was my turn to be coy.

'Maybe a rum and Coke would be nice,' I said.

He laughed. 'Okay, coming right up.'

I ventured into the immense bathroom to check out the complimentary vanity kit, while Luke mixed the drinks. I was reassured to see two white towelling robes hanging by the door as I entered. I could escape my dress, which had become more like a straitjacket as the evening progressed. The vanity sets were impressive too, in cute cases positioned on a shelf above the voluminous sink. I opened one of them to discover it contained all the essentials, including a toothbrush and toothpaste. In fact, I was so distracted by all the premium brands in the kit that I forgot why I was in there, surprisingly, unperturbed by my dishevelled reflection in the mirror. Orange and Bergamot shower gel!

'Even the toiletries are making me hungry,' I called out to Luke, but he didn't reply.

I took a shower and cleaned my teeth. When I slipped on the robe after my shower, I had a dilemma. Should I don the underwear that I had been wearing the entire evening beneath it or stay naked? I opted to stay naked, emboldened by the champagne I had drunk. I smiled at Luke as I left the bathroom and grabbed the rum and Coke that he had mixed for me, setting the glass on the table beside the bed. I had already decided that I was not going to drink it, but it seemed mean not to take it, at least, after all his efforts. Luke took a shower, while I lounged on the bed in my robe, scrolling aimlessly on my phone. I was slightly dizzy.

Luke emerged from the bathroom shortly after, unleashing a cloud of steam into the bedroom. He was also wearing a white towelling hotel robe and was twirling the end of the belt as he approached the bed, grinning like a fool.

'Is that meant to be enticing?' I asked.

'*Is* it enticing?'

'Not really.'

'You're a hard woman to please,' he said, sitting at the side of the bed and rubbing his wet hair with a towel. I sensed that he was nervous, despite his nonchalance, and I was nervous too.

It felt like we were playing out a scene that had repeated itself over generations. Lovers at the threshold of their first encounter. In fact, as I lay there, I imagined a Victorian woman, bound in a torturous set of undergarments, wondering what on earth was coming next. Her plight didn't really help me. The real issue was that I had worked with Luke for some time now, and there would need to be a potentially tricky mental image shift from colleague to lover if this was to go well. Perhaps it wouldn't work out at all, and I would be staring wide-eyed at the ceiling, feeling like I was on a work call as he kissed me? A doom-dream was brewing, and the more awkward the situation became in my head, the more likely it was that I was going to make a fool of myself.

'I guess I should make a camp on the floor,' Luke said. 'It's getting late.'

A silent pause.

'Well, it is a big bed. You could sleep in here.'

'Are you sure?'

'I suppose we might end up in a bed together sometime. You know, when the dust has settled between you and Alice.'

'Sure.'

'So, it's kind of like a test drive.'

'Yeah, I guess.'

'Take your robe off then,' I said, deciding that the best way to navigate my own awkwardness was to make Luke feel more awkward than I did.

'What now?'

'You're not shy, are you?'

'It's a bit embarrassing.'

'Why?'

'I'm not wearing anything under this robe.'

'I've seen a man naked before, Luke! You guys worry about that stuff too much. Come on, take it off,' I said, laughing. I was teetering wildly at the edge of the doom-dream now. My tongue was racing ahead of my thoughts. It was the only way to get through this.

Past performance is no guarantee of future results.

Luke hesitated before undoing the belt of the robe. He hesitated again, smirking at me, before letting the robe slip to the floor.

He had a good physique. He was muscular, but not too toned, despite his gym efforts, which was how I liked my men. I didn't feel too bad about my own body this way. His shoulders were broad, and his torso was quite lean. A perfectly passable specimen to my eyes. He looked so worried, though, and as my eyes lowered to his penis, I couldn't help myself. The doom-dream finally got the better of me.

'I take it back, Luke. I can't do anything with *that*!'

'What the hell!' he said, trying to cover his genitals with his hands. He looked like a startled gazelle, nearly falling sideways in his efforts to protect his modesty.

'It was a joke,' I said, trying not to laugh.

'There are some things you don't joke about!'

'You once said that we should be able to laugh at anything.'

I could tell that he was torn between sulking and feeling horny, and eventually he smiled. 'You're such a dick, Evelyn.'

'Come over here,' I said, pulling back the bedclothes. As he nestled beside me on the mattress, I wrestled my own robe off beneath the covers, tossing it onto the floor beside me. We were lying side by side now, a foot apart on the mattress. Neither of us spoke for a moment, and I could not imagine how we would bridge the gap between us. It felt like the Grand Canyon.

'So, here we are,' I said. 'I'm not really sure what to say.'

'I think it would be best if we didn't say anything,' he said, turning towards me.

207

Despite having a mind that was ever alert and always ready to undermine me at any given moment with inappropriate thoughts, I did not try to reply or be smart, even though these words struck me as slightly melodramatic. I was trembling. I hadn't trembled like this since I was a teenager. Luke's hand rested on my hip, sliding down to my buttock, as he pulled himself closer to me. I could feel that he was aroused as our bodies finally pressed together, with goose pimples rising on my skin. As Luke's lips touched mine, my brain decided to check out of the hotel and leave my body to it. In the space of just those fleeting few seconds, Luke was certainly no longer just a work colleague to me, and that's where I'll turn out the lights to spare everyone's blushes.

Chapter Twenty

If our intimacy was a mistake, then it was a mistake repeated the following morning. After hasty showers, we dressed in the same clothes that we had worn the night before, deciding to grab some food ahead of the journey back with Brian. It was just after eight when we took our seats for breakfast. The breakfast room was a predictably grand space, and a far cry from the buffet area at Frank's hotel, with deep leather chairs positioned around tables beautifully laid out with sparkling cutlery and glasses, sitting on crisp white tablecloths. I appreciated all the little touches, like the silver-plated condiment sets and fresh flowers on the table. We naturally gravitated towards a table at the edge of the room, hiding away from the other guests beneath a magnificent painting of a country landscape. Luke hadn't shaved and was still wearing the same suit and shirt, without the tie. I liked his low-maintenance look.

We were sitting in a perfect position for people-watching. I noticed that the clientele in the breakfast room had a different agenda from those at Frank's buffet. I saw no world record attempts at piling the most food onto a single plate, nor any sign of pastries being slipped into pockets or handbags for later consumption. There were a disproportionate number of couples, though, and I wondered how many had slept together for the first time after the Abacus party. We were like a little club: the first-time shaggers society. Maybe we could get badges and meet up every year here again in our underwear? I recognised a few of the people from the Abacus office, shielding my face with my

209

hand if they looked in my direction.

Under different circumstances, I would have been horrified to have been sitting at the table in my party dress, barely made-up, but I was in a dreamlike state, in no small part stemming from lack of sleep, but there was undeniably something else. I felt different.

The conversation with Luke was different, too. It was relaxed, and lapsed into periods of contented silence, at least, that's how I interpreted it, but that was the very problem. I found myself staring across the table at the man sitting opposite me, his hair sticking up at angles as it dried, second-guessing what he was thinking. I resented him, wondering if we were in this together. My inner dialogue had dramatically changed. I had been so preoccupied with deducing if *I* really liked somebody, recalling how my dad had laughed when I asked him how anybody could be certain. Now, the only relevant thing to know was if Luke really liked *me*.

A waiter disturbed me from my daydream, serving me the pastry selection I had requested. There was pain au chocolat, almond croissant and pear brioche, artistically arranged like a still life on the plate, with a colourful palette of preserves at the side. The tea that accompanied the pastries was my priority, though, and I was desperate to rehydrate after the party. I thanked the waiter every time something new was laid on the table, and there was a lot, forgetting how much that irritated me at Frank's hotel when I was serving. Luke had opted for the traditional breakfast, which was reassuringly similar in appearance to Frank's fayre, though no doubt a free-range, organic version proudly sourced from a farm no more than ten pig-lengths away. Providing Luke didn't mix the scrambled eggs and beans together, I might be able to maintain my sleepy zen forever.

'Are you okay?' Luke asked, reaching across the table to touch my hand. My immediate reaction was to flinch. Holding hands was something couples did. It was somehow more committal than anything that had happened in the bedroom, and the emotional involvement bell was ringing loudly in my head. I didn't move my hand away, but I gave Luke a wry smile that was meant to convey the message, "Okay, we've done this, but it's still only five minutes since you split up with Alice. Can we take a breath?"

'Fine. Are you?' was what I actually replied, not wanting to sully the ambience by going back into it all now.

'Good. Really good.'

We lapsed into dreamy silence again, but I found myself over-analysing his words. What did really good mean? I hadn't considered myself to be paranoid, but perhaps that was simply because I had never cared enough about anyone before. The feeling wasn't nice, even if I didn't really believe any of the negative thoughts.

I had been dragged a long way from my comfort zone. Everything had changed. Who was I now? A writer who hadn't grasped a friend's golden opportunity to complete their novel in India. Not yet, at least. A relationship sceptic, who was sitting at the breakfast table like a lovesick teenager. And, as it turned out, I was a nicey; the very kind of person that I had mocked at the hotel.

I needed to reassess everything.

Significantly, there was no limo on the journey home, and I suspected that the late-night meetings with Storer had gone badly. I nestled beside Luke at the rear of the taxi, while Brian sat at the front, too exhausted to make small talk with the driver

211

or us. His head repeatedly lolloped from side to side as we drove.

I wanted to say *everything* to Luke, and yet there seemed to be nothing useful to say at all. We rumbled home in silence. There was an irrational pressure building inside my head, and I didn't know how to release it. When the taxi finally pulled up outside my flat, I felt like crying, with a mixture of tiredness and emotion almost getting the better of me. Luke surreptitiously squeezed my hand as I shifted on the seat beside him to leave, and this time I squeezed his hand back. I climbed out of the taxi like a robot in the Paris dress, rigidly upright. I was clutching the vanity set I had taken from the hotel, feeling a long way short of the glamour of the brands. I waved the car away before heading inside.

That evening, I decided to take a bath while my flatmates, Katey and Andy, were out. Luke had been messaging me all afternoon. Initially, the messages had arrived as a huge relief and emotional crutch, but as I began to gain confidence in their frequency, I began to push back. Okay, now I was the arsehole, but despite my obvious mixed signals at the hotel, I knew that Luke was still on the rebound, and it was too soon for us to continue our relationship.

The issue was that I lacked my old confidence. As I relaxed in the rose and lemon leaves bubble bath (included in the hotel vanity set), I became increasingly anxious. The candles lit beside the taps in the darkened bathroom were intended to create the tranquillity of a Buddhist temple. As I wallowed in the warm water, watching the flickering flames, they became more of a portent of doom in a witch's coven. How had my response been received by Luke? Had I gone too far in pushing him away?

Just ten minutes into my soak, I ripped the flannel from my face, extinguishing the candles with bubbles dripping from my body, as I launched myself out of the bath, eager to send a more conciliatory message.

Work was always going to be awkward on Monday morning. My nervousness was tempered by the fact that I would see Luke, for a legitimate reason, without all the complications of our personal relationship. I arrived half an hour early, but Brian had already opened the office. He was sitting in the consultation room, beavering away at his laptop, like so many other mornings and evenings when I had seen him. The door was closed, but he waved as I came in.

The air smelt of burnt toast as I entered the kitchen. It was Brian's preferred breakfast, but he had never mastered the timer dial of the toaster. I made myself tea in one of the ridiculous teacups that Brian had purchased to impress Storer and headed to my desk, where the in-tray was, for once, empty after our frantic efforts to process all the applications ahead of the party. Luke arrived just before nine. He made a point of coming straight over to my desk.

'Do you come here often?' he asked, smiling.

'Only when I can't avoid it.'

'Money just can't buy that dedication,' he said, grinning. 'It should be an interesting day in the office.'

'In what way?'

'The fallout of the party. I've heard a lot of people hooked up that night.'

'Let's hope they did for Brian's sake,' I said, ignoring his grin. 'That *was* the intention of the party.'

'Very true. Oh, I bought you a present.'

'What is it?' I asked as he passed the rectangular gift-wrapped box to me. I suspected that it was the real reason he was at my desk.

'Don't worry, nothing too personal. I wouldn't want any more rebound grief from you.'

'Very funny,' I said, smiling.

'Open it then.'

'I'm not good at opening presents in front of people.'

'I'm not people. Open it,' he said, laughing.

As I removed some of the wrapping paper, I could tell that it was a fancy pen. I didn't need to see the brand to know that it was expensive, leaving it half-wrapped. I was embarrassed to look any further.

'Thank you, Luke.'

'Well, you're always saying about writing your novel. You need a decent pen if you're going to write a decent book.'

I wanted to hug him, but I only smiled. This was supposedly an impersonal gift, but I couldn't think of anything more personal to me. I also couldn't recall a time when anybody had bought me a present, apart from birthdays and Christmas. It meant more to me than it should have.

At lunchtime, we headed to a sandwich shop a little way from the office. Luke tried to hold my hand as we walked, but I pushed him away. I then tried to hold Luke's hand, but he pushed me away. The game continued all the way along the road.

As we turned the corner, Badger, our local street musician, was standing on the pavement, mid-song, strumming his guitar. The black and white strands of hair on the top of his head were tied back, with the sides of his head closely shaved. A slight variation on his usual style. He was wearing boots and jeans with a thick red and black striped jumper on top. His familiar woolly hat was positioned on the pavement in front of him. There was one child watching the performance, with a group of adults further along the street pretending not to look. I was smiling in anticipation of a greeting, but to my surprise, Badger smiled at Luke.

'It's still going strong,' Badger said, tapping on the body of his guitar. 'I owe you one, buddy.'

'Better in your hands than mine. Don't worry about it,' Luke said, laughing. Badger noticed me standing beside Luke.

'Hey, you guys better not be an item,' Badger said, smiling. 'It's bad for business. You'll be halving my income.'

'We work together,' Luke and I said in unison. Badger laughed and then continued playing. We walked on.

'You gave Badger his guitar?' I asked.

'Yeah, trust me, you've never heard me play.'

'He is good. I've always wanted to request a song,' I said, when we were out of earshot.

'You should do it,' Luke said, stopping. 'Badger wouldn't mind.'

'Not now, I'm embarrassed. Plus, I'm too hungry.'

The sandwich shop was empty. We had arrived early, before the one o'clock rush, and ordered quickly. There was a chicken club sandwich for me and a sausage bap for Luke. I was shocked by the amount of ketchup Luke poured over the bap. It looked like something from a horror movie, with dismembered fingers poking from the slices. There was no Alice to keep his unhealthy cravings in check. Had I become his enabler? Anyway, I insisted on paying for both of us, despite Luke's protestations.

'This has to stay a secret for now,' I said, as we took our seats. 'We *do* work together,' I added, solemnly. There was no HR department to worry about our relationship at the Abacus, though I was unsure what Brian would make of the development.

Maybe I was just revelling in the secrecy, like a lot of work couples do, to heighten the romance of their relationship, while the rest of the world doesn't actually care. 'Plus, you are…'

'On the rebound, I know,' Luke said, laughing. 'I wanted to ask you about that. How long does this rebound thing last?'

'That's difficult to quantify.'

'A ping pong ball rebounds across a table tennis table in seconds.'

'You're not a ping pong ball.'

'A stock market rebounds in days.'

'Just leave it a little longer,' I said, laughing. 'Until it feels right.'

'It feels right to me now.'

It did to me, too, but there was a voice in my head urging just a little bit of caution.

I knew something was wrong when I saw Brian. He forced a smile as he greeted us, but it was unconvincing. The carefree lunchtime vibe was gone in an instant as we entered the office.

'I need to speak to you both,' he said, gesturing towards the consultation room. He closed the meeting room door as we settled around the table. I gently pushed the camera to one side across the surface. It squeaked loudly, breaking the tension a little. Luke was noticeably quieter than usual.

'Okay, I've been wrestling with what to say to you,' Brian said, folding his hands on the table. 'I'm very fond of both of you, obviously, and so I've decided to go with the truth, warts and all, out of respect.' I noticed that Brian's hands were shaking, and I was uncertain whether I wanted to hear the truth. 'The *Giltie!* party wasn't quite the roaring success that I had hoped it would be. You may have picked up on that during the evening, but Marcus Storer was particularly unimpressed, despite my best efforts to butter him up.'

'So, what does that mean?' Luke asked.

'It's not good,' Brian said, fiddling with his ear, 'but Marcus Storer isn't the bank. Tillon Wright is a respected City financial institution, and it is much bigger than one person. The bank reached out to me initially through other channels, before any discussion with Storer had even taken place. Obviously, it's not helpful that he is no longer onside, but another representative from Tillon Wright contacted me today. To cut a long story short, we are invited to a debrief session in their London offices. Reading between the lines, it's a final opportunity to put our case across for the Abacus to secure investment.'

'I see,' Luke said. 'Will Storer be there?'

'No idea, but we'll have to assume that he will be.'

'When is the meeting?' I asked.

'Three weeks today,' Brian said. 'Which brings me to the more awkward part of this. As you know, I have always been optimistic about the Abacus's chances of success. Some might say too optimistic,' he added, laughing nervously, 'but at some point, we must acknowledge the possibility of failure. I was extremely fortunate that a good friend helped me get this venture off the ground. Sadly, circumstances have changed, and that financial support has been withdrawn.'

'But the number of customers is increasing every week. The Abacus *is* working,' Luke said. 'Why do we need anybody else's help?'

'And that's the really frustrating thing,' Brian said, sadly. 'This is very much a short-term issue. If we could just weather the storm for a few months, then I think we would get over the line, but there are other factors weighing the Abacus down.

There's the debt of the start-up costs to service, along with the repayment of the money the business borrowed from my friend. Alongside the running costs, this all amounts to a considerable sum every month. Far more than the Abacus can turn over.'

'Can't you arrange a business loan to bridge the gap?' Luke asked.

'I have borrowed everything I can,' Brian said, swallowing hard, 'including personally.'

'Personally?' Luke repeated.

'But even that loan is running low.'

'How?'

'Look, I don't want you to worry about me. I'm just warning you that we're skating on very thin ice. You must think of your own careers and situations. It would be wise to start looking around, just in case things don't pan out as we hope that they will. There's no way to sugarcoat it. The meeting with Tillon Wright in the City is very much the last chance saloon for the Abacus. I'm afraid that it's do or die, guys.'

I couldn't look at Luke as we sat at the desk in stunned silence. It wasn't just my career on the line. Brian financing the business personally was insane, with knock-on effects for Luke, too. It was also an unfortunate choice of phrase that Brian had used. The words conjured images of *my* dad, convincing Mum to head to Hollywood where he would make his fortune, back in the Eighties.

I knew how well *that* had gone.

It was late October now, and I was pleased to catch an hour of daylight ahead of the clocks going back at the weekend. The last few fallen leaves blew around my ankles, with a whispering spiral of gold and orange chasing me along the street. My breath condensed on the air, and I pulled my jacket tighter, with the lights of the traffic blurred to my watering eyes. Some of the shops were still open. I was even on time for my bus, sliding back into the old groove, with the same seat, same neighbours and the same conversations about the weather. I was still disturbed by the earlier meeting with Brian. Although it was impossible to ignore the unpredictability of our circumstances, at least there was still hope. Little did I know that there would be another hazard to negotiate before I settled down to sleep that night.

I saw a woman in the distance as I approached the entrance to my flat. I didn't recognise her at first. If I had done so, I would have turned and walked in the opposite direction. By the time I had realised that it was Alice, she had already spotted me. Alice was wearing a long, slim-fitting coat and heels. She looked tall and elegant and was perfectly made up. I was dressed in my work clothes, bleary-eyed and slightly snotty from walking in the cold. Alice made me feel fat and frumpy at the best of times, but my confidence hit a new low as she looked at me now.

'Nice flat,' Alice said. The sarcasm was obvious.

'Have you been waiting here for me?'

'Just for a while.'

'What do you want?'

'It's not so hard to guess, is it? Use your imagination,' Alice said, smiling. I didn't reply. 'Did you know that I have been dating Luke for some considerable time now? Our families are friends. We've taken holidays together, spent Christmas together. I've lost track of all the parties and occasions that we've celebrated as a couple. We've even spoken about marriage and having children. Yes, I would classify it as a *serious* relationship, you know? So, it makes things particularly difficult to accept when a total stranger turns up and tries to ruin everything. Things have changed for us recently, and not in a good way.'

'That's between you and Luke,' I said.

'But it's not, is it? That's exactly the problem.'

'I don't know what Luke has said to you, but I've made it perfectly clear to him that I wouldn't want a relationship unless everything was resolved between you.'

'Resolved. Such a funny word.'

'Call it whatever you like, but you need to sort this out between yourselves, sorry.'

'I see,' Alice said, sniffing. 'Do you know what irritates me the most about you? It's this sense of self-righteousness I pick up on. You act as if this has nothing to do with you. You talk as if *you* have the moral high ground, and *you* aren't the nasty little home wrecker here. But just in case it hasn't occurred to you, you are.'

'I need to go,' I said, starting to walk around her.

'I'm not quite finished yet,' Alice said, stepping towards me. For a split second, I thought that she was going to hit me. 'I don't know what Luke sees in you, if I'm honest. All I *do* know is that if you're fond of Luke, you should be thinking of what is best for him and not just what is best for yourself. Just imagine the life that he would have with me, compared with the life he would have with you,' she added, glancing up at my flat again. 'Don't make him slum it, in more ways than one.'

'That's up to Luke to decide.'

'Maybe, but you should also know that *I'm* very persuasive,' Alice said, smiling again. 'Don't think that this is over. I'm not the kind of person who loses. I'll see you around, Evelyn.'

Chapter Twenty-One

Luke wanted to stay late with Brian the following evening to talk things through, but it felt wrong to leave the office. It had been a week of such mixed emotions, and I just wanted to be there with Luke, whatever the circumstances. He joined me in the kitchen as I washed out my cup, insisting there was nothing I could do to help. Reluctantly, I packed up my things at five and left him to it with Brian. I had developed a habit of working longer, and it was strange to leave so promptly. I hadn't mentioned my encounter with Alice. I was embarrassed about the whole thing, as much as anything. In my heart, I knew that Alice even had a point. I *was* a homewrecker, but it was never my intention.

I was back at the flat at a decent time, and it was a huge relief that Alice wasn't waiting for me in the street again. I was determined to carry on with my novel and quickly microwaved a frozen salmon fillet, feeling too exhausted to cook anything to accompany it. I took the sad-looking piece of fish up to my room on a plate. My flatmate, Andy, whined about the smell as I passed him on the way.

It was getting dark, and I pulled the bedroom curtains closed, dislodging a bluebottle who hadn't realised it was time to die. I tried to ignore his pitiful death throes. My laptop screen was just too bright in the darkened room, and I toyed with the idea of handwriting notes with the pen that Luke had given me. Experience warned me that I would become too comfortable and unproductive if I lay on the bed, but I ignored the nagging voice in my head so that I could play with my new gift. I nestled up against a pillow, sitting on top of the daisy-patterned duvet with my plate and fork, with the pad and pen beside me.

The salmon was bland, watery and already tepid. I pushed the fish around the plate with the fork in disgust. My phone was beside me on the bed. Normally, I kept it out of reach when I was trying to write, but there wasn't a chance that I would ignore it today. Had Alice spoken to Luke, too? I'm not the kind of person who loses, she had said.

The pen felt good on the lined paper of the pad, and I doodled as much as I wrote notes. Luke had left a little note inside the packaging. It read, "Dear Evelyn. Stay a sunset watcher forever. Love Luke x."

I smiled, almost cried, and then pushed the note aside in anger. I wasn't good enough for him. Alice was right. I was just a fraud, like my dad, and Luke deserved better. Would Brian really have lost his investment without Luke breaking up with Alice? I had ruined everything, and the notes I had written in the pad were all shit too. Who was I trying to fool with any of it? If I had stayed under my rock, everybody would have been much better off. I was encouraging Luke to be an impoverished artist and slob, too. Alice was a far better influence. I wasn't designed for any of this. My mobile began to ring beside me at that moment. It was Luke, and I grabbed the handset.

'Everything okay?' I asked.

'Yeah, yeah, everything's good. Are you?'

'Oh, that's a relief. Yes, I'm fine. Just trying to get some writing done.'

'Great,' Luke said, sounding distracted.

'How's Brian bearing up?'

'He's getting his head around things… slowly.'

222

'That's good,' I said, unable to think of anything more optimistic to add. I hated speaking on the phone. It felt like we were on different planets. All subtlety and nuance of expression was lost in the void between us. He sounded odd.

'Yeah, maybe,' Luke said. It was another glib reply, followed by an unfathomable silence, and this time I broke.

'So, what's the problem then?' I was trying to sound as casual as I could. 'I can hear it in your voice, Luke.'

Another pause.

'Well, there is something.'

'Go on.'

'Okay, I wanted to sound you out about it. Honestly, it's not a problem if you don't like the idea. I can always say no, and...'

'Just spit it out,' I said, laughing manically.

'Well, by strange coincidence, Dad's friend, George, called him just after you left the office. It's his 60th birthday, and he's throwing a big party at his house this coming weekend to celebrate. I think George feels a little guilty about how he pulled the plug on the Abacus cash and has invited Dad along. They go back a long way.'

'Did Brian agree to go?'

'Yes, he doesn't like being on bad terms with George.'

'And you're going with him?'

'Well, that's the thing. I am invited, but I don't *have* to go with him. In fact, Dad told me not to bother. It's just that I feel that I *should* go with him, to lend a bit of support.'

'I think that's a nice idea.'

'But Alice will almost certainly be there. I thought that might bother you. Honestly, I don't have to go.'

I didn't reply for a moment, picturing Alice taunting me in the street.

223

'No, you should be there to support Brian.'

'Are you sure?'

'Yes, totally sure. I would be upset if you didn't go because of me.'

'Thank you. I'm not used to that kind of consideration.'

His happiness and relief came at the price of my future misery. I already knew that. My sanctimonious feelings didn't endure long after the call had ended. I tried to get back to writing some notes, but my mind continually wandered to the party. It was fine acting pious, if you really were pious, but I fell more on the side of neurotic and hypocritical than holy. I was horrified that Luke was going to a party that Alice would be attending. Their relationship wasn't over in her mind.

'You stupid cow!' I shouted, banging my legs up and down on the mattress in frustration.

'Are you okay, Evelyn?' Katey called through the bedroom door.

'Fine. Just doing some yoga, thanks,' I called back.

It was clear that I wasn't going to write anything further tonight. I put my posh pen back in its case and laid it on the bedroom floor, beside the dirty plate and fork that I couldn't be bothered to take down to the kitchen. I removed my clothes and turned out the bedside light. I couldn't even face cleaning my teeth. I could see Ganesha judging me in the gloom.

India!

The entire trip had slipped from my mind again. I thought of my sweet friend, Olivia. On top of everything else, I was betraying her, just when she was jumping through hoops to help me fulfil my dreams. Liv didn't deserve this. I was even betraying myself in the process. It was a total mess.

If I thought that sleep would bring a blessed release to all the overthinking, I was soon to be disappointed. The darkness and solitude only magnified my worries and doubts, and Alice, Liv, my job situation and the party played on repeat, like a masochistic remix in my mind: DJ shit-for-brains, featuring the self-delusions. The more I tried to shut it all out, the louder it became. No amount of pillow patting or tossing and turning changed the situation. I nearly texted Luke, but I couldn't retract my holiness. Only exhaustion finally brought some reprieve. My sleepy thoughts became less frantic, but increasingly bizarre imagery replaced them. I ended up fantasising about Luke having a horrible accident. I was the only person who cared enough to look after him. The fantasy became more and more detailed and vivid until it morphed into a dream as I drifted off to sleep.

'Is he okay?' I say to the doctor, standing outside the green curtain draped around Luke's hospital bed.

'I think you should take a seat,' the doctor says. 'It's bad.'

'How bad?'

'He's stable, but I've had to perform a full headectomy. I'm so sorry.'

'That sounds awful. Can I see him?'

'Yes… but he won't be able to see you.'

'I don't care,' I say, ripping back the curtain. 'I'm here, Luke. It's Evelyn.'

'Or hear you,' the doctor says.

'I brought you some grapes, but…'

I stop short, slumping on the chair beside the bed in shock. Luke's hand is poking out from beneath the white covers, and I hold it, staring at the empty pillow where his head should be. An adjacent monitor on a stand displays a heartbeat, racing faster as I squeeze his fingers.

'See, he knows I'm here,' I say to the doctor. 'We'll make this work, Luke. I can be your eyes, ears and mouth. I'll never leave your side, sweet prince. Unlike that bitch Alice,' I add, my fingers playing on the pillow where his hair should be.

'There's something else you should know,' the doctor says, pulling back the covers.

I gasp as Luke's body transforms into the pink salmon fillet I had eaten for dinner.

I wake up.

In my experience, problems seem worse at night, and sleep brings clarity by the following morning, after a spot of subliminal brain housekeeping. Not on this occasion. My subconscious raised two fingers to me today.

You're on your own. This crap is beyond me.

Even though I knew that I should be getting out of bed, I hit the alarm snooze button twice; a short-term indulgence with foreseeable longer-term consequences. It was a cereal bar on the road for me, and not for the first time.

I wasn't certain if I was angry with myself or Luke as I stormed to the bathroom to get ready. I decided that my anger *should* be directed at Luke when my mobile phone started ringing from my bedroom in the middle of a shower. I was dripping wet, and I hadn't even cleaned my teeth yet. Towel wrapped around my body, I grabbed the handset without looking, forgetting that two non-texters called me directly on my mobile. It was the second person.

'Hello, stranger,' Olivia said, her voice taking me by surprise.

'Liv!'

'Is it a good time to call?'

226

'Well…'

'Only I really need to speak to you, and I'm on my lunch break.'

'Yes, of course,' I said, slumping on the bed. I knew that the reckoning was coming. Best to pre-empt it. 'Sorry, I haven't been back in touch.'

'Yes, I thought that was a bit odd. Is everything okay?'

'Kind of.'

'So, kind of not okay too then, I guess?'

'There have been a few complications at my end.'

'Like finding your passport? That didn't sound like the Evie I know. You've always wanted to write your novel in India so badly. I thought you would have battered down the door of the passport office by now,' Olivia said, laughing.

'Yeah, I'm sorry, Liv. I'm a bit crap.'

'So, what's up?'

Silence.

I wanted to reply but found myself crying again. Honestly, I am not a crier, though it was all I was doing these days. I was beginning to realise that my emotional foundations were not strong, and I had simply created a life where those foundations had never been tested. Now it was finally happening, I could feel the fault lines creaking beneath my feet.

'I'm sorry for unloading on you like this. It isn't me. It's just… I met a guy, and I really like him… but everything is turning to shit.'

'Hey, I'm sure it's going to be okay. Do you want to talk about it?'

'Well, I do, especially to you, but not over the phone. Not now. I work with him at the Attraction Abacus.'

'Oh, that's awkward. Even more reason to get yourself out

227

here,' Olivia said, laughing.

I paused.

'That's not so easy either. There are some things I need to do here in the next few weeks.'

'Can't you delay them for a while?'

'Not really.'

'Should I be worried about you?'

'No, nothing serious, but I do need to be here.'

'That's a shame,' Olivia said. 'I don't want to add to your problems, but that's the reason I'm calling. The window is closing on the visa opportunity with my boss. We really need to sort this out. I think it will be too late if you leave it a few more weeks.'

A crackling pause of static.

'I'm not sure that I can do it, Liv.'

'Okay,' Olivia said, sighing. 'It's tricky for me to comment when I'm not sure what is going on. All I will say is that coming out to India and finally writing your novel might be the best thing for you. We would have a lot of fun too. Promise me that you won't dismiss the idea completely.'

'Yes, sure.'

'No, promise me, Evie.'

'I promise,' I said, sniffing.

'That a girl. Look, I don't like to leave you upset like this, but I need to head back to the office. We can speak properly another time if it helps. Even better, we might speak in person on a beach in Gokarna soon,' she said, laughing.

'Yes, thanks, Liv.'

When the call ended, I was now shivering in the damp towel, perched on the edge of my bed. I must have been a wretched sight, red-eyed and goose-pimpled, like a stoned turkey. It wasn't too late to change my mind about the Gokarna trip. Liv was right. It might be the best thing for me. What help was I really going to be with the Abacus? It was still early days with Luke, too. He was better off with Alice anyway. I kicked the posh pen box across the carpet, holding my face in my hands. Why was everything so difficult to decide? I don't believe that God is evil, but I do suspect that God is a piss-taker.

'You're a piss-taker,' I said to Ganesha, sitting on my bookshelf opposite me. His stony silence unnerved me, and I immediately regretted the comment.

That week seemed to fly by. Luke had been right about the Abacus picking up, and there was more footfall in the office than usual. There was also more gossip from our singles, too. The *Giltie!* party had proved divisive, with many customers asking why they hadn't been invited. I couldn't tell them that their Abacus score, the very thing that they were paying for, was the reason for their exclusion, and I fobbed them off by blaming *Giltie!* instead. It was partially true, at least.

I took lunch with Luke every day that week. It was such an odd situation. Our relationship was in a strange limbo, and I found myself constantly wondering if I was ruining his life. I lost that objectivity of thought every night, however, and by the time that George's party came round on the Saturday, I was a mess.

Luke called just before he was leaving for the party to confirm that I was still comfortable with him attending. I couldn't have been more uncomfortable. The thought of Alice being there was awful. I considered faking illness or fabricating some horrible family tragedy to make him feel sorry for me and change his plans, but I decided to persist with the martyr role, again wishing him a nice time. I could tell by his reaction that he was relieved.

Now, I was left in the silence of my room, once again regretting my own stupidity. I was pre-prepared for a difficult evening, stocking up on all my favourite treats. I knew that I wouldn't progress my novel far that night, preferring to jot down notes of my emotions for reference. I would put the sadness to good artistic, future use. Luke's pen gleamed in my hand as I held it up to the bedroom light. I felt like *Hermione Granger*, waving it like a wand to ward off an evil ex.

None of my plans worked.

The notes I recorded in my pad that evening became increasingly erratic and desperate. *I feel sick*, I underlined twice. *I feel dizzy*, was a later comment. Certainly not great inspiration for a novel. I intermittently panicked that the party was taking place *right now*, and I was just sitting on my bed, letting it all happen. I mean, really panicked, to the point that I thought I might hyperventilate. Three times, I pulled a coat over my tartan pyjamas and slipped on a pair of shoes to head to the party before thinking better of it. At least a dozen times, I picked up my mobile to call Luke but put the phone down again. Finally, I started to compose a text, retyping it multiple times over the course of an hour, before ultimately sending, "I hope Brian is okay x."

When Luke didn't reply, I wrote my final note in the pad. *I don't like this.*

Was I experiencing the bittersweet helplessness of being in love, or did I just have trust issues? I didn't have the experience to know.

Chapter Twenty-Two

George's garden seemed different tonight.

It wasn't just the elaborate marquee, stretching the length of the lawn where it met the swimming pool and summer house at the rear of the garden. It wasn't the coloured fairy lights either, strung around the hedges and glowing throughout the mini orchard. It wasn't even the food stations, where hog roasts turned on spits, and caterers served drinks below the helium balloons announcing George's 60th birthday. It was the number of people. Luke had never seen so many people in the garden before. George was fussy about chairs sitting on his manicured lawn, let alone guests dancing on it. Maybe he had mellowed with age.

The DJ was playing easy-listening songs, pleasing nobody, but still, the familiar faces were strutting their stuff. It was that silly placeholder shuffle in little circles for now, until the drinks really started flowing and arms started flying. Luke could see a few of Alice's aunts whooping too enthusiastically as they danced. Their kids were either young enough to think that they were having the time of their lives or old enough to be completely mortified. None of Alice's family and friends had completely shunned him so far. A few looked on in pity, as if he had temporarily taken leave of his senses, but Luke suspected that there was an unspoken consensus that he would return to the fold. Alice's mum, Yvette, plastered in foundation and reeking of perfume, had air-kissed his cheek, leaving a line of lipstick across his skin. It was her universally aloof greeting, and nothing unusual. If truth be told, she didn't really care about anything except herself, and she was refreshingly open about it. Alice's father, George, had raised a Peroni in Luke's direction as they passed on the lawn. Was he flipping the bird with the bottle? Paranoia perhaps. Alice was conspicuous by her absence, and, given the circumstances, he didn't like to ask after her, with nobody offering the information.

Brian was nervous. That much was clear to Luke. The more Brian tried to appear relaxed, the more his discomfort was obvious. He was talking too much and singing along to the George Michael track that was playing, even moving to the music, something that he never did. The intention was to convey the image of a man at ease, enjoying the party. The actual impression was lunatic convulsing with nervous energy. He had almost smoked an entire packet of cigarettes in the first hour.

It was unseasonably warm for the end of October. They had arrived in embarrassingly similar outfits, opting for blue jeans, white shirts and brown shoes. Luke, thankfully, was wearing a different colour jacket to his father, and he fastened it high to disguise the similarity. At some point, they would have to branch out from each other and socialise. There was a loose agreement that they would get wasted to survive the evening, with a cab already booked for the journey home.

This wasn't an alien environment to either man. It wasn't even an alien lifestyle. Luke's childhood home had been smaller than this, but grand by most standards, with Brian reaping the rewards of a financial career that he'd stumbled into through sheer luck, making lots of money without even trying. It had all gone to shit when Brian had screwed up at the bank, of course, and Luke admired him for facing the music tonight, with so many former colleagues attending. That was the main reason Luke had wanted to be there, particularly given the Abacus's ongoing issues. Brian didn't need any crap from these people now. The trickiest people for Luke to confront personally would be his contemporaries. United because of their parents' careers, they had skied together in the winter and sunned themselves in the summer, usually holidaying in luxurious, multi-bedroomed villas that accommodated the entire bank party under one roof. Their little gang became quite incestuous when they were younger. Luke had already spotted two former girlfriends at the party, aside from Alice. They were both now engaged to other members of the clique. There had been a merry-go-round of relationships, with hardly any of the group stepping outside the social circle with their choice of partners.

'Another beer?' Brian said, disturbing his thoughts.

'Sure.'

'I'll grab a couple, but then I should really have a word with George. Will you be okay?'

'I'm a big boy now,' Luke said, smiling.

Once the beer had been relayed, Brian disappeared into the crowd. Despite his bravado, Luke felt awkward on his own. He caught sight of Alice across the garden for the first time, wearing the dress he had bought her the previous Christmas (her specifications had been precise and expensive.) He didn't feel ready to speak to her yet, edging out of view, with the entrance to the marquee forming a barrier between them. There was a group of men and women using their mobile phone torches to illuminate the flower bed at the periphery of the lawn in the gloom beside him.

'Dahlias,' one of the women pronounced. 'George *does* love his Dahlias. They're hanging in well. The first frost is late this year.'

Luke smiled as they noticed him watching, feeling conspicuous standing in the shadows. He was getting hungry now, and the sweet, smoky aroma of hog roast filled the air.

Silhouettes of the other guests played on the backlit wall of the marquee nearby. It was his own personal puppet show. He wanted to check in on Evelyn, but his mobile was almost dead. The remaining juice would be essential for the journey back, and he was annoyed that he had forgotten to charge the phone in his haste to leave the house. Best to leave it for now.

Abba's "Dancing Queen" began to belt out from the speakers nearby. It was at least three hours too early in Luke's opinion. The DJ was a man in a hurry, and he knew his audience. It was the incentive Luke needed to up his drinking pace, grabbing another beer before he had finished the last.

'Hey, Luke. What are you playing at, man?' said a voice behind him. Luke jumped to see a familiar face lurking in the shadows. It was Chris Baxley, a guy he had bonded with on a holiday in Sri Lanka. They had learnt to surf, in between lost hours drinking bottles of *Lion Lager* together on the beach. Chris had small features and big hair that made him look slightly comical.

'Chris. How are you doing?'

'*I'm* fine, but what about you? Jeez, we leave you alone for five minutes and what happens?'

'What do you mean?'

'Dumping Alice and shit. You were always punching *way* above your weight with her, man. Did somebody drop you on your head or something?'

'We're just different.'

'Yeah, she's hot,' Chris said, laughing. He raised his beer bottle to meet Luke's. 'Anyway, it's good to see you, buddy.'

'You too,' Luke said. 'Things going okay?'

'Same old shit, but I heard your old man dropped the ball again,' Chris said, playfully punching Luke's arm.

'Sorry?'

'With the dating stuff.'

'Actually, that's going pretty well.'

'Not what I heard.'

'Well, you heard wrong,' said Luke, laughing. 'Who told you that?'

'I can't remember yesterday, man.'

'You shouldn't believe everything these people say. Their worst nightmare is if Brian makes more cash than they have. The Abacus is going to be the next Google.'

'Whatever,' Chris said, distracted by a group of girls dancing in the centre of the lawn. A few of them looked familiar to Luke. 'Anyway, good to catch up. I'm feeling lucky tonight, and I can't be seen with a loser like you,' he added, laughing, before moving away.

The fleeting conversation had jump-started Luke's social battery, and he moved out of the shadows. It was clear that George or Alice had been slating the Abacus. Maybe both. Luke was determined to launch a charm offensive to counter the rumours. If Brian was going down, it would be in a blaze of glorious failure, not by the death of a thousand backstabbers like this. He'd start with the Robinsons. They were a nice family.

'Are you avoiding me?' Alice said, laughing. She had emerged from the marquee right beside Luke as he passed, nearly colliding with him. She was immaculately made-up as always, a look that Luke knew would have been at least two hours in the making, puckering up in front of the vintage mirror hung above her bedroom dressing table.

'No, of course not,' he replied, far too defensively. 'You look great.'

'Don't I just. You're still dressing like your dad, I see,' she said, smiling. If anybody was going to notice, it would be Alice.

'Why change a winning formula?'

'I'm not sure you're winning, Lukey. Did you miss me?'

'You know it's tricky.'

'You're making it tricky,' Alice said, sliding up the zipper of his jacket until it pinched his neck. 'Anyway, I hoped you'd come along tonight so we could catch up.'

'We've caught up a lot.'

'Don't worry, I didn't come over to give you a hard time,' Alice said, laughing. 'I mean to really catch up. There are a lot of old friends here tonight. It should be fun.'

'Yeah,' he replied. This was an unexpectedly easy let-off. Perhaps tonight wouldn't be so awkward after all. 'Is the birthday boy enjoying himself?' he added, keen to keep the conversation light.

'He's in his element, talking to anybody who will listen. He wants to have a word with you later.'

'Oh...'

'Chill, he isn't going to bust your balls either,' Alice said, laughing. 'It's about business. There could be a good opportunity coming your way.'

'Oh, right. That's nice of him to think of me.'

'You're the son he never had.'

This remark didn't land quite so casually, and Luke decided to quit while he was ahead. 'Well, it's good to see you. I really should find Brian.'

'Yes, you go. I'll catch you later, Luke.'

Luke grabbed another beer as he walked away, ignoring Alice's smirk. Her parting remark sounded like a warning. Stick to the plan and get wasted, he told himself. This night couldn't last forever.

The hours began to slip by harmlessly enough, marked by beers and superficially friendly conversations. Behind the warm words was measurement, as there always had been with this crowd. There was a collective fear that anyone else might be ahead, and everything had to be assessed, evaluating careers, postcodes and relationships with a forensic focus barely masked by the throwaway questions. Luke just drank through it all to make the evening bearable. He was dragged onto the makeshift dance floor around eleven, shuffling half-heartedly around the grass to show willing. A few impromptu rounds of Tequila slammers later, and he was feeling decidedly unsteady on his feet. Perhaps it was time to think about leaving? They had shown their faces. Brian appeared bored talking to another crowd of bank cronies, so it might do him a favour too.

The music stopped at that precise moment.

'Can I have your attention, please?' a voice echoed from the speaker nearby. Luke turned to see George, standing beside the DJ stand, microphone in hand and looking slightly dishevelled. 'I'd just like to thank you all for coming here tonight to help me celebrate the inordinate amount of time I've spent on this planet,' he said. There were a few chuckles, and he paused to milk them. 'Time flies so quickly, and I can hardly believe that ten years have passed since we all met here to celebrate my 50th birthday.'

'You're an old git, George!' a guy shouted. More laughter.

'Thank you, Mark. I love you too. Anyway, I thought it would be a fitting tribute to our enduring friendship to take a trip down memory lane while we're all together again,' George said, switching on a projector that illuminated a large white screen that had been erected beside the DJ stand. 'So, let's take a moment to reflect on the ever-changing lives of the Corfu crew.'

There were cheers from the crowd as the first image

237

appeared. It was a photograph of George and his wife, Yvette, holding cocktails beside a pool, ridiculously tanned and surrounded by friends. It must have been taken at least thirty years previously. They looked like East End villains holing up in the Costa Del Sol. The caption beneath read, "Sexy and sexier".

'You decide which,' George said, winking at the crowd, who cheered and jeered in equal measures. The Corfu crew was a term George had coined on a holiday many years ago, when the Greek island had become a regular summer haunt for the bank brigade. Luke hated the name, as did most of the younger members of their group. The idea of being part of any kind of crew with their parents was horrific enough, ignoring any excruciating dance connotations, and George and co. certainly fancied themselves as clubbers, even now. Was there anything more tragic than a middle-aged man or woman trying to rave? Like it or not, the Corfu crew had stuck. The photographs continued to load thick and fast, each labelled with a cheesy caption.

Body beautiful. More than friends. Tim collapses again.

Luke was beginning to enjoy the show, draining another beer as he watched the years flash by in images. His enjoyment was short-lived, and he nearly choked on the last mouthful, as an unexpected photograph appeared on the screen. It was a shot of himself and Alice, five years younger, fresh-faced and grinning together in sunglasses. Their bodies were entwined on a sun lounger, with Luke trying to push the camera away. The caption simply read, "The Love birds". There was a mixture of "awws" and wolf-whistles from the crowd around him. He felt his face flush, studying his feet in embarrassment until the screen finally changed. Slowly backing away, he nestled beside a bush out of view in case any more unwanted photographs appeared. As he discarded his beer bottle in a recycling box, he felt a pair of arms wrap around his waist from behind.

'Happy memories,' Alice said, whispering in his ear.

'Oh, hi,' Luke replied, twisting away.

'What's wrong? I'm not contagious, am I?' she said, laughing.

'You know the situation, Alice.'

'Yes, I know the situation. I'm still hoping that it's just a phase that you're going through.'

'Let's not go into it again tonight,' he said, mindful that he was slurring now. Alice sounded as if she had been drinking too. This was dangerous territory.

'How can I not go into it? We looked so happy in that photograph. It wasn't that long ago.'

'Alice, please…'

'I just wanted you to know that I may have taken you for granted, that's all. I wanted to apologise.'

'There's no need.'

'Yes, there is. It was too easy to take you for granted. It's too easy to take all of this for granted,' Alice added, staggering slightly as she tried to spin around. 'It *all* comes too easily.'

'We're just different.'

'Are we though? Maybe you're taking things for granted, too. There are a lot of people here who care about you. Are you really going to turn your back on all of us?'

'I'm not turning my back on anyone. Things have changed. It's no reflection on you or them.'

'You're joking, right?'

'Alice, I need to do this.'

'Yes, what *is* it exactly that you need to do apart from screwing your life up?'

'We've spoken about this.'

239

'We've spoken about it, but all I heard was a bunch of crap. Look, I know Evelyn is… different. I like her, and I understand why you like her too, but different becomes the same over time, and when different becomes the same, what would you really be left with? Not all of this, that's for sure. Not me,' she added, manoeuvring closer to him. Her breath smelt of vodka and orange. 'She's not good enough for you, and you know it.'

'Alice, I can't do this now,' he said, trying to ease away.

'You don't even want to think about it, let alone talk about it. It's easier just to dismiss the subject altogether, isn't it? I know what's really happening here. You're making me a caricature in your head. A stuck-up rich girl with no emotions is easier to ditch, right? Well, I do have emotions, Luke. I'm a real person, and you're a coward. You're dismissing my feelings so you can move on with your little girlfriend.'

'It's not like that.'

'So, what *is* it like?' she shouted, drawing the attention of one of George's friends. 'What about the time we've shared together? Doesn't it count for anything?'

'Please…'

'Look, I didn't come over to argue with you,' Alice said, staggering slightly. 'The point is that things can be better for everybody again. Brian needs help with his dating business, and George could help him. I only need to give the word. Why do you think George pulled out to start with?'

'This has nothing to do with Brian or George.'

'Don't be so naïve. I'm *making* it something to do with them. That's how it's going to work, so you'd better start to grasp that concept. George would help you with your career, too. You were doing so well with the auditing course. Christ, George wanted to speak to you about it tonight! You're throwing

240

everything away. For what? You're getting as fat as Brian too, skipping the gym. It's like you've gone fucking insane. Are you guys pre-programmed to be overweight losers?'

'That's not…'

'Look around you. This is where you belong. These are *our* people. It's not that difficult to understand, is it?'

'I think it's better if we discuss this another time.'

'There won't be another time, unless you wake up now,' Alice said, her expression hardening again. 'I won't wait around for you forever to come to your senses, and neither will George. If you and Brian want to hit the self-destruct button, that's up to you. But don't expect me to pick up the pieces.'

She stormed off before he could reply. George's friend blew out his cheeks as she passed, shaking his head. Luke shrugged his shoulders before turning away. It was definitely time to leave the party.

Brian had disappeared to the bathroom. Luke grabbed the bottle of vodka that Alice had abandoned on the grass and took a swig. It had been a mistake to come tonight, and he wanted out. Slumping onto a nearby garden bench to wait for Brian, he stared into the starlit sky. Why was everything so complicated? Alice had made it more than clear that George's investment in the Abacus was inexorably linked to his relationship with her. It was borderline extortion, and Alice was shamelessly manipulative. It only made him more certain that he wanted to be with Evelyn. They would show them that the Abacus could succeed without anybody's help. He needed to message her right now.

His phone dropped to the ground as he pulled it from the pocket of his jeans, and he nearly fell forward as he fumbled for the handset in the grass. He had drunk more than he had realised. There was a text from Evelyn asking after Brian. It was difficult to type a reply, but he kept poking at the screen, one wobbling finger at a time. His head was spinning as he leaned forward to look at it, barely focusing on the screen.

He was crazily drowsy now, and Brian still wasn't back. That was the last thing Luke thought before crashing out in the darkness. What he didn't notice was Alice nestling on the bench beside him as he slept. She positioned his head against her own, wrapping his arm around her shoulder. The flash of her phone camera briefly disturbed him before he nodded back off again.

Chapter Twenty-Three

I hadn't slept. I couldn't sleep.

A message arrived from Luke around two in the morning. I say a message, but it would be better described as the ramblings of a madman, and I couldn't decipher a single word. When I tried to call him back, there was no reply. Perhaps something was wrong? I knew that sleep was totally out of the question now, and so I crept downstairs to make a cup of tea, conscious of every squeaking step as I walked. It was creepy moving around the house in the darkness, and I spooked myself with my reflection in the kitchen window when I turned the light on.

I sent Luke another message, urging him to reply. The most likely scenario was that he was pissed, and I wouldn't hear a thing until the next day. I filled the kettle, trying to ignore the shadowy trees blowing at the rear of the back garden beyond the window. What if it was something to do with Alice?

The mug of tea was cooling on the kitchen table when my phone vibrated beside me. I snatched it from the surface, but the notification was not what I had expected. It was a friend request from Alice. I barely used my social media accounts, though she had still managed to find me. Why now? What was she playing at?

As I squinted at the screen through tired eyes, I could see that Alice had posted some videos and photographs from George's 60th birthday party. I began to scroll through them all, zooming in on every image in detail to look for Luke. George's garden looked more like the grounds of a stately home. Luke moved in circles that I could barely imagine. Eventually, I saw a photograph of Luke as I continued to scroll. He was swigging from a bottle of Tequila, surrounded by a group of guys obviously playing some kind of drinking game. The pissed theory was more than just credible now.

The photographs made me jealous. It wasn't the fact that Luke looked so happy. I didn't begrudge him that part, though I had knocked an hour off my life worrying about him that night. Rather, my jealousy was centred around the world that he was part of, full of glamorous friends and flamboyant parties. It hit me in my weak spot. Things became worse as I continued to flick through the photographs. I paused on a shot of Alice, who looked stunning in a black dress. She obviously knew it too, pouting at the camera. I had already witnessed her immaculately formed stomach first-hand, but she had elegant shoulders to match. It seemed incredibly unfair that God should grant her both a good back and front. I swiped the image away. There were several more photographs to wade through, and I saw Luke in the background of a couple of them. He was holding a different drink in each one. This was, without doubt, the cause of the garbled text I had received from him.

A slideshow followed the photographs, labelled "The Corfu Crew, now and then". I was slurping my tea faster now as I flicked through the images, no longer worried about Luke's safety, but fixated by the new world that I was seeing. Many of these photographs were historic, and the first few stills dated back many years before the party. There were some shots of George, with far more hair than he had now, posing in a pair of skimpy swimming trunks by a pool. He clearly fancied himself back in the day. Alice had taken the time to add captions to each of the images, and I took twisted pleasure in the clumsiness of the puns.

The gloating smile slipped from my face when the last two photographs loaded. My mug was frozen at my lips as I studied the images, side by side, unable to register what I was seeing. The left photograph depicted Luke and Alice a few years younger, looking blissfully happy together on a holiday abroad somewhere. They were cuddling together on a sun lounger. The caption read, "The Love birds". The right photograph had clearly been taken that evening, with several of George's birthday balloons visible in the background. Luke and Alice were sitting side by side on a garden bench. Luke's arm was around her shoulder, his face pressed against hers. They appeared to be kissing. The caption read, "Times may change, but some things stay the same".

I returned to bed around four in the morning but didn't sleep. I felt numb rather than sad, though my emotions often deceived me in the heat of the moment. In the past, I had been mistaken for not caring about things at all. I understood and acknowledged that easily drawn conclusion. There was a definite disconnect between my face and my feelings, with an invisible gap between the two that had to be bridged before even I knew what the hell was going on inside. The things I said at the time were often inappropriate, too, so it was better all around if I locked myself away to reflect on how I really felt. With that in mind, I switched off my phone and stared at the ceiling, trying to decipher my feelings.

When I made breakfast later, all that persisted was a sense of resignation. Alice had warned me that she didn't lose. I had been deluding myself. Luke was out of my league, in every way.

Those doomed relationship genetics, passed from Mum, had finally taken me down. It was inevitable. My toast fell butter-side down onto the floor, and at that precise moment, I decided that I was going to India. The greasy stain that the toast left on the carpet was almost India-shaped through squinted eyes.

I returned to my room, nodding to Ganesha. You were right all along, I thought. My passport really did seem to be lost, though. I kept my important documents in a biscuit tin at the bottom of the wardrobe, and it was only on a third search that I found that it had slipped inside an envelope of old wage slips from Frank's hotel. Thankfully, it was still in date.

My email to Olivia was succinct and not as friendly as our usual exchanges. I was wiped out by lack of sleep and had no energy for any niceties. On the positive side, emailing her on my laptop meant that I didn't have to switch my phone back on to face any messages from Luke. I opened the bedroom window slightly to aerate the stuffy room before curling back up in bed around two in the afternoon. Sleeping was a total waste of a weekend, but there wasn't a chance in hell that I was going to achieve anything else that Sunday. I'd had my ups and downs over the years, but I couldn't recall ever feeling this lost before.

I started to cry and didn't stop.

Chapter Twenty-Four

When I awoke, I thought I had slept through to Monday morning. The room was gloomy, and the house was silent. My head was swimming, as if I had crashed out for days, but only three hours had passed since I had retreated under the duvet. I flipped open the lid of the laptop, still refusing to switch my phone back on. There was already a reply from Olivia in my inbox. I was almost too embarrassed to read it, with the tone of her message far friendlier than my original email. She had tried to call me, but, unsurprisingly, she hadn't been able to get through. Liv deserved the courtesy of a truthful reply at least, even though it was the last thing in the world I felt like doing.

Yes, my change of heart *was* due to the guy I had met at the Attraction Abacus. No, I wasn't sure that I was doing the right thing. I wasn't sure about anything at all, but I just wanted to escape. Yes, this was my current passport number, and I would wait for visa confirmation before booking flights.

As I read the message back, I realised how self-centred it all sounded, and I added a few lines to the final paragraph, telling Liv how much I appreciated her and how much I would love to spend a year with her in India. She wasn't just a second-best option, and, once my head was straight, I would be back in touch to explain everything fully. The effort was exhausting, and I pushed the laptop away across the duvet once the email was sent. I still couldn't face seeing anybody, had no interest in writing, and couldn't even be bothered to grab the TV remote from the table. Instead, I wallowed in self-pity, reprising my detailed critique of the bedroom ceiling.

Another hour passed before I heard knocking at the front door through the partially opened window. Andy barely made a sound as he descended the staircase to answer it, with just the faintest hiss of his skinny legs rubbing against nylon joggers audible. He would have made an excellent serial killer. I froze when I heard the voice from the street as he answered the door. It was Luke.

'Evelyn, it's for you,' Andy shouted up the stairs. He sounded pissed off that he had wasted the trip to the front door.

'Can you tell him to fuck off, please?' I shouted back.

A pause.

'Do you mind fucking off, please? Not my words, friend.'

'I can hear her,' Luke replied, before shouting up at the window. 'Evelyn, I'm not leaving until I speak to you.'

Another pause.

I stewed silently on the bed, contemplating my next move. For a few seconds, I thought that I might just leave Luke standing on the doorstep all night until a wave of fury washed over me. The hell I would! We were going to have this out right now.

I leapt off the bed, yanking up my tartan pyjama bottoms. My left foot was trapped in the leg opening, and I stumbled sideways, now livid. Once upright, I pulled the waist cord of my dressing gown so tight that it nearly bisected me. Luke was going to pay for showing up here like nothing had happened.

I hated myself for doing it, but I checked my reflection in the mirror before leaving the bedroom. I looked like shit; a pale, smudged marshmallow face stared back at me. What did it matter anyway? Storming down the staircase, I passed Andy in the hall, who recoiled in fear. Even Luke took a backward step as I

248

reached the open doorway.

'You've got some front turning up here,' I said, sounding like an extra from *EastEnders*.

'What's wrong? I've been trying to call you all day.'

'Are you serious?'

Luke appeared convincingly confused, and this additional deception infuriated me. 'I don't know what has happened, but I can tell that you're angry,' he said.

'Wow, you really are Sherlock-fucking-Holmes, aren't you?'

'Well, it seems not. I have no idea what's wrong, and I've got a raging hangover.'

The cheek of the man! He was doubling down on his innocence. This was how players played.

'Maybe we'll start with you lowering your gaslight setting.'

'What are you talking about?'

'I mean, you're good,' I said, shaking my head. 'If I hadn't witnessed the evidence with my own eyes, I would be starting to think that I was crazy.'

'For the record, you sound crazy.'

'I see,' I said, folding my arms. 'You're going all in on this. Presumably, you'll be claiming some kind of memory loss because you drank too much at the party.'

'Evelyn, please. I really don't know what you're talking about.'

'Fortunately for you, your girlfriend has posted a little *aide-memoire* on social media, so feel free to review that at your leisure.'

'What? I assume that you're talking about Alice. Whatever she posted is irrelevant. I told you that it's over between us.'

'You should check it out. It doesn't appear to be very over.'

'I don't care what it appears like,' Luke said, getting angrier now. 'I thought you trusted me. I thought we had something going on here. I'm telling you nothing happened at the party.'

I had never seen Luke angry before. That was the point that I started to lose my confidence, but I couldn't back down, pulling my dressing gown tighter as I shivered on the doorstep.

'Well, this is all just messed up anyway, isn't it?'

'What do you mean?'

'You, slumming it with me. We come from totally different worlds. I saw the party.'

'Are you serious? This isn't *Pride and Prejudice*. Anyway, it's been a long time since I fitted in with those guys. You know the world of trouble that Brian has got himself into. Do you really think that I'm in a better place than you?'

'That's easy for you to say. Even your troubled is better than my normal. You're blinded by your own privilege.'

'That just sounds like self-pity to me.'

'Maybe I am feeling sorry for myself, but I know when something isn't right. I don't think that it will work out between us.'

'You won't try to make it work. No, you're *scared* to try to make it work. Let's talk about the real problem here.'

'What's that supposed to mean?'

'I mean the chip on your shoulder. You're scared to do anything in case you fail.'

'That's incredibly insightful. You've got all the answers, haven't you?'

'Just an observation.'

'Well, why don't you take your observations somewhere else, along with your serial womanising?'

'What? You *are* crazy!'

'Maybe I am. Even more reason for us to call it a day.'

'Is that what you really want?'

'Yes, just go, please.'

'Fine,' he said, hesitating for a second, before turning and marching off down the street. As he walked away, I was already regretting my words.

I called in sick on Monday morning. Whatever had been lurking beneath the surface now engulfed me, and I felt as though a heavy blanket had been thrown over my head. Luke had hit a nerve about the chip on my shoulder, and I knew that he was right. So, what? What did any of it matter anyway? That morning, I was overwhelmed with the utter pointlessness of everything. I pictured myself in X-ray vision. I was a ludicrous skeleton moving around the house in meaningless circles.

I cleaned my teeth. Why bother?

I ate breakfast. Why bother?

I got dressed. Why bother?

I even visualised my skeletal self, sitting at my desk, trying to write my pointless story about a pointless relationship that might lead to a pointless new career. My stupid, grinning skull looked so pleased with itself in the daydream, despite the ultimate futility of it all.

I had promised Liv that I would sort out my jabs for the India trip, though a cursory online check revealed that I should have sorted this out way earlier. Six to eight weeks before travelling ensured maximum effectiveness for the inoculations, it seemed, but maybe I could take a chance on partial effectiveness. Some of the jabs even seemed optional, like rabies, so I could really spin the health wheel of chance. In all honesty, falling between the jaws of a rabid dog sounded quite relaxing by this point.

251

To my surprise, the important jabs were provided free by the N.H.S. Better still, according to my doctor's surgery, I was fortunate with my timing, and there was earlier availability than there would ordinarily be at the time of year. The universe was telling Luke where to go.

I don't know how many times I looked at Alice's post from the party. Perhaps the angle of the photograph could be misconstrued, but Alice certainly didn't drag Luke onto that bench to sit with her. I just couldn't be bothered to think about it any longer. I did feel bad for Brian. I knew that it was the worst possible time to be taking sick leave, but I just could not face seeing Luke in the office. There were only two weeks remaining before the big City showdown, and I knew that he would need all the help he could get. He should blame his lothario son for the problem.

Chapter Twenty-Five

Things change quickly, particularly confidence.

I missed Luke badly. I cared about him deeply. Whatever I had been trying to tell myself to the contrary was a lie. The panic I had felt on the night of the party was becoming a recurring hysteria during the day, and I felt dazed, almost drunk, most of the time. I had pushed Luke away, and he could be doing anything now without me, while I just let it all happen.

I was still going through the motions of planning the India trip, but my heart wasn't in it. Finally, on the Wednesday after the party, I decided that I could no longer live in self-denial and would return to work. To my shame, there was no part of me that was worried about the Abacus or Brian. My thinking had funnelled into a one-dimensional obsession, and I needed to see Luke. It was now that I realised the true depth of my insecurity, and I felt a complete self-loathing. I wanted Luke back at any cost. I was prepared to put up with any shit that had happened at the party. I couldn't admit the truth to Olivia in our emails and continued to enthuse about the India trip. I was a total fraud.

Luke wasn't at his desk when I arrived at the office. That wasn't unusual. He could be slack with his timekeeping, whereas I was entirely punctual. His intermittent appearances were often down to coursework obligations, I told myself, though my disappointment was difficult to swallow. Maybe he was back following Alice's gym regime?

Brian waved through the window of the consultation room,

phone to his ear, as I entered. Busy as always. It was a relief that I would have time to compose myself before talking to him. I still hadn't decided which flavour of sickness had overcome me in the last couple of days, mindful that Brian may have spoken to Luke, so I couldn't afford to be too creative. A stomach upset was favourite. There were no obvious outward symptoms, and Brian wouldn't want to discuss the finer details.

It was strangely alien sitting at my desk. I had only missed two working days, but it felt like a whole lot more to me. My in-tray was chaotic, both in the volume of applications and in the manner that they had been tossed on the pile with complete abandon. Brian or Luke must have been really pushed for time in the last few days. I straightened the tray before doing anything else, unable to bear the mess in the corner of my eye. Brian finally emerged from the consultation room around eleven. He stood in the middle of the office, scratching his head, visibly uncertain what he was going to do next. He looked tired, although he had a face that readily embraced careworn.

'Ah, Evelyn,' he said, finally remembering that I was there. He turned and marched towards me, stopping in front of my desk. 'Thank God, you're back. Things have been crazy.'

'I can see.'

'Yes… sorry, how do you feel?'

'Better, thanks.'

'Great news,' he said, scratching his head again. 'Well, if you can wade through the backlog, that would be amazing.'

'Sure,' I replied. No further quizzing about my sickness. Perfect. Ask no questions, tell no lies. 'No Luke today?'

'Oh, no, Luke isn't in this week.'

'Must be busy with his course, I guess?'

'Yes, yes, his course,' Brian said, his face flushing.

'Anyway, I really need to crack on. Great to have you back.'

I knew Brian well enough to know that he was squirming, but the question was, why? There wasn't a chance in hell that Luke was absent because of his course. Brian was no poker player, and he had nearly choked on his words. Why was he being evasive, and where was Luke?

Working was good for me. Wading through the pile of applications and keying them into the system occupied just enough of my brain to stop me from overthinking. If my mind wandered too far, I made errors, and the repetitive keying proved therapeutic, like a slow-burning lobotomy. It also gave me a pitiful sense of achievement to see the pile dwindle. That's how low my self-esteem had sunk. There were a couple of visitors to the office in the morning. I was too drained to worry about being overheard in the consultation room when I processed their applications.

Lunchtime felt lonely. I had been spending lunch with Luke recently, and our sandwich shop was empty and soulless without him. Even Badger wasn't about. I checked Alice's social media for any recent posts, but there was nothing. She was, however, showing as offline. Could she be somewhere with Luke? I knew that I was jumping to conclusions, but it made perfect sense. I couldn't stop myself from thinking the worst.

I had almost cleared the application keying by two o'clock and was starting to worry about what I would do next. Three hours sitting at my desk with nothing to keep my mind occupied was daunting. The door of the office opened, interrupting my thoughts. A middle-aged woman entered. She wasn't our typical customer, being slightly older and more glamorous than our regular demographic. Her blonde hair, almost certainly dyed, was cut into a geometric bob, and her make-up was strikingly bright. She wore a bold, floral-patterned dress. Expensive, I suspected. It was the kind of garment you would need to pick up from a charity shop with prior knowledge, for fear of handling an unexploded fashion bomb. I knew that she had that *exact* knowledge just from looking at her. The woman was smiling at me. She had an inquisitive, pixie face.

'Is Brian around?' she asked.

'He just popped out to buy some cigarettes. He should be back any minute.'

'He still has that filthy habit then,' the woman said, smiling. She walked towards me, and I stood from my chair. 'I can wait for him. You must be Evelyn. I'm Sarah, Luke's mum.'

'Pleased to meet you,' I said, shaking her extended hand. 'Sorry, Luke isn't here today.'

'Yes, I know.'

How did she know?

'I've never actually been *in* here before,' Sarah said, looking around her. 'I've walked past a few times. Brian really did get his venture off the ground then.'

'Yes, the Abacus is amazing. It has grown so much in the time that I've been here.'

'Well, I certainly can't fault Brian for lack of ambition, that's for sure. Perhaps his execution has left something to be desired in the past,' she said, smiling. I pretended not to know what she was talking about.

Making tea avoided awkward conversations, and when I shortly emerged from the kitchen, posh cup and saucer in hand, Sarah was studying the cut-out scientist standing in front of the consultation room.

'Luke designed that,' I said, as Sarah took the cup from my

256

hand.

'He always was artistic.'

'Yes, strange that he ended up studying to be an auditor.'

'We already have one dreamer in the family. I think Luke came to appreciate the value of a good job. At least he did for a while,' she added, smirking at me. What did she mean? There was an awkward pause, and Brian bundled through the door at that moment. He froze when he saw us standing together, looking from me to Sarah in confusion. It felt as if he had burst in on us having an affair.

'I've just made Sarah a tea,' I announced, as if that explained everything.

'Great,' he said, still frozen in the doorway. 'Nice to see you, Sarah.'

'You too, Brian. I hope it isn't a tricky time to call in?'

'No, not at all,' he said, finally advancing into the room. They hugged awkwardly. 'Just unexpected.'

'Evelyn was showing me around. It's all very impressive.'

'Yes,' Brian said, looking about the office as if he was seeing it all for the first time, 'and Evelyn's a real star,' he added, placing a hand on my shoulder, before thinking better of it and slowly withdrawing his arm.

I felt a sudden sadness as I saw them standing together, smiling at me. They seemed nice. They could have been my in-laws in a different universe.

'I'd better get on and leave you guys to it,' I said.

'Thanks, Evelyn,' Sarah said.

'Yes, thanks,' Brian said. 'Shall we step in there?' he added, ushering Sarah towards the consultation room.

The walls of the consultation room were never quite thin enough

257

when I wanted them to be. After a painfully silent morning, when any background noise would have been more than welcome, there were now roadworks in progress outside the Abacus. I cursed every time a pneumatic drill drowned out the conversation within. For an estranged couple, Brian and Sarah laughed a lot, and I wondered if I had misinterpreted their situation. I was really listening in for clues about Luke, of course. I heard his name mentioned early in their conversation, but the drill clattered over the end of the sentence, much to my annoyance. It was a recurring theme, and the drill thundered away every time I picked up the thread of their discussion again. This just wasn't working.

I stood from my chair, tipping the last dregs of tea from my mug into the bin beneath my desk, and positioned the empty mug against the partition wall, with my ear pressed against the bottom. Their conversation was much clearer now. Brian and Sarah were talking about friends and old holiday escapades. It was mildly interesting, but it wasn't what I was here for. I also wasn't certain how long I would be able to hold the position if they didn't say something more revealing soon.

The main door of the office opened, and I almost fell to the floor, sliding the mug away from the wall with a clatter that Brian and Sarah must have heard within the room. I froze as they stopped talking for a moment, before they carried on chattering away like before. The familiar guy who entered the Abacus didn't seem to notice any of it, and I straightened my skirt, trying to smile.

'Hi, Toby.'

'You remember me,' Toby said, beaming. My lip was curling in disgust at the unnecessary interruption as I tried to smile back. Toby had hit on me multiple times when he had visited the office, which was a weekly occurrence, and his act was getting old.

'Of course, I remember you. How can I help?'

'I was hoping to have a word with Brian,' he said, peering into the consultation room.

'Brian is busy this afternoon.'

'Do you know when he'll be done?'

'Not for a while, I suspect. What's the problem?'

As I asked the question, I heard Luke's name mentioned within the office. Sarah said that Luke was "too much like Brian", or something similar. My eyes were focused on Toby, but my ears were pinned back like a rabbit to catch the other conversation.

'I just wondered if there had been any system problems,' Toby said. A pause as I tried to listen again.

'Why do you think there have been problems?' I managed to spit out, though my brain had little to do with the sentence.

'I haven't had many dates arranged recently. Can you check?'

Luke's name was mentioned again from the room, and this time I was convinced I heard Sarah mention Alice's name too. What were they talking about?

'Err…'

'So, could you?' Toby said, looking at me in confusion. I was smiling inanely, but my lights were out.

'It might be better if you come back another time. Brian is… more familiar with your details.'

'Could you just check quickly while I'm here?'

I could check, but I'm certain that you have repulsed every woman within a thirty-mile radius, including me.

'Sure,' I said, returning to my chair. Think of the job.

As I began to type, I froze with my fingers touching the

keyboard. I heard Luke's name mentioned again from the room next door. Seconds later, Brian clearly said, "He wants to give it another go with her." The drill drowned out Sarah's reply, but there was absolutely no way that I had misheard Brian. His words were too clear and too devastating.

I couldn't look up, but I sensed that Toby had moved closer to my desk. I had to say something to stop myself from attacking him or bursting into tears.

'Yes, we do seem to have system problems. Looks like you'll have to come back another time, sorry.'

'Are you sure?'

'Definitely. Things will be better another day,' I said, though the strange reply was more for myself than Toby.

So, it really was over.

Luke was going to make another go of it with Alice. Our relationship had gone full circle, and the only role left for me to play was one of twisted stalker. Lying on my bed that evening, it was difficult to accept it all. I had treated myself to fresh cream chocolate eclairs for dinner, and I was systematically working through the box of four, feeling sicker and more shameful with every mouthful. There was cream around my lips and chocolate on my fingertips as I tapped at my laptop, trying to find more information about Luke and Alice in the virtual world.

Luke, predictably, had added nothing. He was even less active than I was online, so nothing was strange there. Alice's posts were conspicuous by their absence. Scrolling through her history, she couldn't take a crap without sharing that fact with the rest of the world, but there had been nothing posted from her at all in the last few days. I hadn't noticed her final entry previously. It read, "Taking some time out from my socials. Be safe and always be the best you."

My fanciful theory that Alice had gone away with Luke now seemed a certainty. I found myself scrolling backwards through her timeline to better understand my love rival, with a grim sense of resignation. The narcissistic selfies of her posing in various states of undress became repetitive, along with the motivational captions that accompanied them.

Winning every day. Chasing perfection. One life, one chance.

More interesting were the photographs taken when Alice was younger. There was a sadness in her eyes that I hadn't noticed before. One particular image drew me in. Alice must have been in her early teens, with a silver medal on a ribbon draped around her skinny neck, standing wet-haired beside a swimming pool with two other girls. She was staring wistfully into the distance, away from her rivals. What Alice was staring at was unclear, perhaps nothing, but there was something strangely moving about the photograph. A series of congratulatory comments and emojis were listed beneath the post, but, amongst them all, one message caught my eye. It was from George, her father. It read, "Second place is first loser. Try to forget it. Every day is a new opportunity to improve." The message was followed by a presumptive thumbs-up emoji.

I looked up from my laptop, realising where I had heard those words before: Luke had used that exact phrase at my welcoming meal at the Abacus. The words were a toxic baton that had been passed from George, to Alice, to Luke and finally to me, weighing heavily on the bearer. This was why Alice had spent her entire life fighting to improve. George had a lot to answer for, preaching from his arrogant, high-flying position. I would have felt sorry for Alice, but finally she had her gold

261

medal. I had never stood a chance.

Where were they now? Finally, luxuriating in that Dorset hideaway? I doom-dreamed a scene where I leapt from my hiding place in the bushes to confront the pair of them cavorting in the hot tub. Luke wasn't laughing about me now as I shovelled horse shit into the bubbling water beside them. In my doom-dream, Luke breaks down in tears, saying how ditching me had been such a huge mistake, while I stand and just nod, shovel in hand, manure steaming off my arms.

My thoughts became increasingly bizarre until reality finally took hold, and I snapped myself out of it all. I was being ridiculous. The only person who would be upset if I confronted Luke and Alice in real life was me. My ugly crying would only make *me* a figure of ridicule or pity, and after a few glib platitudes from Luke, I would be packed back off again, no better off.

It was the mistake of all forsaken lovers to seek closure. Closure had already happened. I simply wasn't part of it. Nobody changes their mind in these situations, and I was better off maintaining my dignity. This is what I told myself. The only way to make your ex-lover regret anything is to thrive, though I didn't feel like the thriving type as I stuffed the remaining half of a chocolate eclair into my mouth to finish the box.

There was an email waiting for me from Olivia. I had seen it previously in my inbox but hadn't felt ready to open the message. It was time to take the India trip more seriously now, and the decision about my future had been taken out of my hands. Still distracted by my thoughts, I read the first paragraph. Liv was asking how I had been, and her words made me realise how much I had unloaded on her already. She was a good friend, and I felt guilty that I had been so focused on myself. I couldn't face replying about the break-up and instead began to plan how I could make the India trip successful as well as fun. I had written most of my romantic comedy, but the novel seemed to have reached a premature and unsatisfactory conclusion. Kris Harper would be horrified by my flagrant disregard for the genre conventions. In India, I would have all day, every day to write. There would be more than enough time to start a new novel. Maybe something completely different, like a thriller? I felt more like a murderer than a lover in my current mood.

I refocused on the email, only pausing when I reached the unexpected last paragraph. Olivia's boss, Michael, was coming to England on a business trip, and he wanted to meet me ahead of the visa arrangements. Liv insisted that there was nothing to worry about, and the meeting would be nothing more than a routine confirmation that I could join her in India. I just needed to bring all my personal documents and answer a few questions. It would take no more than a couple of hours to run through everything.

I blew out my cheeks, slumping back on the pillow. Michael wanted to meet that week, but I really didn't feel like doing it. The address was way out of town, and it seemed ridiculous that the appointment had to be face-to-face. Surely, a video call would suffice. Ridiculous or not, there didn't seem to be any other option than to attend, but it felt like one more unnecessary complication in a week that had been horrific enough already.

Chapter Twenty-Six

Luke's absence from the office made it bearable to carry on working at the Abacus that week. Although Brian didn't broach the subject, I knew from his conversation with Sarah that he was aware of Luke's situation, but I couldn't blame him for not mentioning it. Brian had been forced into an awkward situation through no fault of his own. In fact, I struck up a better rapport with him that week than I had ever done in the past. He needed my help to prepare for his big City meeting, and, for me, it was nice to have somebody to talk to about other things.

When the office was quiet, Brian came over to my desk and discussed his ideas for the meeting with me. I became more confident in my opinions, with nothing really to lose, and I think he appreciated my honesty. Just like the meeting with Storer in the Abacus office, my biggest fear was that Brian's presentation would become too rehearsed and robotic, and I told him so. Although Brian seemed to take this advice on board, he continued to rehearse little quips and anecdotes that he always tested on me first. I'm not a huge fan of joke-telling or stand-up comedy, so most of his lines fell flat, though I tried not to show it. However, I could not fault Brian's work ethic that week, and he was still grafting away whenever I left the office. On Thursday evening, I grabbed some shopping after work, and when I passed the Abacus on the way back an hour later, I could see Brian in the consultation room, still packing in the hours. What could there possibly be left to do? I had input all the applications for the day, and there had been more than enough time to prepare his presentation and business plan for the following week. Again, I nearly popped in to tell him to go home but decided against it.

On Friday, Brian seemed to relax, and he felt that he had prepared sufficiently for the meeting. This was fortunate, as I had booked the afternoon off to meet Michael, Olivia's boss, and I couldn't be his sounding board later. I always dressed smartly for work, but that day, I made an extra effort, and even Brian noticed.

'You don't have an interview, do you?' he said, laughing, but then his expression changed. 'I mean, of course, I wouldn't blame you, Evelyn, but don't give up on the Abacus just yet.'

'It's not the kind of interview that you're thinking of,' I said mysteriously. We had shared a few nice days, but Brian was keeping his secrets, and I was going to keep mine.

I agreed the meeting arrangements for the following week with Brian, but Luke wasn't mentioned, so I had no idea whether he would be attending. I decided that it would be better not to raise the subject, but it was difficult to believe that Brian would not want his own son there. I had noticed some system updates under Luke's profile during the week, so wherever he was, he was still working remotely occasionally.

'Just make sure you don't tombstone at the meeting,' I said, laughing, on Brian's final visit to my desk.

'What do you mean?'

'You must have seen the videos online? You know, when somebody gets up to speak and freezes. Check it out.'

My comment was meant to be a bit of Friday fun, but as I left, I could see Brian scrolling through screen after screen of videos, looking whiter and whiter.

I took the train to meet Michael that afternoon. It had been wishful thinking that he would meet me locally, but his chosen venue was unexpected. It was a spa hotel on the South coast. The hotel seemed an odd choice for his business trip. I would have been nervous meeting a total stranger there, but Michael's connection with Olivia reassured me, and the journey was worth the effort if it meant I could stay in India longer. Liv had made me promise three times that I would attend that week.

The train was surprisingly busy for the time of day, but I managed to grab a forward-facing seat with a table — the Holy Grail of rail travel. There were some particularly unruly children running riot in the carriage, and their father had little interest in controlling them, apart from the odd half-hearted reprimand that they duly ignored, while he continued to message on his phone. I could see that other passengers were more irritated by it all than I was.

I had never imagined getting married, let alone having children, and the chaos in the carriage made me feel strangely positive for the first time that week. I might never have to run around after annoying little kids. Maybe it was just the autumn sun warming my cheek through the train window, but I felt almost happy. Perhaps being single was just my natural state. Cat-lady wasn't a possible future, due to allergies, but maybe I could keep a few goldfish in my writer's pad? Fish weren't too judgemental, and if I did screw up, they would have forgotten about it within the hour. I could travel wherever I liked, whenever I liked, unhindered. India might only be the start of my globetrotting.

Luke had laughed at me and said that this wasn't *Pride and Prejudice* when I had confronted him. He was wrong. Class differences were still there, even if they weren't quite so obvious.

Maybe it was Mummy and Daddy buying your first car. Perhaps they found the deposit for your house. I would never be able to do that, but Luke and Alice wouldn't break a sweat. We were different, and I was better off sticking to my own swim lane.

I walked to the hotel from the station. It was a bright, crisp day, and I fancied the exercise. I had even remembered to wear flatter shoes. Ridiculously, I was nervous, though Liv had assured me that the meeting was nothing more than a formality. Why bother then? I suppose Michael needed to check that I wasn't a complete psychopath, or perhaps he just needed to check that I existed at all. I didn't like the idea of answering questions all the same, especially when I had no idea what they might be. My passport and inoculation appointment details were safely stored in my handbag, along with every other form of ID I might need, including my library card for good measure.

Fortunately, there was a message waiting for me at the hotel reception. Michael expected me at least. The Tuscany suite, a private conference room on the first floor, was to be the location of our meeting. I followed the receptionist's directions, up a winding flight of stairs, and knocked lightly on the door before entering. There was a man sitting at one of the chairs around the wooden table. He had dark hair and downturned eyes set into his rugged complexion. He was casually dressed in jeans and a white T-shirt and wore a pair of white trainers. Not what I had expected.

'Michael?' I said, smiling.

'Actually, no, I'm his translator, Mirek,' the man replied, with a slight accent that I couldn't place.

'Oh…'

'Did Olivia explain that Michael doesn't speak English?'

'No, she didn't.'

267

'I see. Apologies for any confusion. Michael isn't his real name at all. It's just a convenient alias for English-speaking clients.'

'Oh, okay…'

'But don't worry, I can still help with your visa process. Michael apologises that he is currently held up in traffic, but he will join us shortly. I'll call him in his car now so we can save some time. Please take a seat,' Mirek added, gesturing to the chair opposite him.

I smiled and lowered myself at the table. Mirek dialled a mobile number and began to speak in a language that I didn't recognise. I caught the odd word, like my name and then a longer name, which I presumed to be Michael's real one. Mirek paused, holding the handset to his chest mid-call.

'So, you want to go to India,' he said, smiling.

'Yes, I've always liked the idea.'

'You've always liked the idea,' Mirek repeated, nodding. He then relayed the translation over the phone to Michael.

'Michael asks what you would bring *to* India?'

'I'm sorry?'

'What would you bring to India… as a person?'

I froze for a moment. Olivia had told me the meeting was just a formality, and I hadn't prepared any answers.

'I think I'd bring a good work ethic.'

Mirek nodded and then translated my reply into the phone.

'But Michael points out that you wouldn't be working.'

'Well, I'd be working on my own projects.'

'Which are?'

'I write. I'm a writer in my spare time.'

'I see,' Mirek said, nodding his head again. The muffled response to this at the other end was longer. Mirek held the phone

268

to his chest again.

'Michael asks how your writing benefits India?'

'It doesn't, I suppose,' I said, laughing, 'but it keeps me out of trouble.' It wasn't a considered reply, and I almost stopped Mirek from repeating it. I was too late, and Michael's response was delivered faster.

'Michael asks if you need to be kept out of trouble?'

'No, I was just being flippant.'

Mirek translated for Michael.

'So, you're flippant, Michael asks?'

'No, I'm not flippant,' I said, shifting in my chair. 'I was *being* flippant.'

Mirek rose from the table, gesturing with his hands as he spoke to Michael. He then lowered the handset again.

'Michael doesn't quite grasp that distinction,' Mirek said, clearing his throat, 'but do you have any other personal attributes that might benefit India?'

A pause.

'I can't think of any. Mirek, can I be honest?'

'Please do.'

'I was led to believe that I would be granted this visa as a… companion to Olivia. So, as such, I hadn't really considered my worth to the subcontinent of India.'

'I see,' Mirek said, nodding his head again. There were a few indecipherable words exchanged on the phone. 'Michael says that you *are* correct, but he is still responsible for authorising this visa. So, for his peace of mind, please indulge him. Can you think of any other way you might benefit India?'

My mind was blank. I couldn't think of any way I benefitted anything. For a moment, I just smiled at Mirek.

'I've been told that I'm an honest person. Sometimes, I'm

too honest for my own good.'

Mirek smiled back, and then there was another phone conversation between the two men.

'Michael says that is an interesting statement. He asks if anybody really can be too honest for their own good?'

'I would say they can,' I replied, my face flushing.

'Anything else?'

'I think that I'm a good friend.'

'Yes, yes. Olivia speaks very highly of you. I'm sure she would agree on that point if she were here. I don't think that Michael would dispute that. Anything else?'

'Mirek, perhaps we could try a different approach. If you tell me exactly what Michael is looking for, I'll give you an honest answer.'

'Sure, sure,' he said, babbling away on the phone again for a moment. He paused, smiling at me. 'Do you dance?'

'I'm sorry?'

'Michael asked if you dance. During his time in India, Michael has become very fond of Bollywood movies. He finds the dancing entirely captivating. In fact, he has asked me to play this song,' Mirek said, scrolling through his phone. 'Here,' he said, selecting a track. A Bollywood theme began to play in the echoing conference room. 'He asks if you would like to dance now?'

'No, I'd rather not.'

'Michael requests a small dance to demonstrate your prowess?'

'I don't think this is the right occasion.'

'How can you resist,' Mirek said, swinging his arms from side to side.'

'Mirek, this isn't really appropriate.'

270

'Sure, sure,' Mirek said, stopping the music. 'I'm certain that you have other abilities that you are being too modest to talk about.'

'Olivia said that Michael needed to see my documents. Perhaps we should focus on that for the moment?'

'Fine. Do you have your passport with you?'

'Right here.'

'That's great,' he said, sitting again. 'We can apply for your visa at the end of our meeting, if all is well. I just need to collect a few more details,' Mirek said, lifting a pen from the table. He paused to explain our conversation to Michael. 'Your full name, please?'

'Evelyn Gloria Foster.'

'Gloria?'

'Yes, it's a family name. Is Michael laughing on that phone?'

'No,' Mirek said, listening to the handset. 'Michael is coughing, not laughing…' The sound was louder still, and I swear that it was laughter. 'What is your date of birth?'

'March 15th, 1996.'

'A Pisces, I believe?'

'That's correct. Hopefully, there is no prejudice against Pisces in the visa system.'

'Absolutely not. A fine star sign,' Mirek said, nodding yet again. 'A water sign. Water signs are renowned for their creativity.'

'I don't pay much attention to astrology.'

'Of course not, of course not. Hold please,' Mirek said, listening to the phone. 'Michael asks if you would like to compose a short poem?'

'Mirek, please, can we stick to the visa details?'

'Sure, sure,' he said, studying the form in front of him. 'You

271

are currently employed at the… Attraction Abacus?'

'That's correct.'

'And you would continue to be employed there during any spell in India?'

'No, I intend to resign from the job.'

'No sabbatical?'

'I haven't explored that possibility.'

'Please hold again for a moment, Evelyn,' Mirek said, relaying the information on the telephone. 'Michael asks why not? Is your boss that unapproachable?'

It was a strange thing to say, and it took me by surprise.

'No, but the Abacus is a start-up. It would be unfair to even ask. I think it is highly unlikely that would work in practice.'

'I see,' said Mirek, conversing on the phone again. 'Michael thinks that you are making a huge assumption, if you don't mind him saying.'

'Can we just continue, please?'

'Of course,' Mirek said. 'Only two more questions, I promise. Firstly, Michael would like to know if there are any relationships that might… compromise your stay in India?'

'What do you mean?'

'Issuing a work visa for a year is quite a commitment. Do you have a partner that might complicate your time there?'

'No.'

'You're not in any kind of a relationship at all?'

'No, I recently ended a relationship.'

Mirek exchanged a few words on the phone.

'But it could be rekindled, Michael supposes? He says that we rarely turn our backs completely on a good thing.'

'Mirek, that is none of Michael's business. Or yours.'

'Okay, okay. Well, we have covered the groundwork. This is

great timing. Michael has just arrived at the hotel, and the last details of your U.R.E. must be discussed face-to-face anyway. Perhaps I might take you to him?'

'Thank you, Mirek,' I said, rising from my chair and following his gesticulation towards a second door at the far end of the conference room. The visa application process was far more convoluted than Olivia had suggested, and I had no idea how a U.R.E. fitted into it all, or what it even was. Surely there was nothing left to discuss. The second door had the word "Terrace" written above it. I paused with my hand on the handle, turning towards Mirek. 'You mentioned that there were *two* final questions,' I said.

'Ah, yes, apologies, Evelyn. Michael also asked for three words to describe how you feel right now?'

I was already opening the door as I processed what Mirek had just said. I can't remember exactly what I noticed first when I walked out onto the terrace; everything seemed to hit me at once. A cool breeze felt very welcome after the stuffiness of the conference room. It was getting dark. The terrace overlooked the sea, with a string of lights suspended from the roof above the balcony wall. There were a few people walking along the shingle beach beneath, and a single kite surfer battled against the angry grey surf in the distance.

Guitar music was playing nearby, and I half-recognised the song, though the rasping vocal was at odds with the gentle melody. I turned towards the source, where a familiar face confronted me. It was Badger, though more accurately I should say Badger's head — because his suited body threw me off completely, so accustomed to seeing him in his long jumpers, jeans and boots. He smiled when he saw me watching, and I finally recognised the song: "Someone Like You" by *Adele*. My favourite song. Badger continued to sing, nodding towards the area further along the terrace. I followed his eyes to where Luke was standing, smiling at me.

'Luke?'

'I trust that you were fully briefed, Evelyn. A U.R.E. can only be delivered in person.'

For a moment, I was lost for words. Tears were forming in my eyes.

'Mirek did mention that,' I managed to say.

'It's a unique romantic experience, in case you are wondering. I only hope that you are still open to receiving it from me.'

'I see,' I said, stepping towards him, the tears now flowing down my cheeks.

'I also hope that this is the song that you always wanted to ask Badger to play.'

'Isn't it a breakup song?' I asked, laughing through my sobs.

'No, it's just a beautiful thing,' Luke said, taking my hand.

I was disoriented for the next hour. I just remember laughing and talking a lot with Luke. It felt almost like a dream. Mirek apologised for his deception when Luke grabbed a couple of Cosmopolitans from the hotel bar. Well, Mirek half-heartedly apologised, at least, between his giggles. It transpired that he actually worked at the hotel in the kitchen. I wasn't sure if I should be furious, amused or just happy.

Luke promised to explain everything as we settled on the terrace. The drinks were on "Michael", Luke said. It was getting darker now, and we sat beside a patio heater, looking out to sea. Badger continued to serenade us, strumming his guitar beside the table. Badger's performance was repayment for the gifted instrument, Luke said.

Olivia had contacted Luke through the Attraction Abacus website earlier in the week. Apparently, Liv was worried about me, and she wanted to try to help. She only knew that I worked at the Abacus and that I was involved with somebody else who worked there. Luke answered her email, and, after a few "frank" discussions between them, they had hatched the visa plan. Olivia's real boss, Michael, was still safely in India, none the wiser. He spoke perfect English, too. Liv had a lot to answer for!

Luke had told Brian that he wanted to make another go of it with me (a message I now realised that I had partly overheard relayed to Sarah and misinterpreted as referring to Alice.) He had been working remotely to give me some space that week, with Brian's agreement.

'This was the only way I could be certain that you would come today. The last time we spoke, it was… difficult,' Luke said, smirking.

'I'm not over that.'

'Understandably,' he said, instantly changing his tone. Grovelling didn't suit him, and this time *I* tried not to smile. 'I've seen the post, and Alice was way out of line. I was asleep when she took that photo. Honestly.'

'I believe you.' I did believe him, too. I had always wanted to believe him, but now, sucker or not, I really did. I hesitated for a moment, listening to Badger's song. 'So, what now, Luke?'

'So, you go to India and write your book. Olivia is still arranging the visa for you. I can't believe that you didn't mention any of this to me, by the way. Did you think that I would try to stop you? I hope that you wouldn't have even *let* me stop you. That's not how we roll, Evelyn.'

'No… I don't know, but I was confused. I'm still confused. Anyway, what about the Abacus?'

'You can't plan your life around the Abacus. *If* things somehow go well next week, I'm sure there would be a job waiting for you when you get back. That's a huge *if*, though. You need to plan your own future. I do too.'

It all sounded so simple. Too good to be true. I could hear the waves crashing onto the shingle beach below in the gloom, above the strains of Badger's guitar. It was perfect, and I felt perfectly happy, yet there was still something in the back of my mind dragging me back to reality. Though I hated myself for doing it, I had to clear the air.

'And what about us, Luke?'

'So, there is an us?'

'We could see how it goes. The India trip is an obstacle, though.'

'A year's not so long. I could come and visit.'

'I'd like that.'

'I would too,' he said, taking my hand across the table.

'So, maybe we'll try again then,' I said.

'We really should.'

'But no guarantees.'

'Absolutely not. If someone comes along with a 70-plus score on the Abacus, I can't promise anything.'

'Completely understandable. I fall short of *Giltie!* standards.'

'Yeah, you don't seem to have much to offer India, either. You should have danced.'

'Hilarious.'

'Anyway, short-term, this hotel is booked for tonight,' Luke said, grinning again. 'Great spa treatments. I have held a couple

276

of slots for tomorrow morning, just in case.'

 'How many rooms are booked for tonight?'

 'Just one. I couldn't be sure that you would stay.'

 'You've tried that trick before.'

 'As I recall, it worked.'

 'Don't push your luck, Luke.'

Chapter Twenty-Seven

The big day had finally arrived. It was time.

Could Brian go into the meeting with a half-viable business plan and walk away with enough money to make all our dreams come true? Was the impossible remotely possible? It was slightly surreal sitting in the reception area of Tillon Wright with Luke and Brian. The glass-fronted offices surrounding us, full of industrious-looking executives, felt like a hall of mirrors. The entire floor of the investment bank was slick, modern and very beige. We were waiting on a set of leather sofas, arranged in a loose circle, with a low, ceramic table separating us. Brian and Luke were both wearing dark suits and ties, and I had opted for a plain charcoal dress. We looked the part, at least. I hadn't seen Luke since we left our seaside spa hotel (yes, I had stayed with him.) We were taking things one day at a time, so the old cliché went, but this meeting had always been planned as an emotional amnesty.

Tillon Wright were keeping us stewing. Brian took the opportunity to fire up his laptop, reaching out at arms-length down to the impractical table. He muttered to himself as he reviewed the business plan, though the last-minute preparation didn't appear to be doing him any good. His face was flushed, and his hands were shaking.

'I just need to use the bathroom,' he said, after a few minutes of frantic tapping.

'Brian needs to calm down,' I said to Luke as he wandered

away.

'He's convinced that he's going to freeze in the meeting. I don't know why he kept watching those videos.'

'Yes, not the best idea,' I said, feeling guilty for my introduction to Brian's current obsession. Luke was little better, with his head darting in different directions like a sparrow every time somebody emerged from one of the offices. I needed to intervene. 'Three words to describe how you feel right now?' I asked, smiling at him. Luke ignored me for a second, until my message finally penetrated his anxious stupor.

'Shitting myself.'

'That's two.'

'Who's counting, Evelyn?'

'Well, we are. That's the whole point.'

'Not now, please.'

'That's more like it,' I said, though I think he missed the pun and looked away without replying, leaving me grinning at the back of his head. I knew that he was distracted and that I was being irritating, but I needed to do something to prevent myself from being sucked into the communal meltdown. Staying present helped me, even if it didn't help Luke.

We were called into the meeting room about twenty minutes later. Brian had commented how much he needed a cigarette at least five times by that point, and it was just a relief not to hear those words again. There were three men and a woman sitting around the elongated oval-shaped table that stretched the length of the conference room. The interior was certainly higher tech than the Tuscany suite I had shared with Mirek, with individual video conference points at each seat and a huge screen at the end of the room.

The meeting began with Tillon Wright's smartly dressed

team introducing themselves. The only woman, Anya Kapoor, had some kind of marketing role that I didn't quite grasp. She reminded me of a newsreader, smart and polished in her introduction and corporately glamorous. The guy next to her, Roman Kvisty, was an out-and-out money guy. He was older, with beady eyes that had studied too many business plans. Opposite him was Rupe Fotherington. Slightly younger, Fotherington was cut from the same cloth as Marcus Storer — square-jawed, smooth and hopelessly in love with himself. I imagined the pair of them rolling off the same conveyor belt, with "twat" stamped on their foreheads. At the end of the table was an older guy, mid-sixties at least, who was slightly built and wore an ill-fitting suit. His name was Joseph Flatt, and he introduced himself simply as the boss, a label he clearly found joyous, though not so much his colleagues, who smiled along through gritted teeth. Flatt was an obvious creep and shamelessly stared at my breasts while he waffled on.

We briefly introduced our little team, though I could barely look at Brian as he spoke. His voice wobbled like an awkward teenager's. This nervous energy seemed contagious, and Luke went full falsetto at one point in his introduction, too. I managed to spit out my few introductory sentences, face burning, but I was more concerned for the others. Perhaps the presentation would provide focus and a release from their tension?

Brian was soon to dispel that hope as he struggled to connect his laptop to the Tillon Wright conference system. It was as if the HDMI lead was alive in his hand, and I wanted to squash it with my handbag to put an end to the suffering. Finally, after much fumbling, Brian's presentation appeared on the huge screen. The images were graphically impressive at the magnified size, with our much-loved scientist sporting his heart-adorned lab coat, test tube in hand, beside the Abacus logo; it was almost like having another friend in the room. There was little reaction from the Tillon Wright guys, though, not even a smile, and I felt as though a trump card had fallen flat.

Maybe this lack of reaction unsettled Brian, but as the entire room watched him in anticipation, his cheeks flushed to a worrying shade of purple, and he just sat there, frozen. When Brian eventually opened his mouth to begin the presentation, nothing happened. After a horrible delay, only one word was uttered. It sounded like "kwarr", and he just pointed towards the big screen, as if that helped. He was staring madly.

Fotherington coughed, and after a few seconds, it was clear that Brian wasn't going to continue, still frozen at his desk. His eyes were trying to speak, but his lips were no longer playing ball, fixed in a strange, twisted smile. Luke stared at the desk in front of him, unable to watch. I had to do something. Brian was tombstoning for real.

'Apologies, everybody, I missed my cue,' I said, smiling to the Tillon Wright representatives. 'I'm a little nervous, sorry. I forgot that Brian wanted me to run through the introduction. He'll pick up on the clever stuff later.'

Brian only nodded, still grinning inanely, and I continued to explain the basics of the Abacus. I don't know if the Tillon Wright guys bought my story, but they seemed happy to let me run with it. We had reviewed the presentation at length in the Abacus office, so I was painfully familiar with the content. I was surprised how easily it all rolled off my tongue. I even found myself throwing in a few of Brian's awful jokes, though they landed just as badly with the investment team as they had done when he practiced them with me. Somewhere around the third slide, Brian regained his composure and began to contribute. By the end of the fourth slide, he was back at the wheel, and Luke was chipping in too. We had completed the overview in time for the scheduled tea break.

'Nice intro,' Fotherington said dismissively, as we wrapped up, 'but we knew most of this already. We're more interested in a little exercise we'd like you to complete over the break.'

'We want you to calculate *our* Abacus scores,' Flatt said, interrupting him.

'That's a great idea, but there's a lot of data we'd need to capture to give you that information,' Brian said, trying to wriggle out of it.

'We have it all here,' said Kapoor, holding up a familiar-looking set of paperwork in her manicured hands. 'Marcus Storer forwarded your Abacus application forms. You've all met Marcus, right? He apologised that he couldn't be here today, but he gave us your Abacus forms, and we filled them in earlier.'

'So, I'm thinking that we break now and reconvene in about half an hour,' said Flatt. 'That should give you enough time to key the data and run your algorithm, I would think. There are only four of them, after all, and I'm sure that you're used to dealing with hundreds. We can't wait to see how the Abacus scores us.'

'Sure,' Brian said, trying to smile, though he looked totally devastated.

There was only one laptop, and it made sense that I entered the data. It was my regular day job to process the Abacus application forms, so I would be much faster keying them than Brian or Luke. I knew the entry screen layout like the back of my hand. Tillon Wright had allowed us the use of a small office to complete the exercise, and Brian and Luke hovered beside the desk as I worked.

'How long will the keying take?' Brian asked, pacing the room.

'Ten to fifteen minutes,' I said, keeping my eyes fixed on the screen. Every second counted. 'How long do you need to run the algorithm?'

There was a pause.

'Longer than you think,' Brian replied.

When the keying was complete, after exactly 12 minutes, Brian suggested that we take a break while he ran the figures. Tillon Wright had left a tray of drinks in the room, and I grabbed a cup of tea. Luke opted for coffee, though I was worried about how the caffeine would affect him after his earlier performance. We sat back on the familiar sofas in the reception area. Luke looked frazzled.

'Well, that was spectacular,' I said.

'It could have been so much worse. Thank you for stepping in.'

'That's okay. I know that you were about to do the same.'

'Yeah, right,' he said, smiling grimly. 'It's difficult. Brian is too invested in all this, and I'm too worried about him.'

'He'll be fine. We'll get through it together,' I said, trying to reassure Luke with a smile, while secretly wondering if Brian would leave the building in an ambulance.

There were only five minutes left until we were due to reconvene in the meeting room. We finished our drinks, but there was still no sign of Brian. Luke suggested that I check in on him while he returned to the Tillon Wright crowd to stall the meeting. I agreed.

Normally, I would have knocked on the office door before entering, but I was so flustered that I didn't. Brian didn't hear me come in either. He was fixated on the pieces of paper scattered around the desk, which he was annotating with a biro pen.

'Brian, we only have a few more minutes. How's the algorithm running?'

Brian jumped, trying to cover the pieces of paper with his hands. I had never seen him move so fast, and a few of the sheets gusted to the floor in his haste. As I looked down at the page nearest to my foot, I could see his writing scribbled on one of the Tillon Wright applications. There looked to be some kind of scoring system scrawled in the margin, too. As Brian looked up from the piece of paper to me, eyes full of guilt, I was confused. He had manually calculated the Abacus score on the form.

'Why are you doing this by hand?' I asked. He paused for a moment, still staring at me.

'There isn't any other way to do it, Evelyn,' he said, swallowing hard. 'There never has been.'

'What?'

This was why Brian had looked so despondent at the end of the meeting when the exercise had been set. There was no way to hide the truth now. *Toto* had pulled back the curtain, and here he was, the great and powerful *Oz*, with his fake dating algorithm.

'I'm sorry. I feel terrible,' he said.

'No algorithm at all, huh?'

'It's a chicken and egg situation, Evelyn. Without the investment, I couldn't develop the algorithm, but without the algorithm, it seems that I can't secure the investment. I mean, I know what I want the algorithm to do, but…'

'Does Luke know?'

Brian shook his head sadly, and I looked away.

Suddenly, *everything* made sense.

284

All those nights that I had seen Brian working late in the office were no longer quite so mysterious. He had been manually calculating the Abacus scores from the data input that day! Brian himself had suggested the best date activities for our singles, not some algorithm. He was a professional matchmaker. There had been so many applications entered over the weeks that it must have taken him an age. My mind was swirling with questions, but of all the things I should have asked him at that point, only one sprang immediately to mind.

'Why 67?'

'Sorry?'

'Why is my Abacus score 67?'

'*Your* Abacus score? You were never in the system, Evelyn.'

'Yes, I was. Luke arranged dummy dates for me, remember?'

'Ah, those,' Brian said, the penny dropping. 'You had a test profile set up for the dates, but it was never updated with a real score. I enter *all* the profiles with a default score of 67 before I review them. It's a number that doesn't draw attention if I miss an update. Nice and average. Not that any of that really matters now. I seem to have been found out.'

It may not have mattered to Brian, but it mattered to me a great deal. I felt a sudden surge of confidence through my body at the realisation. Maybe I was a B grade, like Luke, or even a B+!

'I'll go and tell the Tillon Wright team the truth,' Brian said.

'No, wait. We've gone too far to give up now,' I said, collecting the applications from the desk. 'Don't say a word, and I'll deal with this when we get back.'

Luke looked mightily relieved as we returned to the meeting

room. The Tillon Wright team were already assembled, and the creepy old guy, Flatt, gave us a withering look as we took our seats.

'So, what have you got for us?' Fotherington said, leaning back in his chair, bulging arms folded behind his head. I could tell that he was anticipating a huge score.

'Actually, we have a problem,' I replied. 'The Abacus algorithm has calculated your scores, but during the input process, it was apparent to us that you had supplied real data. This isn't something we had anticipated.'

'Of course it was real. And?' Fotherington said.

'Well, this becomes a data protection issue. We are the custodians of the Abacus data, and because you are all present in this room at the same time, it would breach our privacy policy to share your scores while you're together.'

'I'm sure that we are all happy to waive our rights on that account,' Flatt said. The others nodded their agreement.'

'Unfortunately, it's not that simple. We would be exposing ourselves to the possibility of future litigation if any of you became disenchanted with Tillon Wright at a later date.'

'This is ridiculous,' Flatt said.

'As Evelyn correctly states, it *is* our privacy policy,' said Brian.

'You are all exceptionally high-scoring individuals on the Abacus scale,' I said, trying to smooth things out. 'I think I can safely reveal that fact, without breaching any data confidentiality. Each of you excelled in different criteria that pushed you all into our higher percentile during the algorithm calculations. And that's the beauty of the Abacus. Everything is considered, from impressive financial status,' I said, looking at Flatt, 'to exceptional physical attractiveness,' I added, now

286

looking at Fotherington. 'Huge personal talent and ability also form part of our calculation, as does high intellect,' I said, now looking from Kapoor to Kvisty, 'but our algorithm distils all of these factors into a single number, that in this case, indicates that you are *all* quite the catch, in dating terms.'

There was silence for a moment. Had I gone too far in trying to appeal to their egos? The Tillon Wright team looked at each other, and it was impossible to predict which way the meeting was heading.

'It's unfortunate that we can't proceed as planned, but this needn't be a showstopper,' Flatt said, rifling through the paperwork in front of him. 'Roman has reviewed the business plan, Brian, and you have achieved impressive numbers in the short time the Abacus has been up and running.'

'Thank you,' Brian said. I met Luke's eyes, and he smiled back.

'However, Tillon Wright does have reservations. At this point, I'd like to patch in Marcus Storer. He has offered to join us remotely from the US,' Flatt said.

My heart sank.

This time, I did not look at Luke, but I could see Brian slumping in his chair as Flatt dialled the number. The phone rang unanswered for quite some time, and for a glorious moment, I wondered if Storer was unavailable. No such luck. There was a pause, then crackling static over the conference system before Storer appeared before us on the huge screen. He was wearing sunglasses and was sitting beside a pool in a pair of shorts and a T-shirt.

'Hey, Marcus. Good afternoon… sorry, good morning,' Fotherington said, grinning.

'Hi, Rupe. Hi guys, how are you doing?'

'All good. We have the Abacus team with us today. I believe that you've met them before?'

'Sure have. Greetings Brian, Luke and Veronica.'

'Evelyn…'

'Sorry, Evelyn. You remind me of a Veronica.'

'Yes, you said,' I replied, smiling through gritted teeth.

'So, I won't take too much of your time today,' Storer said, 'I just want to run through my findings after our first Abacus/*Giltie!* collaboration event.'

'Go for it, Marcus,' Fotherington said, settling back in his chair. 'We'd all love to hear about it.'

I disagreed. Our Abacus team certainly didn't.

Storer said that he didn't want to take much of our time, but he covered the *Giltie!* London party in minute detail, and most of that detail wasn't complimentary. From his initial struggles to compile a guest list from the Abacus candidates to the perceived lack of quality of our high-scoring guests on the night, Storer didn't pull his punches. No negative episode was ignored, including the fight between our intellectuals and the near riot that occurred when our singles were turned away from the *Giltie!* lounge. Brian tried to counter some of the negativity, but his arguments were roundly dismissed. In fact, Storer's findings were, in total, a complete assassination of the Abacus and our management team. With every new point raised, the Tillon Wright team exchanged ever more worried looks until the hatchet job was so complete that nobody could look anybody else in the eye.

'In summary, the Abacus is a cute idea but proved to be way short of the quality required for a feed to the *Giltie!* dating service,' Storer said.

There was stunned silence in the room. Brian swallowed

hard. Anya Kapoor was the first to speak, shuffling her paperwork, as if it were the end of a news bulletin.

'Well, I don't mean to be rude, but I have another meeting in forty minutes. Perhaps we could start to wrap this up soon?'

'Yes, certainly,' said Flatt, clearing his throat. 'Anything further to add, Brian?'

A shocked pause.

'Not really,' Brian mumbled. 'I think we covered all the salient points.'

As I looked from Luke to Brian, it was just too sad to witness. We had come so far, for it all to end like this. For some reason, at that precise moment, I recalled the conversation with Brian in the pub, after one of his failed appointments. Brian had asked if I was a predator or prey, confessing that both he and Luke were prey. It had seemed such a strange thing to say at the time. Now, it made sense. As I scowled at Storer's arrogant face on the screen, I knew without doubt that I was a predator. This wasn't over yet.

'I'd like to add something,' I said. There were a few disgruntled mumbles from the Tillon Wright crowd. Kapoor looked pissed off that she wouldn't get away early.

'Go on,' said Flatt.

'What we have here is a classic case of the tail wagging the dog.'

'What do you mean by that, Evelyn?'

'You said that the Abacus business plan looked promising. Your very own Mr Kvisty reviewed the numbers,' I said, looking from Kvisty to Flatt. 'But that's the whole point. It was the *Attraction Abacus* business plan that Mr Kvisty was reviewing, not a *Giltie!* plan. When Marcus Storer first introduced *Giltie!* at our local office, his analogy was that *Giltie!* was the River Nile, and the Abacus was a tributary that would feed it. I now see that Marcus Storer had the whole thing the wrong way round.'

'What do you mean by that?' Storer growled over the conference system.

'The Attraction Abacus *is* the River Nile. I am sitting in a room full of high-scoring, intelligent businesspeople. Can you believe that Marcus Storer wants to extract the top twenty per cent of our client base as a feed to the *Giltie!* service and ignore the majority? What I *mean* is, what businessperson in their right mind would discard eighty per cent of their client base, and only focus on twenty per cent? Only a financial fool championing a vanity project would do such a thing.'

I could see that Storer was livid on the screen. His lips were moving, but the call had lost sound at the vital moment.

'So, what are you proposing, Evelyn?' Flatt asked.

'The undoubted failure of the collaboration party in London was ultimately down to the flawed concept of *Giltie!* itself, not the Abacus. I'm proposing that the Abacus should be the *only* project considered worthy for future investment. We know the business plan is solid, as Mr Kvisty expertly identified. *Giltie!* is a dead duck.'

'Marcus?' Flatt said.

A crackle of static, with Storer's voice, unintelligible on the line.

'We can't hear you, Marcus,' Flatt said.

The room was quiet again. I could see Storer still silently raging on the screen, sunglasses askew. He looked like a mime artist with bullet ants in his shorts. My heart was pounding in my chest, and as I glanced from Flatt to Kvisty, I could sense that something had changed in just those few moments. They had listened. They were considering what I said, at least. There was a chance that I had saved the Abacus, and now the eyes of the room were all on me.

Then it happens.

In my moment of greatest triumph, a doom-dream is brewing.

Not just any doom-dream, but the ultimate doom-dream.

Katy Perry's "Roar" begins to play in my head. The definitive anthem of female empowerment.

The doom-dream is so intense, so vivid and complete, that I have no way of distinguishing it from reality. I am convinced that this is happening.

Past performance is no guarantee of future results.

I am possessed.

I climb up onto the conference table, hitching up my dress.

In the centre of the table, I lower my underwear, squatting low to cover my modesty. I smile at everyone, before peeing all over the magnificent mahogany surface.

The feeling is liberating. The sound is disturbing.

Katy Perry belts out her triumphant chorus, as the puddle grows bigger and bigger beneath me.

I join in with the chorus, singing at the top of my voice.

The Tillon Wright team recoils in horror.

Luke covers his mouth with his hand.

That dirty old pervert, Joseph Flatt, likes it all too much.

I lunge across the desk, screaming, knickers around my ankles, and begin to throttle him in his chair — his sick old head wobbling from side to side.

'Are you okay, Evelyn?' asked Flatt.

'Fine,' I said, realising that I was now standing, with my dress pulled halfway up my thighs. The others were watching me with concern. I smiled awkwardly at Luke before smoothing my dress down and slowly lowering back to my seat. 'I'm just passionate about the Abacus.'

Brief silence again.

'Well, you certainly made a strong case,' said Flatt. 'I suggest we take another break so our team can consider the proposal.'

Chapter Twenty-Eight

Luke had never visited my room before. I had only screamed at him from the doorstep of the flat. I spent all morning tidying everything in preparation for his arrival, but my recent slump meant that there was far more to tidy than usual. It was more of a room reconstruction project, if truth be told.

Luke was slightly early. Andy, my flatmate, was uncharacteristically vigilant and beat me to answering the front door. I could hear the passive-aggressive tone in Andy's welcome, eternally irritated to waste energy. Luke was already climbing the stairs as I bundled the last of my dirty clothes into a carrier bag and stuffed them into the bottom of the wardrobe. A temporary fix, no harm done. I straightened my skirt, checked my reflection in the mirror and met Luke in the doorway to my room. He was holding a small, plastic-wrapped bouquet.

'For me?' I asked, smiling.

'Garage forecourt flowers,' he said, grinning. 'You mentioned that you had never received any before. I felt that you needed to experience the *real* thing at least once. I had to pass four perfectly good florists to buy them.'

'Oh, they are impeccably wilted, just like I always imagined.'

'I even left the price sticker on for the full experience.'

'Reduced for quick sale too. What can I say? I feel complete,' I said, taking them from Luke's hands. 'Such contrasting colours too. I've never seen that blue in nature

293

before.'

'That blue doesn't exist in nature. There *is* a radiation risk keeping them in your bedroom.'

'They are perfectly imperfect, thank you.'

'Just like us,' he said, kissing me.

I gave Luke the grand tour of my room. He was very polite and constructive, carefully considering each object as if it were an exhibit in the British Museum. He hesitated beside my ornament of Ganesha, running his hand over the surface. They were finally face-to-face. I felt as though I should leave the room so the guys could resolve any differences.

'Olivia bought me that,' I said. 'It's my inspiration for the India trip.'

'Very apt. She's a good friend, isn't she?'

'The best,' I said, smiling.

'Any news on the arrangements?'

'The visa is moving along. It's exciting in a way, but I'm still conflicted about the timing.'

'It won't be forever. I'm excited *for* you.'

'That's sweet, Luke.'

Next, he sat at my desk, surveying the familiar view from the window. I resisted the temptation to point out all the subtleties that he might miss. They were *too* subtle, even nondescript, after all.

'So, this is where the magic happens,' he said.

'Can you taste the procrastination in the air?'

'Seems to me that you are doing just fine,' he said, noticing the box on my desk that I had carefully positioned earlier. 'Oh, you still have the pen I gave you. I thought that might have been a casualty of recent events.'

'It suffered a little abuse, but I would never have parted with it altogether,' I said, smiling.

We lay on the bed together shortly after, our bodies entwined, just talking. It was an unfamiliar experience to me, and I nestled closer to Luke, closing my eyes. So much had changed, and it barely felt real. My ear was pressed against his chest, and I listened to the low rumble as he laughed. Despite my happiness, my mind wandered to Alice, picturing the sad photo of her as a child, staring wistfully into space. It was never my intention to hurt her, and I felt bad. When Luke popped to the bathroom, I was idly scrolling on my phone when I decided to check Alice's socials, still feeling awful. There was a new post from her. A shirtless man, with an abdomen as chiselled as her own, stood beside her in the gym, posing for a joint selfie. Alice was wearing a crop top and ludicrously tight Lycra leggings. The caption read, "Finally winning. Lost the unnecessary weight."

On the face of it, the comment was innocent enough, but I knew that Alice was more than capable of a darker message and wondered if Luke had seen it. I closed the app as Luke returned to my room, sliding beside me on the bed, and didn't say a word about it.

'A question,' I said, resting my head on his chest again as he settled.

'Shoot...'

'You remember when we were on the hotel terrace with Badger?'

'Of course.'

'I guess that you were asking me out... officially?'

'I guess so.'

'That means that you are my boyfriend.'

'It does.'

'That may not sound weird to you, but it does to me. Even

295

weirder, I am your *girlfriend*.'

'I can just call you my latest squeeze if you prefer?'

'That's beautiful, Luke. I'd like that.'

We rambled on about nothing for another hour. Both of us had studiously avoided the subject of the Abacus. It was as if mentioning it at all might bring bad luck, but we couldn't avoid it forever.

'So, when do you think that Brian will hear back from Tillon Wright?' I asked.

'He said that they are still completing their due diligence, but it's looking hopeful. He thinks that there will be a decision in the next week or so. Dad only tends to hear the positive, though.'

'That's a nice trait,' I said, smiling.

'It is, but it has landed him in a shit load of trouble in the past,' Luke replied, laughing.

'A lot like my dad.'

'Yes, sorry. You must miss him.'

'In some ways, though, I became accustomed to not missing him a long time ago. Anyway, do you think that Brian and Sarah will ever get back together?'

'Who knows? I hope so, obviously, but I want them both to be happy.'

'I think they will.'

'Oh, you do, do you? You seem to be our resident love guru these days. What happened to that sceptical girl I met?' he said, laughing.

'Some idiot gave me a flyer in the street, and it all changed from there.'

We were talking well into the evening. I hadn't even noticed the time.

'Would you like to go out and do something?' Luke said, eventually.

'We're doing something right now, aren't we?'

Luke sat bolt upright at that point, looking at me as if he had never seen me before. There was a huge smile on his face. The biggest smile I had ever seen.

'Yes, that's exactly it, Evelyn. We *are* doing something right now.'

Chapter Twenty-Nine
Six Months Later

Luke looked good in a suit, I decided, as he walked towards me in the office. I would never tell him as much. He'd be too much of a dick about it, but he looked good all the same. The Attraction Abacus offices were now situated out of town, on a popular new business park. The three-storey building, glass-fronted and sleek, befitted an up-and-coming tech company. I missed the intimacy of the old place, but Tillon Wright's money had to be spent somewhere. Their investment was partly down to me, after all.

We had an authentic algorithm now, developed by a software house in Brighton to Brian's original specification. I ran my profile through the system to calculate my actual Abacus score, but I can't tell you what the number was. That would be contrary to the company's data privacy policy, but I was pleased. There was even an Attraction Abacus app now, so gone were the days of scanning faces in the office and weighing people. Singles could do all those things for themselves now in the comfort of their own homes.

'Hey,' said Luke as he approached.

'Hey, yourself,' I said, kissing him. We were the bosses now, so I didn't care what HR thought about our office relationship. It was still early days, anyway.

'I bought a couple of sandwiches for our lunch. Ham and pickle or salmon tartare on pumpernickel?'

'That's a trap!'

'Make your choice.'

'Salmon tartare on pumpernickel.'

'How millennial! You won't afford a house like that.'

'I'm relying on my rich boyfriend to sort all that out.'

'He must be a sucker.'

'Yeah, I've got him wrapped around my little finger, the big dope.'

'Funny,' Luke said, handing me my sandwich. 'Well, the time has come. How do you feel?'

'It's only six months.'

'I know. You'll love it,' he said, squeezing my hand. 'Brian has bought you a cake. I said that you'd swing by his office later.'

'Sounds good,' I said, kissing him again.

I was such a kisser these days.

Brian looked so content sitting in his spacious office when I visited him around four. The gold-lettered sign on the door read, "Brian Asquith, Chief Executive Officer." His vast leather chair was a little bit over the top, but who could begrudge Brian a few luxuries after all he had been through?

'Ah, here comes the great adventurer,' Brian said, as he saw me enter the room.

'It's only six months,' I said, smiling. It was my new mantra.

'Thank God! You can't get back soon enough.'

'You'll hardly notice that I'm gone.'

'That I doubt. I bought you a cake,' he said, pointing to an elaborate fondant masterpiece in the corner of his office, with "Good Luck" piped around the bottom.

'Is that the Taj Mahal?'

'Yes, I know that the Taj isn't in Gokarna, but I didn't know any other landmarks.'

'Did you bake it?'

'Absolutely not.'

'It's perfect, thank you,' I said, giving him a hug. Brian had crossed a line into father-in-law territory now. 'I just need to sort out a few things in my desk before I leave. All my appointments have been rearranged. I think everything is looking good.'

'Great, thank you. I'm sure we'll find a way to deal with any problems if they arise. You just look after yourself.'

'I will do. You too.'

'Oh, and before you go, some big news at my end, Evelyn. Sarah left me a message today. She was very enthusiastic about meeting up. Very enthusiastic indeed. I think she must have caught wind of the Abacus upturn.'

'I'm sure that's not the only reason she was in touch. You two still seemed to have it all going on when she popped into the old office.'

'You remember that? Maybe. Anyway, I might let her sweat a bit before returning her call.'

'Even better, arrange to meet her at Victoria Falls and don't show up.'

'I like your thinking,' he said, laughing.

I had a few things to pick up from my own office before I left. There was a huge part of me that was unsure about the forthcoming sabbatical, particularly after the eventful last few months. My ever-developing relationship with Luke made it tougher to leave, even temporarily. Luke had insisted that I should still go, and I knew that I might regret it if I didn't. The sabbatical was now only planned for six months rather than the original year. Liv was delighted, and it felt like a good compromise. Even so, I didn't like the idea of saying goodbye to

300

Luke at the airport the following day. Even as I thought about it, my phone began to ring as I stood in the corridor. It was Olivia.

'Liv?'

'Hey, you! I thought I'd better call just to make sure that you're still going to show up.'

I laughed. 'How could I not after everything you've done?'

'Yeah, you're lucky to have a friend like me.'

'Don't I know it.'

'We are going to have a lot of fun, Evie.'

'I can't wait,' I replied.

'But we have been friends long enough for me to know that you will be feeling a little sad about leaving Luke right now.'

'Yeah, I'm used to having the idiot around these days,' I said, laughing. 'It's only six months, though.'

'Well, you have a lot of writing to do, along with all the partying with me, so the time will fly. That's the other reason I'm calling. I've managed to rent you one of those beach cabins you always spoke about for a few months.'

'What!'

'I know, I'm just *too* good to you. It was an extra incentive to get you on that plane,' Olivia said, laughing.

'I didn't need it, but that's amazing, thank you so much, Liv.'

'You can make it up to me when you're here. Anyway, it's late. I need to shoot, but I'll be there to pick you up at the airport. In India!' Olivia added, dissolving into a scream. I screamed back.

I was still smiling about the call as I reached my office. I ran my fingers over my own gold-lettered nameplate on the door as I entered. It read "Evelyn Foster. Vice President of Client Relations." The title was ridiculous, but Brian had insisted that I deserved something grand. My office was modest, however, with just a small desk and chair and my certificates on the wall. The spider plant, cascading from the cupboard in the corner of the office, was the survivor from the old office. I had lovingly nursed it back to full health. My nostalgia extended further to the scientist cardboard cut-out — Luke's original design — that I had rescued from the clear-out of the old premises. It stood in the other corner of my office now. The Abacus marketing was more sophisticated these days, but I liked to keep this simple reminder of the early era.

I was sitting at my desk, sorting a few things in my drawer, when a young woman appeared in the doorway. She knocked lightly on the frame, even though the door was open, but didn't enter. Her face was familiar, but I couldn't recall her name. I sat upright from the drawer.

'Evelyn?'

'Hi,' I said, smiling.

'You won't remember me. I'm Diya Desai.'

'I *do* remember you,' I said, feeling relieved to finally make the connection. 'What can I do for you, Diya?'

'Well, I know that it's late, but my dating hasn't been going so well lately. You previously said that if I ever had a problem, I should come and talk to you about it. So, here I am.'

'Yes, of course. Please close the door and take a seat.'

Diya settled in the chair opposite my desk, looking nervously around the room. She had been one of the first women I had added to the Abacus system in the old office, and I had been as anxious about it all as she was way back then. I really needed to head off and pack, but I felt a certain bond with Diya because of that early shared experience.

'So, what's the problem?' I asked.

'It just doesn't seem to work out with the guys I date. No matter what I try to do, and I have tried a *lot* of different things, the relationship always ends badly. I just wondered if the Abacus was selecting the wrong kind of men for me, or you could suggest what I should try next.'

'I see,' I said, coughing lightly. 'Well, the Abacus is based entirely on science, Diya. I'm a scientist. That's my diploma on the wall from the British Society of Relationship Theory,' I added, clearing my throat. 'But, if I'm entirely honest with you, the actual *science* isn't that strong. Let's forget the whole Abacus thing for a moment. I'm going to give you some woman-to-woman advice with some sound logical reasoning behind it.'

'I'd appreciate that, Evelyn.'

'Someone once said to me that there is never any point in making an effort. They said that if a guy is into you, you can do no wrong. They also said that if a guy isn't into you, then you can do no right. There *is* some truth in that, but it ignores something else that's very important.'

'What's that?'

'People change. *You* can change. Therefore, my advice to you is to *always* make an effort, because that guy that you dislike, sitting across the table from you, might turn out to be the person you care most about in the world.'

303

Epilogue

My second laptop battery was running low.

The first was long exhausted, but that was the price I paid for working from a simple, stilted cabin, sitting on a pristine beach south of Gokarna. The wooden doors were ajar, inviting a spectacular view of white sand and the Arabian Sea glittering beyond them. The afternoon was particularly humid, and my personal battery was pretty much drained, too. It was a good time to stop. Still, the novel was reaching a conclusion, and I was feeling relaxed about my progress. I had decided against writing a thriller. It was far too chilled here to worry about all that murdering stuff and what I would do with a body. In fact, I think I would just dump the sucker under the nearest bush and take a nap. No *Poirot* required. Instead, I owed it to Luke to complete the Attraction Abacus. It was *our* story, and we had almost made it through to the end.

I packed up my things and locked up the hut. The sand was burning beneath my feet, and I danced into the sandals that I had left in the shade, wrapping a mint sarong around my swimsuit. A wide-brimmed straw hat kept the sun out of my eyes as I strode across the beach.

I made the trip from the town to the cabin and back again on foot every day. I used to struggle with what to think about when I walked, but my thoughts were clearer now, and I always looked forward to the journey. Maybe it was the pace of life in India, but I think, more significantly, I had changed. I found myself looking forward, rather than backward. Not in the discontented way that Dad had done, always believing that tomorrow was going to be better than today, just because today hadn't delivered an unlikely miracle: I wasn't deluding myself, like Dad. Instead, I could see a future that didn't scare me. You can get older without growing up, and if I looked at my life objectively, that had been my own sad little progression path, until the last year at least. I was ready to become an adult and take responsibility for my own life. It was time to stop blaming other people for my own shortcomings and to accept who I was. There had been no bad relationship genes passed to me. My fate was my own.

I rested in the shade of a coconut tree. It was cooling, but I was conscious that I was only seconds away from a potential concussion. There was a distant cry of a monkey, or was it a bird, screaming through the lush foliage. Everything sounded so exotic here, and always the sea roared in the background. I loved this place, and I wanted to share it with Luke. I really missed him. We called each other regularly, but it wasn't the same. I'm no phone-smith, and the conversations made me feel even further away. Even video calls, which constantly broke up, and where we talked over each other because of the time lag, were little better.

Loneliness wasn't the issue, as such. I was four months into my trip and had been disciplined with my writing in the beach cabin, always too focused to let negativity spoil my progress. The evenings spent with Liv were amazing. My sweet, wonderful friend Liv! I told her every day just how much I appreciated her and what she had done for me. I had been so caught up in my problems that I hadn't thanked her nearly enough before. She told me not to worry about it, but I did.

We laughed like we had done when we were younger, drank

too much, and partied even more, but at some stage of the night or early morning, we had to go to bed. Understandably, Liv was mindful of work the next day, but I always wished for our time together to last longer. That was when I really missed Luke the most: when I was alone in my bedroom. The air conditioning was never quite powerful enough, the room never quite dark enough and my mind never quite still enough to sleep. It was these nights that made me long to go home.

I continued along the beach, waving to a guy who was pulling a fishing boat ashore. He had sold me a whole red snapper when I first arrived. I didn't like to say no and walked all the way back to town with the huge fish, with no idea of what I was going to do with it. The locals were openly pointing and laughing at me. My wave to the man was more of an apologetic "not today, thanks".

I followed the trail edging the sand to a wider expanse of beach, where I stopped, contemplating a swim. A swim was always tempting, but I rarely remembered a change of clothes, like today, and walking the rest of the way back to town in a wet swimming costume could be uncomfortable. I talked myself out of it and gathered my things to continue. Surprise checked my step as I slung the rucksack over my shoulder. There was a man walking in my direction along the beach. He was tall, wearing a pair of Chino shorts and a white linen shirt. His gait was familiar. His face was even more familiar. It couldn't be. Surely not. And then I saw his stupid grin and absolutely knew that it was.

We ran along the beach towards each other, and I jumped into Luke's arms, just like a movie. We kissed. The kind of kiss that I had always been jealous of — long, lingering and totally inappropriate in public. I didn't want to let go, and for quite some time I didn't, clinging to Luke like a koala. When we did release each other, we stood face to face, studying each other for any clues of what we had missed in the last four months.

'You look brown and thin,' he said, 'like a *Twiglet*.'

'You look pale,' I replied. 'Pale and handsome.'

'I wanted my visit to be a surprise. Liv told me where to find you.'

'You and that girl, always plotting.'

'I really wanted to see you.'

'I couldn't be happier that you came.'

'Plus, Michael said that I have a lot more to offer India than you do.'

'You can tell Michael where to go from me, next time you see him!'

'Forget your visa extension then,' Luke said, laughing. How I had missed that laugh! 'By the way, I haven't come here to ruin your writing plans. I'm planning to do a bit of painting myself. Dust the old acrylics off. You must get on with your story. It's just a holiday for me.'

'You're not ruining anything,' I said, kissing him again. 'I've almost finished the book, anyway. Only the last little bit to write.'

'Do you know how it's going to end?'

'I think I do now.'

We swam in the sea together.

I was in no rush to get back to town, and though I wanted to thank Liv, once again, for what she had done, I didn't want the afternoon to end. The sun was getting low now, casting an orange sheen over the warm Arabian Sea lapping around our bodies. Waist height in the water, clinging to each other again, we gazed out towards the horizon, cheek to cheek.

'Looks like we are sunset watchers after all,' I said.

'We were always destined to be,' he replied, kissing me.

I had never felt so happy. It was crazy how much my life had changed in such a short space of time. How much *I* had changed in such a short space of time. I really had found the guy who made me want to tear up my dating checklist and toss it over my shoulder. Everything felt possible, and I didn't want that feeling to end.

Nobody knows what tomorrow will bring.

Perhaps I'll tread on a poisonous coral, or Luke will wake up with third-degree sunburn. Maybe that rabid dog will finally catch up with me. I'm not naïve. There will be many arguments to come, but, hopefully, just as many making-ups to follow them. Real life is not a romantic comedy, and good times don't last forever. Happiness is a slippery fish; just when you think you have hold of it, it's gone again. Bad times don't last forever, either, though. It all just depends on where you choose to end the story.

So, with joy in my heart, like my teenage dad, dressed in his leather jacket as *Danny Zuko*, flying away in a cardboard car with *Sandy* at the end of his *Grease* school production, I choose to end the story of the Attraction Abacus right here: Luke and I, wrapped around each other, watching the sun set over the sea. I think Kris Harper would agree that it meets his genre conventions.

Three words to describe how I feel right now? Happy. Ever. After.

A note from the author

Thank you so much for buying this book, and I hope that you enjoyed reading it. This book was independently published, and it is only through people like you that books like this can flourish.

Independently published books do not have vast marketing budgets, but they can still become successful. If you did enjoy reading this book, please tell your friends about it. Word of mouth is still the best way for a book to grow. If you have time to leave a quick review, that would be amazing too. You don't have to write a huge amount. A few words or just a star rating make a big difference in helping the book reach a wider audience.

Thank you again for reading.

Also, from Heptagon Books

The Path of Good Response
By S. Frogley

What if there was a way to make a perfect decision? If poor choices, even addictions, could be controlled from within the mind.

Schelldhardt is the largest company in the world and will do anything to grow. When Joe Massey is unexpectedly offered a role aboard Schelldhardt's luxurious corporate headquarters at sea, his main priority is Rachel. Joe has trailed Rachel through school and university into the workplace and cannot imagine life without her.

Realistic dreams disturb Joe's sleep as he is drawn deeper into a dark corporate world. As an inexperienced graduate, his opinion seems far too important to Schelldhardt. Why is he really there? The deposed CEO, Arnold Shendi, may have Joe's answers, though Shendi has secrets of his own.

A new speculative thriller, set aboard a vast ship at sea.

The Gap
By S. Frogley

The gap is the place where our intentions meet our actions.
The gap is the place where our failings are exposed.
All humanity exists in the gap.
The gap is the next global battlefield, and the war has already begun.

Two organisations are locked in battle to control the mysterious gap. Schelldhardt, the largest company in the world, is using its powerful online reach to divide the global population. The Friary is a secretive institution aiming to stop them.

Lana Carter is a young woman searching for her sister, Grace. Grace was working for Schelldhardt before her sudden disappearance. Enlisting the help of another former Schelldhardt employee, Joe Massey, Lana must unravel Grace's fate and shape the ultimate destiny of the gap.

A new speculative thriller, and sequel to *The Path of Good Response*.

Printed in Dunstable, United Kingdom